INTO THE FIRE

Van Buren spoke. "Okay, here's the situation. In our area of operations, an enemy mechanized brigade is attacking from north to south. Our mission is as follows: On order, Team Cobra defends Battle Position Charlie to destroy enemy reconnaissance and lead elements of the mechanized brigade to prevent penetration of Phase Line Crush. Red team will use artillery to destroy enemy recon assets to deny him the opportunity to locate our main defensive belt. We will use a combination of direct and indirect fires to destroy the remainder of his forces. When the enemy reaches Phase Line Volcano, artillery will be shifted, and the focus of all fires will be on enemy armor. Questions?"

Hansen, Gutterson, Thomas, and Ryback finished making notations on their overlays. "No questions, sir," Hansen said, after a quick glance to the others.

The captain reached out, shook all of their hands. "Gentlemen, you're the best I've ever served with, and the pleasure has been all mine."

Hansen's eyes burned. "Thank you, sir."

Van Buren grinned, just staring at them for a moment more. Then he shouted the words they had all been waiting for:

"Let's get some!"

ARMORED CORPS

PETE CALLAHAN

JOVE BOOKS, NEW YORK

THE BERKLEY PUBLISHING GROUP
Published by the Penguin Group
Penguin Group (USA) Inc.
375 Hudson Street, New York, New York 10014, USA
Penguin Group (Canada), 10 Alcorn Avenue, Toronto, Ontario M4V 3B2, Canada
(a division of Pearson Penguin Canada Inc.)
Penguin Books Ltd., 80 Strand, London WC2R 0RL, England
Penguin Group Ireland, 25 St. Stephen's Green, Dublin 2, Ireland (a division of Penguin Books Ltd.)
Penguin Group (Australia), 250 Camberwell Road, Camberwell, Victoria 3124, Australia
(a division of Pearson Australia Group Pty. Ltd.)
Penguin Books India Pvt. Ltd., 11 Community Centre, Panchsheel Park, New Delhi—110 017, India
Penguin Group (NZ), Cnr. Airborne and Rosedale Roads, Albany, Auckland 1310, New Zealand
(a division of Pearson New Zealand Ltd.)
Penguin Books (South Africa) (Pty.) Ltd., 24 Sturdee Avenue, Rosebank, Johannesburg 2196,
South Africa

Penguin Books Ltd., Registered Offices: 80 Strand, London WC2R 0RL, England

This is a work of fiction. Names, characters, places, and incidents either are the product of the author's imagination or are used fictitiously, and any resemblance to actual persons, living or dead, business establishments, events, or locales is entirely coincidental.

ARMORED CORPS

A Jove Book / published by arrangement with the author

PRINTING HISTORY
Jove edition / April 2005

ISBN: 0-515-13932-7

JOVE®
Jove Books are published by The Berkley Publishing Group,
a division of Penguin Group (USA) Inc.,
375 Hudson Street, New York, New York 10014.
JOVE is a registered trademark of Penguin Group (USA) Inc.
The "J" design is a trademark belonging to Penguin Group (USA) Inc.

PRINTED IN THE UNITED STATES OF AMERICA

10 9 8 7 6 5 4 3 2 1

ACKNOWLEDGMENTS

My editor, Tom Colgan, brought this project to me and as such deserves a heartfelt thank you for the opportunity.

Shawn T. O. Priest describes himself as a "Gulf war veteran with the First Cav who spent seventeen months in Korea at Camp Casey as part of First Tank. Too much of a smart-ass to keep his trap shut, he was widely regarded as Command Specialist of the Army for the five years and eight months he held that position without demotion or promotion." Shawn's sense of humor, tutelage, and enthusiasm were incredibly helpful. He helped me build this series from the ground up, provided keen insights into the plot development, read and responded to every chapter, designed maps, and even helped to compile the book's glossary. I am deeply in his debt.

Captain Keith W. Wilson, commanding HHC/1–72 AR BN, took this manuscript into the field, spent many hours thoroughly critiquing every line, and provided me with the kinds of insights that only someone currently serving in Korea would know. His advice and significant contributions have been invaluable and are greatly appreciated.

Major Mark Aitken rescued me from the throes of my fictional battlefield by helping me to define the enemy force and to plan many of the battle scenes. Moreover, he designed maps and provided me with dozens of photos from his tour in Korea, spent many hours on the phone with me answering questions, and became someone I am deeply honored to call my friend.

Lieutenant Colonel Jack Sherman, AR, USAR, Operations Officer 5th Joint Task Force, read the chapters and reflected upon his own experiences abroad as well as offering not only technical advice but philosophical and psychological insights into the nature of war and its effects on soldiers. His timely responses and enthusiasm lifted my spirits during some long days.

Lieutenant Colonel Tom O'Sullivan, U.S. Army (Ret.), served as a platoon leader in C Company First Tank (Second Platoon Leader). Tom willingly pored over every sentence of this manuscript, making both technical and stylistic suggestions as well as sharing some joyous and tragic moments of his long and distinguished career. His efforts were as welcome as they were inspirational.

Major Phil Corbo, CFC, C1 Plans Officer, Korea, read and critiqued chapters, provided me with orders of battle, and sent invaluable information regarding the 1–72's gunnery procedures.

The following people offered technical assistance or helped me reach those who could. They are many, and this is a testament to the generosity of the U.S. Army community:

Sergeant First Class Timothy L. Gray, 1/66 AR (4th Infantry Division)
Staff Sergeant Jason Frisk, Delta Co., 1–72 AR
Major Jeffery Price, S3, Support Squadron, 2 ACR
Lieutenant Colonel Michael Johnson, USAR (Ret.)
First Lieutenant Ivan Torres, Training Officer, 3-112 AR TXARNG
Sergeant Major David Maciborksi, U.S. Army (Ret.)
Master Sergeant Jeffrey W. Letcher
Gary Lapp, U.S. Army (Ret.)
Scott Cunningham (www.armorinaction.com)

Lieutenant Colonel Steven A. Boylan, Public Affairs, 8th
   U.S. Army, Korea
Bruce E. Zielsdorf, Dir., Army Public Affairs, NY Branch
Charlotte Bourgeois, Managing Editor, *Armor* magazine
David Manning, Editor, *Armor* magazine
Joseph S. Bermudez, Jr., author of *Shield of the Great
   Leader: The Armed Forces of North Korea*

  The listing of these individuals is my small way to say
thank you and does not constitute an "official" endorsement of this book by them or the United States Army.

For Shawn, Keith, Mark, Jack, Tom, Phil,
and all the other tankers who have proudly served . . .

And especially in memory of Private James R. Williams

It is soldiers who pay most of the human cost. In war it is extraordinary how it all comes down to the character of one man.

—GENERAL CREIGHTON W. ABRAMS, JR.

CHAPTER
ONE

AN ARCTIC AIR mass dubbed by forecasters as a *Siberian express* had been blasting through the rugged valley of Rodriguez Range for the past week, driving temperatures into the subzero digits. Second Lieutenant Jack Hansen had only been in country for three months and had never experienced one of Korea's brutal winters. As he stood inside the tank commander's hatch of his M1A1 Abrams, he swore inwardly over the wind and the flurries obscuring his view. With a shudder, he adjusted the chin strap on his combat vehicle crewman's helmet, lifted his binoculars, then scanned the horizon for pop-up plywood tanks and personnel carriers or for the plastic targets simulating sets of enemy troops.

Nothing yet.

He lowered the binoculars, wiped his eyes, and hoped the wind wouldn't play havoc with the targets again. More resetting delays might break the crew's tempo.

It was only 1350, yet the sky loomed like a sheet of gunmetal, and pockets of shadows were already gathering near

the snowy mountains ahead. Hansen had to forget about
the weather and the gloomy atmosphere, about his discomfort, about everything save for the task at hand. He and the
men of the 1st Battalion, 72nd Armor were conducting a
Level I Gunnery qualification. The semiannual training involved all five companies of the battalion deploying for a
month to the recently renovated Korean Training Center, a
U.S. range complex just a short distance from the border
separating their forces from those of their closest enemy,
the North Korean People's Army. Currently, they were
conducting Tank Table VIII, the Super Bowl of tank gunnery, and they were doing it so close to the northwest line
of the demilitarized zone that in some areas they could fire
into North Korea.

That morning at 0600, lined up on a stretch of ice-slick
concrete, Hansen and the rest of Charlie Company had attended the range safety briefing conducted by the man su-
pervising the gunnery, Battalion Master Gunner Sergeant
First Class Jerry Zorn. "This is what we tankers live for—
to shoot big bullets. But this is where we find out who
knows his business—and who does not. Lest I remind you,
we are First Tank, gentlemen, the most forward deployed
American armor unit in South Korea. What does that
mean? It means there is no second best. Everybody quali-
fies. Everybody fights. Nobody quits. Good to go?"

Hansen and the rest of the Charlie Company Cobras had
boomed their acknowledgment.

The pressure was on, all right. And the stakes were even
higher for Hansen. This was his very first gunnery, and he
wanted nothing more than to prove to his men and to the rest
of the company that despite being a butterbar from West
Point, he was one of them: an armored warrior, a tanker.

But he had to make it through the gunnery first. Tank
Table VIII was usually comprised of six day and four night
engagements, each worth up to one hundred points. A perfect score of one thousand would give Hansen and his crew

bragging rights and the honor of being Top Tank, while nine hundred and above would earn them the distinguished rating, and eight hundred to nine hundred would rank them as superior. All crews needed a minimum of seven hundred points to qualify as combat ready. The obvious goal was to qualify your tank Q1 by racking up the seven hundred points as quickly as possible. Being Top Tank was a secondary goal, and Hansen needed to remember that, even though he and the boys of Red One, riding aboard the tank named *Crimson Death,* had taken down every target during the first five engagements and may have racked up an impressive, head-turning, five hundred points. That alone would be a remarkable feat, especially after having sat in their tank for nearly four hours, anxiously awaiting their turn on the range.

Hansen drew in an icy breath, then called into the boom mike at his chapped lips. "Crew report."

Specialist Rick Gatch had the best seat in the house, tucked all warm and snug inside the diver's hole beneath the turret. Although Hansen could not see Gatch, he knew that the NASCAR fan from Daytona Beach was reclined in the chair, gripping the T-bar with the motorcycle-like throttle, and checking the tank's fuel levels, engine temperature, and rpm. Those readings were obviously okay, because the heavily tattooed twenty-seven-year-old responded, "Driver ready!"

Next came the loader's turn to check in, and Hansen pictured Private First Class Victor Deacon at his station on the left side of the turret. The nineteen-year-old hillbilly muscle head from North Carolina known to all as Deac had taped a gatefold of a bikini-clad babe to the turret wall because "Y'all know that the only thing better than bombs is boobs." Deac hit the knee switch, opening the tank's ammo door. He adjusted the ammo to fill the tubes he had emptied during the last engagement. "Give me one!" he cried, then satisfied, he added, "Weapon safe. Sabot loaded. Loader ready!"

Finally, it was the gunner's turn, and Sergeant Lee Yong Sung, a painfully polite KATUSA—or Korean Augmentee to the United States Army—soldier serving his mandatory two-year active duty commitment with U.S. forces, made a slight adjustment to his thermal sights, switched back to daylight, then nodded approvingly. The twenty-two-year-old's indicator light showed sabot. The computer was set for the ammo loaded. "Sabot indexed. Gunner ready!"

Hansen was about to radio the control tower looming high above the range. He wanted to ask what the delay was, but it was better to simply report that they were in Ready Condition One and keep the bitching to himself. "Charlie Niner Two, this is Red One," he began, using the familiar call sign for the tower. "REDCON-1, over."

"Red One, this is Charlie Niner Two," responded Sergeant First Class Zorn. "Scouts report enemy armor in sector. Bound to Phase Line Bravo. Engage and report, out."

Hansen knew that up in the tower, Sergeant First Class Zorn was signaling the tank crew evaluator, Staff Sergeant Stan Jackson, from their sister battalion, 2-72 AR, to be ready to begin timing the run. The battalion used external evaluators to provide unbiased evaluations and scoring. Zorn knew Jackson from their time together as tank gunners at Fort Stewart, Georgia. The TCE would start the clock as soon as the targets rose, and he would stop the clock once all targets were destroyed. That time would be a primary factor in the crew's score.

"Driver, move out," Hansen ordered.

Gatch brought the sixty-eight-ton, four-speed automatic beast forward. With the 1500 horsepower turbine engine reverberating through the tank's steel-encased, depleted-uranium armor, and the tracks churning up rooster tails of mud and snow in their wake, Hansen allowed himself a grin.

He was just twenty-three years old.

His life had just begun.

And he was already living a dream, perched atop one of

the most powerful combat vehicles in the world and feeling equally powerful. He was the leader of First Platoon, in charge of four tanks and fifteen other men. He had come a long way from that week at Fort Knox, where as a second-year cadet he had first climbed aboard an Abrams for driver training. His Mustang GT back home on Long Island had absolutely nothing on the M1, and by week's end he had stood in the TC's station and had uttered aloud, "This is the shit."

Those words echoed in his head as the tank rolled on and Gatch brought them up to a stable speed, making it easier for Lee down at his gunner's station to pick up targets.

Hansen grew more tense, squinting as he aggressively searched the hills. All of the targets rose on computer-operated lifters and would remain up for forty to fifty seconds, with main gun targets located between 1,200 and 2,000 meters downrange. Knowing that didn't help much, though. Those simulated enemy forces could be anywhere.

And there they where! "Two tanks!" cried Hansen, spying the wooden tracks about 1,500 meters out while laying the main gun tube on target. "Stationary tank first!"

For a second, a cloud of windswept snow obscured the enemy forces, but Hansen was confident that Lee had already picked them up on his thermals. He would press one of two thumb buttons on the gunner's power control handle, or GPCH, to fire a laser, which allowed the ballistic computer to calculate the exact distance to the target. Then he would guide the reticle back into the center of the half-hidden tank and announce, "Identified!"

Which is exactly what he did.

"Up!" Deac reported, having lifted the arming lever for the 120 mm smoothbore main gun. He no doubt sat in his loader's seat, clear of the gun's thirteen-inch path of recoil. Were he within that deadly zone, the gun would kick back and crush his chest in a nanosecond.

Hansen balled one hand into a fist and shouted, "Fire!"

"On the way!" replied Lee, who squeezed his trigger on the Y in way.

The tank rocked back as the sabot burst from the main gun's barrel with a boom that would make anyone nearby piss his pants, not to mention anyone staring down the barrel of said weapon. The round, technically known as an M829A2 Armor-Piercing, Fin-Stabilized, Discarding Sabot-Tracer (APFSDS-T), resembled an inverted conelike projectile consisting of three aluminum petals attached by a plastic ring. Behind those petals lay the extremely dense and slender depleted-uranium long-rod penetrator. Once fired, the round's cone ensured the initial stability of the penetrator rod as it exited the gun tube to achieve speeds in excess of 1,600 meters per second. As the round raced toward its target, the three petals would fall away by the force of the surrounding air, leaving the six-finned penetrator rod to continue along its deadly path.

Although Hansen and his men were using the lighter, less-expensive training rounds whose penetrators were made of a softer metal than the service rounds used in actual combat, those rounds still earned tankers' attention and respect.

In a flash, the long, bulletlike projectile punched a neat hole in the plywood tank, then hit the berm behind, tossing up a cloud of dirt and snow as the round's aft cap dropped with a metallic clang to the bottom of the turret. Hansen hollered, "Target!" to acknowledge that they had made a direct hit.

The crew's every move had just been recorded on video by Zorn and Jackson, who were also eavesdropping on their intercom system and monitoring their progress on computer screens. As Zorn had earlier reminded them, "The days of 'you call it' are over. We're leaning over your shoulders, scrutinizing every fire command and every moment's hesitation. You screw up? There's no way to hide it."

And if Hansen screwed up, not only would he embarrass himself, but he would be letting down his crew, his platoon, his company, his entire battalion.

No, that wouldn't happen. Couldn't happen. But there was still another tank out there, trying to escape. "Moving tank!"

Gatch kept them rolling smoothly while Lee targeted the tank and shouted, "Identified." Deac withdrew another training round from its ammo tube, slid it into the main gun's breach with his fist, then let his arm rise on the breach block as the round locked into place. He threw up the lever to arm the main gun, rolled to his seat, and with perfect timing as the ammo door closed shut, he announced, "Up!"

His gaze riveted on the fleeing tank, Hansen could barely contain his excitement. *C'mon, c'mon, let's kill this bastard.* "Fire!"

"On the way!"

Again the tank rocked back as the main gun spat another sabot that, in the blink of an eye, traversed the 1,500 meters to the escaping tank.

Were the round to strike a real tank, the depleted-uranium penetrator would drive straight through the armor, and as it entered, heated fragments of metal would fly off in all directions, hitting anyone and anything inside. For now, though, it was enough that the penetrator struck the wooden target dead center as Hansen roared, "Target!"

The crew whooped and hollered.

But the engagement wasn't over, and if Hansen did not follow protocol, he could easily forfeit every point the crew had just earned. "Cease fire! Cease fire! Crew report."

"Driver ready!"

"Weapon safe. Sabot loaded. Loader ready!"

"Sabot indexed. Gunner ready."

"Charlie Niner Two, this is Red One. Engaged and destroyed two T-72s. Continuing mission, over."

"Red One, this is Charlie Niner Two. Good job. Clear all weapons systems and advise when clear, over."

"Roger that, Charlie Niner Two. Clearing weapons, out." The tension in Hansen's shoulders began to loosen.

Had they done it? A perfect run? The other five engagements flashed through his mind. He could not remember a mistake. "Driver? Stop."

"That was some badass shit!" Gatch cried, bringing the tank to a halt. "Badass!"

"Chill, Gatch," Hansen ordered. "We don't know."

"We hit every one, sir," said Deac. "Even a dumb coon hunter like me knows what that means."

IN THE TOWER, Jackson lifted his gaze from his stopwatch and glanced to Zorn. "This'll be a short debrief, Jerry. Kid comes out of nowhere. First gunnery. Scores a perfect six for six. What do you think? Is he a natural or just lucky?"

Zorn snorted and began rewinding the tape of Hansen's run. "He's got a good crew, especially his gunner. A KAT-SUA has to be damned good to sit in that seat. Lee's earned it."

"Yeah, but what about that Gomer Pyle and that biker dwarf Hansen's got in his turret?"

Cocking a brow, Zorn stood, bringing himself to his full height of five feet, five inches. In a mock-serious tone, he asked, "Biker dwarf?"

"What? You got a politically correct term for it?" Jackson shook his head and smiled. "Now don't you find this interesting?"

"What?"

"We have two crews with a shot at Top Tank."

"*If* Hansen doesn't choke and bolo." Zorn pressed Play and began watching the tape. "You know what the night run can do to people."

"Yeah, but look at that," Jackson said, placing a finger on the TV screen. "Center of mass every time."

"Oh, those boys will qualify . . . but Top Tank? No way."

"I don't know, Jerry. That crew's in the zone. Keyman's got some real competition this time."

"Keyman rides his crew harder than anybody in country. He'll take it again—because his men will be scared shitless if they don't."

WITH THEIR RUN completed, Hansen received orders to return to the admin push radio frequency and to move to the baseline, keeping his main gun clear and pointed downrange at all times until they left the area. Lee engaged the pair of hand grips referred to as the Cadillacs after the company that manufactured them, Cadillac Gage. Gatch whipped the tank around, and to those watching from the tower, the turret remained seemingly motionless while the hull turned under it.

Once they reached the baseline, Lee traversed the gun over the front of the tank as Gatch steered them toward the ammo pad upon which stood a honeycomb of storage units for the training ammo. The combat ammo was stored nearby on a separate pad, guarded by armed soldiers.

Before Hansen could give the order, Deac popped his hatch and dismounted to give hand signals to Gatch. Once the tank was in position on the ammo pad, the loader climbed back on board to begin off-loading aft caps and small arms brass. While some officers wouldn't bother to help, Hansen shared in the grunt work, and he knew the men appreciated that.

When they were finished with the off-loading, they began rearming the tank for the four night engagements. A member of the range detail arrived to ensure that they did not load more rounds than they were allotted, and, wearing a ridiculously innocent expression, Deac tried to sneak an extra sabot on board. However, he was summarily stopped by a hard tug on the shoulder. "Oh, that's it? Well I'm sorry, Cooter. Lost track of the count. What do y'all expect from a dumb-ass tanker?"

"Don't mind him," Gatch said to the humorless sergeant. "His left nut's been frozen for a week, and there's some kind of fluid backup thing that's putting pressure on his brain."

"Do we have a problem here?" Hansen asked, widening his gaze on his men as he hopped down from the tank.

"No, sir," Deac snapped, heading off to return the sabot.

"Sir, we are fully loaded and ready to move out," reported Gatch.

"Good. And hey, nice job out there."

"Thank you, sir. But like I say, don't thank me—"

"Thank me and Dale," Hansen finished with a knowing grin.

"Yes, sir. Me and Dale. Don't leave home without him."

The Dale to which Gatch was referring was none other than Dale Earnhardt of NASCAR fame, who had been tragically killed doing what he did best. According to Gatch, the spirit of Mr. Earnhardt watched over him every time he dropped into the driver's seat. Gatch even had an In Memory of #3 Dale Earnhardt bumper sticker placed on the inside of his driver's hatch.

Hey, if it worked for Gatch, Hansen would not argue.

Within a few minutes, they were rolling again, heading for the motor pool. During the short drive, Deac could not keep his mouth closed. "Y'all might think we'll do it, but I *know* we'll do it. Top Tank's ours, and we're going to shove it right up Keyman's ass!"

"We should accept the honor with grace and dignity," Lee said softly, his English much better than most KA-TUSAs. "The warrior who is not humble has a short life."

"That some Korean proverb?" Gatch asked from the driver's hole.

"No, but I think it is true," Lee answered.

"I think we all need to calm down and stay focused," Hansen warned them. "Otherwise, we'll prove them right and barely qualify tonight. Do you understand?"

Their replies echoed over the intercom.

Once they reached the motor pool, Gatch complained about the lack of valet parking, then steered them into their space. He revved the engine, then shut down master power. Hansen, Deac, and Lee climbed out of the turret. To avoid slipping, they kept at least three points of contact on the beast: their feet and at least one hand. Gatch crawled out of his hatch and worked his way across the hull. Once on the ground, Deac nearly fell on his ass as his boot hit a patch of ice, but Hansen caught the teetering loader.

The five-minute walk to the debriefing tent would have been bearable back in September or October, but in December? They double-timed the whole way there.

Inside the tent, Hansen found his platoon sergeant, Sergeant First Class Matthew Abbot, waiting to shake hands. Affectionately and traditionally known as the platoon daddy, Abbot was a stout tanker of thirty-six, a Marlboro man gone gray whose voice was burred by a lifetime of smoking. He had soft blue eyes that when widened revealed an intensity that Hansen could only dream of possessing. Abbot had been a tanker for over sixteen years and had braved some rough battles in Iraq, the kind of stuff you didn't see on TV. He was the most experienced tanker in Red Platoon and as such served as a mentor to Hansen and the other men. His incredible patience, along with his ability to diplomatically criticize, made him the best teacher Hansen had ever met. After spending the last three months with the man, Hansen had learned much more than just tank operations; he had learned how to better deal with the people who made everything happen.

"Well, I guess you da man, LT," Abbot said.

"Thanks." Hansen cocked a thumb over his shoulder. "But these guys helped a little."

"Yeah, just a little. Come on. I don't want to let the cat out of the bag, but I heard Jackson say you went six for six. Congratulations."

Hansen muttered a "Yes!" as Abbot led him and the others over to the other side of the long tent, its poles rattling against the wind.

Captain Mitchell Van Buren, the company commander, sat before a flat-panel video display, along with Zorn and Jackson. They were watching one of Hansen's runs and nodding their approval. Standing behind them were the company's XO, First Lieutenant Randy Chase, and the company's First Sergeant, Thomas Westman.

Van Buren, a handsome officer of just thirty-two who looked like a Sears catalog model but who spoke like a hard-core tanker, rose as Hansen and the rest snapped to. "At ease, gentlemen. Well, I'm sure one of these hens already told you, so congratulations. You scored six hundred."

"Thank you, sir," Hansen replied too quickly.

Zorn cocked a brow. "Don't let it go to your head."

"No, I won't."

"Now then, even with a perfect score, there are a few things you could've added, like more MRS updates during your first engagement," Jackson said. "Let's start with them."

The tank crew evaluator was referring to muzzle reference system updates that accounted for the slight movement of the gun when the gun tube heated up. They were accomplished via a computer and were like doing a quick boresighting to make sure everything was aligned properly. If that had been the crew's biggest mistake, then Hansen was still satisfied with their accomplishment. He listened open-mindedly and attentively, even as he noticed that while two of his other tank commanders, Abbot and Staff Sergeant Richard "Neech" Nelson were present to support him, Staff Sergeant Timothy Key, the infamous Keyman, was not present. Hansen had, of course, attended Keyman's after-action review and had congratulated the staff sergeant for a perfect day run, but Keyman was not there to do likewise. As far as Hansen was concerned, he had done nothing wrong in the past three months to incite the man—nothing wrong except being a butterbar from West Point. Hansen had heard through the grapevine that Keyman did not trust officers, especially West Point graduates. He thought they were arrogant and had their asses padded all of their lives. His arrogance and his unwillingness to sit down and hash it out with Hansen had turned the two into fierce competitors. And maybe that wasn't so bad. Keyman's self-importance kept him and his crew well-honed, and given the battalion's "fight tonight" state of readiness, having a total asshole on your side could help when heavy fire lit up the skies.

But in the end, it hurt, if only a little, that one of Hansen's own TCs had not shown up for the review.

They left the tent and followed the well-beaten snow path back toward the motor pool. Abbot tipped his head, drawing Hansen to the back of the group. "I'm sorry he didn't show up, sir."

Hansen shrugged. "Did he at least have an excuse?"

"He said he's been having problems with his GPS. The reticle's been drifting. Said he needed to have it checked out."

"You believe him?"

"Well, I think the timing is a little coincidental. I'll talk to him."

Hansen shrugged. "You think you should?"

"Maybe I'll wait until you beat him and he blows a nut."

"You know, I'm damned if I do, damned if I don't here."

"What do you mean?"

"I beat him, and I light his fuse. I lose, and he's still pissed that I'm in charge."

Abbot nodded. "He's a big boy. Either way, he'll have to deal with it. I'll check in with you later. Good luck tonight."

"You, too."

As Abbot hustled off, Hansen hurried to catch up with his men, and when he reached them, Deac said, "Well, sir, I guess Keyman couldn't bear to look us in the eyes."

"That's right," said Gatch, his breath frosty on the wind. "He's all threatened and scared now. Somebody's finally giving him a run for his money. And that somebody is us."

"Why would he run for his money?" Lee asked.

"All right, guys, that's enough," Hansen said. "Let's go over to Ajima's for ramen and Cokes. I'm buying."

"So you are making a run for your money?" Lee asked, his frown deepening.

Hansen just winked and turned off the trail, leading the crew along a broad ridge as the booming of 120 mm guns resumed in the distance.

A few minutes later, they sidestepped their way down to the base of a hogback where Ajima, loosely translated as *Aunt,* had set up her tent. Most units in South Korea had *ajimas* who followed them around and sold ramen, coffee, Cokes, and other fresh food. The middle-aged Korean women would even extend credit to soldiers in the field, but come payday, you would find them in the orderly rooms, looking to collect.

The 1-72's *ajima* was a gruff old woman whose skin had gone to leather and who took no shit from anyone. If you touched before you bought, she would slap your hand and shout, "Money first!" And if you wanted to know something about the unit, say, exactly when the next training exercise would take place, old Ajima could tell you. She knew more about the unit's comings and goings than most tank crew members. Sometimes she would arrive at a highly classified assembly area even before the tanks did, although she was hardly a security risk.

Moreover, from what Hansen could tell, she was on the up and up. Some *ajimas* were part of the black market, paying soldiers for MREs, Jim Beam, and Chivas Regal. If

Ajima engaged in those activities, she kept her dealings away from the average tanker.

As they approached her tent, the scent of steaming noodles was so strong on the breeze that it seemingly warmed the air and most definitely made Hansen's stomach groan.

"Oh, you cold and hungry," Ajima said, winking at Hansen as he ducked inside and approached the makeshift counter constructed of old fruit crates.

"How you doing today, Ajima?"

She gave an exaggerated shudder. "Hansen, you nice guy. So I tell you. Keyman come here. Call you asshole to other men. Okay?"

"You hear that, LT?" Deac cried. "That bucket of slop's talking behind y'all's back!"

Hansen gave Deac a hard look, then faced Ajima. "Thanks for telling me. We need Cokes and ramens for all of us, please."

As Ajima crossed back to a large pot atop her portable stove, she said, "Don't worry, Hansen. You do good on night run tonight. Kick Keyman's fucking ass."

"Right on, Ajima," Gatch said. "Right on!"

CHAPTER
TWO

SERGEANT CLARK WEBBER shook his head in disgust, pushed off from the tank he had been leaning on, then looked the other gunner straight in the eye. "Brophy, it ain't my fault you wanted to party before payday. You came begging for the money. You agreed to my terms. Now it's time to pay your principal—plus your vig."

"My vig?" the gunner asked. "What are you, Webber, the fucking Mafia? You're not even Italian for chrissakes!"

Webber grabbed Brophy by the collar of his Nomex coveralls. "I'm not kidding you, Brophy."

"Hey, man, I was drunk. And I came here to tell you face-to-face that I'm not paying you a goddamned cent."

"Listen, fat boy, you think because you're the battalion commander's gunner that you can get out of this?"

"Get out of what? I didn't beg for the money. You talked me into the loan. And at a hundred percent interest? Are you nuts?" Brophy ripped Webber's hands from his collar, wiped his own hands on his hips as though they had been soiled, then started off.

"You walk away, you'll be sorry!"

Brophy swung around, looking incredulous, even stunned. "You're lucky I came. You've been scamming people for too long, Webber—you and your loan-sharking and get-rich-quick schemes. It's about time somebody made *you* the victim. Give you a taste of your own medicine."

Webber sighed, raised his palms in truce. "All right, look. I'll cut you some slack this time. Just give me the hundred bucks, no vig."

Brophy's lips curled in a lopsided grin. "Come on, Webber. You're a businessman. You should know all about profit and loss. Write it off on your taxes. See ya." With that, the gunner marched off.

"You motherfucker," Webber muttered, still in disbelief. He reached for his Zippo and pack of smokes, already considering his revenge, when he heard boots hit the snow behind him.

Damn it. The asshole was awake. And just a few minutes too soon.

"You going AWOL or what?"

Webber steeled himself, took a step forward, then turned to face Keyman.

The tank commander had his CVC helmet tugged down over his bald pate, and while he almost always wore a frown, his brow had furrowed even more into a scowl. Staff Sergeant Timothy Key did an expert job of intimidating the other guys on the crew.

But not Webber. As a kid, Webber had been bullied through elementary school, tormented really, called Clark Kent because he had worn glasses. Then one day in the fifth grade he had snapped and had beaten a kid into a bloody pulp.

Which was to say that bullies and Webber went way back, and he would not abide them. Not ever.

"I asked you a question, Sergeant." Keyman's bloodshot eyes widened as he tongued the lump of chewing tobacco between his cheek and gum. He craned his head and spat, then resumed his scowl.

Webber took in a long breath through his nose. "Just getting some fresh air. Glad you could join me."

"Bullshit."

"About what? Getting the air or being happy to see you?"

"You got the right name, you know that, Webber? What a tangled web we weave when we are a fucking liar." Keyman sniffled, then spat again.

"I don't know what you're talking about, Sergeant. I really don't."

Keyman brought himself to full height—all six feet three inches of it. "Don't be making deals on my time. Do you read me?"

Webber stood tall himself, five feet ten inches of insubordination waiting to happen. He answered from the corner of his mouth. "I read you, Sergeant. Like a book."

"You'd better. Now go tell Smiley and Morbid that we're going to boresight again."

"Again?" Webber's heart dropped.

"What? Did I say it in Korean?"

Of course he hadn't, but he couldn't be serious. Webber had to voice his protest, not just for himself but for the others. "You're doing this because of Hansen. He got lucky. But we'll beat him."

Keyman bared his stained teeth. "We'll beat him if this track is perfect. And we'll show him and everyone else that I shouldn't be his wingman—he should be mine."

"Hey, man, why do we always have to win? To keep you on the fast track for E-7? You really want it that bad?" Everyone knew Keyman was hoping to make sergeant first class in the next round of promotions.

Lowering his voice to more menacing depths, Keyman answered, "Yeah, I do. And you're going to help me. Now move out."

Fuckin' psycho, Webber thought as he dragged himself

under the barrel of the main gun, where the words *Cold Steel* had been stenciled in bold white letters. He resignedly mounted the tank, climbed up on the turret, and stuck his head past the open loader's hatch. "All right, ladies! We're boresighting again. Let's move!"

In the meantime, Keyman was already unpacking the boresight device, a cylindrical tube about a foot long with an eyepiece jutting from one end. The device would be inserted and locked into the main gun's tube. Sadly, while boresighting was an extremely important job and insured that the gun's primary and thermal sights were looking at exactly the same thing, redoing the process would not make it any better.

Corporal Segwon "Smiley" Kim glanced up at Webber from down in the loader's station, his eyes a bit foggy from boredom. He did manage to turn on the dumb-ass smile that had earned him his nickname. "Hey, Webber. What up, dude? We just boresight two hour ago. He wants again?"

Webber took in a deep breath. "Yup. Let's go."

Smiley's trademark grin faded.

Within two minutes the loader was standing at the end of the gun, shivering his ass off and staring into the bright red peep sight, guiding Webber via hand signals to the prearranged point on the panel. "Okay, you on!" Smiley hollered.

At his station, Webber adjusted gun data in the computer. "Okay, ready to do it again."

Outside, Keyman removed the boresight device, spun it 180 degrees, then reinserted and locked it into the tube. Once more, Smiley guided Webber until he was on again. Webber then compared his first set of numbers with the second set and split the difference, entering the result into the fire control computer. Meanwhile, the tank's driver, Morbid, whose real name was Specialist Anthony Morabito, had squeezed in behind Webber to watch. "I have a bad feeling about tonight's run."

"You would."

"No, I mean it. I just had a dream that we lost."

"Go climb back in your hole and have another dream that we win, okay?"

"I can't. We're going to lose. And then he'll go ballistic, and we'll be paying for it."

"Not on my watch."

"I almost want us to lose."

Webber turned and jutted an index finger into Morbid's face. "Don't ever say that around him, do you hear me?"

Morbid nodded vigorously.

"Now go on outside. I'll bet he loosened a Wedge-Bolt just to test you. Go check them out, all right?"

"Yeah, okay. And hey, Webber, man, thanks. Two more months of that bald fucker. That's all I got. Then it's good-bye Keyman, good-bye Korea, and good riddance to both."

"You got that right. And oh, yeah, before you go. Have you thought about that opportunity?"

"Yeah, but I can't risk that kind of money."

"Like I said, there's no risk. You front me the cash. I charge the hundred percent interest, which we split sixty/forty in my favor, of course, because the contacts are all mine."

"I don't know, Webber . . ."

"Come on, bro, where the hell are you going to find a forty percent return on your money? And you'll be helping out a fellow tanker in need. It's all about cash flow, you know? I just took a hundred dollar hit, and I could really use the help. One hand washes the other? I'll keep Keyman off your ass?"

"Jesus H. Christ!" Keyman screamed from outside. "Morbid? Get out here now!"

Webber hoisted his brows.

And Morbid winced. "All right, Webber, you got a deal."

* * *

SECOND LIEUTENANT SUH Jae Sung and the crew of his T-62 medium tank sat behind a berm draped in ice and snow. They were about thirty kilometers north of the DMZ within a central region of the peninsula known by the Americans as the Chorwon Avenue of Approach. They had just completed an alert, and, needing some air, Suh popped his hatch and rose into the cold. He gazed out past the gun tube, reflecting on the moment as a crow squawked overhead.

Suh and his men were part of the NKPA's II Army Corps and part of a mechanized brigade of ten battalions and five companies whose manpower and equipment never ceased to awe the twenty-two-year-old Korean. Three battalions of mechanized infantry included over one thousand men aboard both the BTR-60 and the VTT-323 Armored Personnel Carriers with troop capacities of eleven and thirteen respectively. The BTR-60 was armed with 7.62 mm machine guns, while the VTT-323 had 14.5 mm machine guns and/or an AT-3 antitank guided missile system.

Two battalions of motorized troops numbering over 850 combatants could be moved via a host of Soviet-made trucks, while a dismounted battalion of light infantry stood at over 400.

Suh's own tank battalion was comprised of thirty-one T-62s divided into three companies of ten tanks, with one HQ track. Two tracks within each company were equipped with plows for breaching obstacles. The battalion also had two Type 62 light tanks, eighteen 2.5-ton utility trucks, and one T-34 tank retriever. Over 200 personnel worked on or supported all of those tracks.

Artillery support was the job of two howitzer battalions (122 mm and 152 mm) with eighteen guns in each. Personnel in those battalions also had access to nearly 150 SA-16 shoulder-launched, fire and forget, IR surface-to-air missiles in addition to 6 ZSU 23-2 towed, twin 23 mm antiaircraft machine guns.

And no, the firepower did not end there. A company of six BM-21s provided deadly multiple rocket launcher capability. Each truck was fitted with forty launch tubes arrayed in four rows of ten, and the 122 mm rockets could be launched from the cab or fired remotely from up to forty meters away at a rate of .5 second per projectile. Those rockets could carry smoke or fragmentary, incendiary, and even chemical agents.

Yet another battalion of antiaircraft artillery was ready to roll out with twenty-four ZSU 23-4 self-propelled, quad heavy machine guns whose tracked platforms resembled tanks, along with three SA-7B shoulder-launched IR SAMs.

As their name implied, the brigade's recon company of ten BRDM-2s would, were they to head into battle, spearhead the pack. Three of those reconnaissance vehicles were distinguished by their conical turrets, which mounted 14.5 mm and 7.62 mm machine guns, while the rest had their turrets removed in favor of the ATGM launcher equipped with deadly AT-5 SPANDREL missiles. The BRDM-2s carried crews of two, with a troop capacity for six, and they represented the fangs of the great beast that would penetrate enemy lines.

Of course, the brigade relied upon a company of engineers, a chemical company, and a supply company for its very existence, and Suh, like every other tanker, understood their importance all too well.

As a whole, the brigade was a complex and formidable military unit that boosted the confidence of men like Suh, men who faced an equally formidable enemy.

Once again, as intelligence had indicated, the members of the 1-72 Armor had left their home of Dragon Valley in Camp Casey and had headed off to Rodriguez Range for their external evaluation (EXEVAL) and tank gunnery. The brigade was well north of the range complex, but Suh wished they were much closer. He would like to see for himself how much sharper his enemy was becoming.

Knowing that the Americans were out there training with their KATSUAs, training to kill men like him, made Suh want to burst from his position, roll down to that range, and take on an entire company single-handedly (forget the technicality of breaching the DMZ).

After expressing that to his men, Suh's new driver, Corporal Kang Ho Lim, tried to comfort him by saying that the marijuana-smoking, morally corrupt GIs manning those tanks were incapable of hitting their marks. The nineteen-year-old boy was quite naïve about American tankers and their M1A1 Abrams main battle tank. In fact, Kang had admitted that before he had gone to tank school, he had assumed that the Americans had been issued the M1A2 SEP tank, which was a superior upgrade to the older model, with second-generation forward-looking infrared radar, thermal imagery system, and too many other improvements to remember. Fortunately for Platoon Leader Suh and the two other tanks under his command, the Americans had spread their forces too thinly throughout the world, and the Korean theater was always last on their list to send new equipment.

However, recent intelligence indicated that within eighteen months the Americans might replace their M1A1s with A2s, and that would further tip the technological scales in their favor.

Occasionally, Suh and his crew would debate the prospect of war, and Suh's gunner, Sergeant Yoon Jeong-Seop, considered himself a student of history and often made the argument that they would never invade the south. According to Yoon, the Democratic People's Republic of Korea had already ignored three windows of opportunity for invasion. The first one had opened between 1965 and 1972, when U.S. armed forces were heavily committed to the Vietnam War. And then again, between 1973 and 1981, American military intervention in Korea would have been politically impractical because of postwar pacifism. Finally, from August 1990 through February 1991, the American campaign to liberate Kuwait involved a substantial portion of the U.S.'s ground and air forces. "Any one of those windows would have provided an excellent chance for the DPRK to finally unite the Korean peninsula under one government," said Sergeant Yoon.

On the other hand, Suh believed that a new window had opened during the past decade, one that their dear leader in Pyongyang would not ignore. The U.S.'s war in Afghanistan and Iraq, coupled with its war on terrorism, had placed a considerable burden on the country and its resources. While the world's attention continued to be focused on nations of the Middle East, North Korea's dear leader in Pyongyang would seize the chance to act. Suh had felt certain of that, and his suspicions were confirmed by the many alerts that had been called during the past week. Rumors indicated that the U.S. was accusing their dear leader of selling nuclear weapons to a fundamentalist group in Syria. While the dear leader denied the claim, Suh believed such a sale had occurred, and now, if the dear leader waited too long to act, the U.S. would divert forces to the region and invade, just as they had in Iraq.

Indeed, the window was wide open.

"So-wi," called the loader, Private First Class Bae Jung Hun. "The soup is ready."

"Ah, yes, *Il-byong Bae*. It smells excellent." Suh lowered himself down, inside the tank.

The young man smiled and offered Suh a small bowl. *"So-wi,* I am concerned about my family."

"Concentrate on your job. On our mission."

"I will. But it is difficult. I have been thinking about our conversation this morning."

"The United States will never use nuclear weapons against us."

"I know, *So-wi*. I am not worried about them. I am worried about the dear leader. Do you think—"

"I don't know, *Il-byong*. He has lost the support of China. It seems the Chinese are more worried about their economy than their border. So he is alone. And he may choose to use all weapons at his disposal."

"But if he uses them here, we will die from radiation poisoning. They say the tank will protect us. But I do not believe them."

"Trust me, *Il-byong*. If we are going to die, it will not be at the hands of poison. We will go up in a great fire, taking the enemy with us."

"Yes, *So-wi*."

Suh set down his soup, removed one of his gloves, then felt his icy nose. "It's getting even colder outside."

"Yes, *So-wi*. It is very cold."

AS THE SIXTY-EIGHT-TON behemoth known as *Cold Steel* hurtled down the course road, Webber's thermal sight was right on the money, and his ammo indicator light showed HEAT—a high-explosive antitank round. He had already spotted the plywood target, an enemy armored personnel carrier, before Keyman had opened his trap.

"Two PCs. Stationary PC!"

"Identified!" Webber pressed the thumb buttons on his Cadillacs, and the range appeared in his sight: 1,350 meters.

That data was transferred directly to the tank's fire control computer, which also automatically accounted for the lead angle measurement, the wind velocity and direction measured by a sensor on the turret's roof, and the data from the pendulum static cant sensor located at the center of the turret roof. That little fire control computer was a pretty amazing device, but Webber still had to manually input data on the ammo type, as well as the temperature and barometric pressure before the main gun would be ready for engagement.

And *Cold Steel* was ready to engage, all right.

"Up!" yelled Smiley.

"Fire!"

"On the way!" Webber squeezed the trigger.

Boom! The HEAT round screamed away through the night. Were they using the actual go-to-war service round, an impact sensor would connect with the target, igniting an explosive that melted surrounding copper while a shape charge concentrated the molten metal and hot gases into a narrow blast that would cut through armor. However, since it was only a training round, a large concrete-filled cylinder struck the plywood target, leaving a clear hole in the wood.

A large dust cloud appeared in the greenish glow of Webber's thermal sight, a cloud that quickly dissipated, providing the necessary confirmation.

"Target," confirmed Keyman. "Moving PC."

Webber quickly acquired the next target, glowing bright in the thermals. "Identified."

"Fire!"

"On the way."

The tank rocked. Another concussion. Another dust cloud. Another kill.

"Target!" Keyman repeated. "Cease fire! Troops!"

Webber swung his sight and spotted the single set of plastic targets that was supposed to be a squad of advancing troops. "Identified!" Never taking his gaze from the sight, he switched the firing controls to the coax, a 7.62 mm M240 machine gun mounted in-line or coaxially with the main gun.

"Fire!"

"On the way!" Gritting his teeth, Webber cut loose a killing burst, firing in a Z pattern and dipping into the 4,000 rounds of ammo stored in the gun's huge bin. His targets dropped before he had time to take another breath.

"Target! Target! Cease fire! Cease fire!" Keyman ordered. "Charlie Niner Two, this is Red Two. Engaged and destroyed two BMPs and one set of troops. Continuing to attack, over."

"Red Two, this is Charlie Niner Two," responded Zorn. "Occupy Firing Point 2 and report when set."

"Roger, Six."

With three out of four night engagements completed, and Webber feeling certain they had earned all three hundred points, Top Tank should be in the bag. Just one more engagement to go, and that would undoubtedly take place on the course road between Battle Position 2 and Battle Position 3, about twenty meters north of Phase Line Charlie.

Part of Webber wanted them to win so they would maintain their reputation as the company's top tank; yet another part wanted to see Keyman get bested by a rookie lieutenant. The staff sergeant needed to learn humility, and such a defeat would either humble him or harden him even more, if that were possible.

"Driver, stop!"

Morbid abruptly hit the brakes at the point on the course marked Firing Point 2, and Webber banged his forehead on the eyepiece. "Jesus . . ."

Keyman went on unfazed, lest he betray Morbid's heavy foot. "Charlie Niner Two, this is Red Two. We are set at Firing Point 2. REDCON-1. Over."

"Red Two, this is Charlie Niner Two. Your gunner is dead. Prepare for three-man operation and report when REDCON-1."

Webber set his hands on his hips and smiled. Time for the TC engagement, wherein Keyman would do most of the work. From his station, the staff sergeant would identify targets through the TC's extension, seeing the exact same things Webber would see through his sight; then he would fire the main gun from his station.

"Loader? Battlecarry sabot," Keyman barked, ordering Smiley to load the main gun. Next, Keyman got a crew report from all but Webber, sitting quietly in the gunner's seat as a simulated casualty.

"Charlie Niner Two, this is Red Two. We are prepared for three-man operation, over."

"Roger, Two. Scouts report enemy armor in your sector. Attack to Firing Point 3. Engage and report, out."

"Driver, move out!" Morbid throttled the tank forward, rapidly accelerating down the course road. As the turbine engine settled into gear, he eased back slightly, and the tank became a steady firing platform, primed for the kill.

All right, Keyman, Webber thought. *It's all sitting on your shoulders now—just like it should be. You want this more than any of us, so go get it, if you can.*

But for the sound of the engine and the telltale sound of the moving track, a tense silence followed as Keyman scanned for targets. Five seconds. Ten—

There it was: a plywood tank rising steadily from the target pit. It locked into position before beginning its slow trek down the tracks, giving the impression of a moving tank with its flank exposed.

"Load sabot!"

Smiley got to work, then called out, "Up!"

"On the way."

Muffled thunder rocked the turret, and Webber peered through his thermal sight, realizing in disbelief that the penetrator had landed well in front of the target.

"Short!" Keyman said, stunned himself.

There were only two things that could have happened: the proper ammo setting was not selected, or Keyman had received a bad distance to the target with the laser range finder. The ammo indicator light glowed for sabot. It wasn't that. It had to be the range.

Webber looked back inside the sight, and the range showed 1,240 meters. Meanwhile, Keyman realigned the reticle on the target and squeezed the button. He got a reading of 1,380 meters. Since they were moving, his first reading had the target almost 200 meters closer—a bad lase.

Smiley loaded another round, but he remained silent.

Keyman was quick to adjust to the problem. "Loader?"

"Up!"

"On the way!"

Boom! Keyman's round drilled the tank. The aft cap clanged to the floor. "Target! Cease fire."

With machinelike precision Keyman had destroyed the enemy, but not before destroying his own chance of achieving a perfect score. That was unfortunate for him but more unfortunate for Webber and the rest of the crew.

"Charlie Niner Two, this is Red Two. Engaged and destroyed one T-72. Continuing mission, over."

"Roger that, Red Two. At this time, clear all weapons systems and report back to this station."

NO ONE SAID a word as they left the range and returned to the ammo pad. And even there, Keyman only gave the necessary orders, ignoring Webber's attempt at small talk regarding the platoon sergeant's run, which they had just monitored over the radio.

By the time they reached the motor pool, Webber had grown quite used to the silence and was even enjoying it. He shut down everything at his station and dismounted to find Smiley, Morbid, and Keyman waiting for him on the packed snow.

Then Keyman suddenly blurted out, "Before we go in the tent, I just want—" He broke off, staring at the snow.

Morbid glanced to Smiley, who in turn glanced to Webber. "What do you want, Sergeant?" Webber asked.

"You know what . . ."

Webber gripped his chest and shivered violently. "Sergeant? Can we get to the point?"

"We'll get there when I say we'll get there!"

"We might die of exposure first," Webber mumbled.

Keyman stepped forward, tipped his head, and got directly into Webber's face. "You wanted this to happen, didn't you?" He shifted down the line to Smiley. "And you? You're loving this, too."

About a half-dozen meters behind them, Jackson and Zorn were hustling down the path, heading back toward the debriefing tent. Although Keyman did not see them, Webber did, and he noticed how Jackson paused a moment to listen to Keyman's screaming before rejoining Zorn.

"I say again. You're loving this, aren't you?"

As Smiley struggled to find words, Webber dragged his arm beneath his runny nose, then said, "Sergeant, are you trying to apologize?"

Keyman stood there, seething a moment, the air jetting from his nostrils like the 1-72's mascot: a fire-breathing dragon. "You think this is funny, Webber?"

"No, Sergeant. Not funny."

"Oh, really? Then what is it?"

Webber smirked, then slowly shook his head. "Nah. I won't even go there."

"You people need to get your priorities straight, you know that? You people don't understand how important this is. You don't get it at all. Move out!"

Webber fell in behind Keyman as they marched their sorry and frozen asses to the debriefing tent.

There, they met up with Lieutenant Hansen, who, along with Abbot, offered congratulations. Keyman took Abbot's hand, but when Hansen proffered his, the sergeant only nodded and uttered a curt, "Lieutenant."

Some platoon leaders would have taken great offense, but not Hansen. The guy just returned the nod and said, "Excellent job out there."

The review began, and Keyman listened quietly as Zorn and Jackson went over the first three engagements, complimenting each member of the crew for a job well done. Then Jackson asked, "So what happened during the fourth engagement?"

Keyman hesitated, drew his lips together, then scratched his glistening head. "Bad range. I could have sworn I had a good lay on the target when I lased to it." Keyman leered at Webber and the others. "I could have sworn it."

Jackson nodded. "So you just got a bad range in the computer?"

"It would seem so."

"I would have reminded him that the engagement standards call for the target to be between fourteen hundred and sixteen hundred meters, but I was dead," Webber pointed out, winking at Morbid and Smiley.

That ignited Keyman's glare.

"Well, the missed shot cost you four points," said Jackson. "Still a good engagement—but not perfect."

"I figured. But we're going to work on that. I can assure you that will *never* happen again."

"Look, Keyman. I'm going to say something, and it's going to remain inside this tent," Jackson began. "We all know you're disappointed. And you're a man. You can deal with it. But don't take it out on your crew. Enough said?"

Keyman echoed through his teeth, "Enough said."

"Now then, you've earned a 996, which up to this point is the highest score in the company. Congratulations."

Keyman could not have looked more disappointed. "Thank you."

Shit, thought Webber. *He's going to be on the rag for months.*

Once again, Hansen and Abbot went around to offer their pats on the back, and Webber was keen on watching Hansen confront Keyman once more.

"You're going to be tough to beat," Hansen said, thrusting out his hand in an exaggerated offer to shake.

For once Webber watched Keyman get intimidated as

he took the lieutenant's hand and said, "Actually, sir, I was hoping to be impossible to beat."

"I know you were. But I wouldn't complain. I'd take your score any day of the week."

"I guess so, sir."

Hansen frowned. "Staff Sergeant Key, why don't you and I sit down and finally—"

"Damn," Abbot said, stepping between the men. "You boys got attitude. Too bad you don't got dicks to match. You Hansen?" Abbot raised his hand, holding his thumb and forefinger about an inch apart. "See that? That's about the size of your main gun barrel." Then he turned to Keyman. "And you?" The platoon sergeant brought his fingers even closer together.

"Yeah, well, I hear you got trouble elevating your gun," Keyman told the older man.

"Hey, now. It just takes a little extra lube grease—"

"And a whole lot of Viagra," Hansen finished, grabbing his crotch and grinning.

"Yeah, but we don't grow 'em small in Texas," Abbot boasted. "So are we okay here?"

Hansen looked to Keyman, who turned to Webber. "Yeah, whatever. Hey, Webber, let's go get some chow."

"I'm not hungry."

"Then be back at the tank by twenty-one thirty." With that, Keyman marched toward the exit, where Smiley and Morbid were waiting.

"You're dismissed," Hansen called after him.

Keyman fired back a halfhearted salute.

"From what I've seen, he's not the type to make mistakes like that," Hansen said, watching Keyman leave.

"No, LT, he's not," said Webber.

"What's up with him?"

"I don't know. Past couple of months he hasn't been sleeping real good. Wakes up a lot. Says he has dreams."

"About what?"

"About you, sir."

"Excuse me?"

"Let's pray they ain't wet dreams," Abbot said.

Under the heat of Hansen's gaze, Webber could only shrug. "I don't know anything else, sir."

"Well, thanks for that, Sergeant. Will you keep an eye on him for us?"

"No problem, sir."

CHAPTER
THREE

"TANK!" HANSEN CRIED.

"Identified!"

"Up!"

"Fire!"

"On the way!"

The gun's reverberation worked into Hansen's arms as the sabot screamed away from the tank like a javelin thrown by God. Almost instantly a hole appeared in the plywood tank, and the penetrator burrowed into the mound of earth and snow behind it. "Target! Cease fire!"

"Now that's what I'm talking about," said Gatch. "That's *exactly* what I'm talking about!"

After taking a few seconds to catch his breath, Hansen keyed his mike. "Charlie Niner Two, this is Red One. Engaged and destroyed one T-55, continuing to attack, over."

"Red One, this is Charlie Niner Two. Move to Firing Point 2, battlecarry HEAT, and report when set."

Hansen needed to ensure his tank was at the designated

point on the course road before beginning the next engagement, which again would be on the offensive.

He took a deep breath. This was it! He called down to Deac. "Loader? Battlecarry HEAT."

In just a few seconds, Hansen's order was filled: "HEAT loaded, loader ready."

Hansen received a crew report, then once they were in position, he informed Charlie Niner Two that they were REDCON-1.

"Red One, this is Charlie Niner Two. Scouts report enemy light armor with troop support in sector. Attack to Phase Line Delta. Engage and report."

"Roger, Charlie Niner Two. Attacking to Phase Line Delta, out."

To tankers everywhere that call meant that Hansen and his men would be facing one PC and two squads of infantry. Instead of throwing the TC engagement at him last, as they had for Keyman, they had moved it up first. Hansen wondered if Jackson and Zorn had deliberately chosen that order. Were they trying to downplay his success?

Or was he just being paranoid and overreacting to the situation? The latter was probably true.

Tensing, Hansen probed the windswept hills with his thermal sight as they reached a sharp curve in the course road, heading toward their next firing point. Gatch hit a patch of ice, and the tank began to slide right. "Driver?"

"I got it!"

The M1A1's engine roared as Gatch increased throttle while turning hard to point them forward. If he wasn't careful, snow and dirt might build up between the track and the sprocket, causing him to throw a track, but Hansen felt confident that Mr. NASCAR would pull them through. Although Gatch had chosen to join the Army instead of doing time for assault and battery, he loved military service, had reenlisted for another six years, and was, for the most part, squared away. He even boasted that after five years as a tank driver, the only thing he had ever thrown was *up* after a long night of drinking.

Gunning the engine once more, Gatch did, in fact, get them past the ice and onto a level stretch of dirty snow crisscrossed by dozens of shallow track trenches.

Though Hansen could not explain it, his neck began to tingle, and suddenly—before they reached the firing point—a stationary personnel carrier emerged from behind a small berm about a thousand meters out.

Hansen was a half second away from giving his fire command when he saw troop targets shoot up, just five hundred meters out. "PC and troops. PC first!"

"Identified!"

"Up!"

"Fire!"

"On they way!"

The stationary PC took a direct hit, tossing up a temporary wall of dirt and debris.

"Target! Cease fire! Traverse left! Near troops."

"Identified!"

"Fire!"

Lee put the coax to work, letting loose a steady stream of 7.62 mm ball and tracer ammunition. The tracers created an eerie stream of red, laserlike glow that pierced the plastic soldiers, turning them into Swiss cheese before dropping them flat. Two targets down.

Beating a fist into his palm, Hansen mouthed a silent *Yeah!* then screamed, "Target!"

"Identified far troops." Lee hollered over Hansen's confirmation.

"Fire!" ordered Hansen, having been caught off guard by the sudden appearance of the second set of troop targets. He had been thinking too much in pairs. He shouldn't have made that mistake. At least Lee hadn't, and it seemed the gunner was about to save their asses.

Indeed he did by releasing quick thunder and even quicker death to the simulated infantrymen.

"Target! Cease fire! Check your work."

Taking nothing for granted, Hansen probed the sector for another minute until he felt confident they had eliminated all targets. "Charlie Niner Two, this is Red One. Engaged and destroyed one enemy PC and two infantry squads. Continuing to attack, over."

"Red One, this is Charlie Niner Two. Good job. Clear all weapons systems and report when clear."

With a weary grin, Hansen issued the routine order, then cleared his throat and gathered his thoughts. "Gentlemen, no matter what happens when we get back, you have to admit that everyone here is already a wiener."

"Wieners, yeah. But it'd still be nice to win," said Deac.

"Yeah, it would," added Gatch.

Hansen continued: "A TC's only as good as his crew, and you did me proud. Now I know you were all bummed knowing this was my first gunnery. But you hung in there and trusted this butterbar from West Point. Hooah! Good for you!"

"Hooah, LT!" Deac boomed. "Hooah!"

"Thanks, Deac. And Lee? You da man, tonight!"

"Thank you, sir. This gunnery was the most enjoyable of my career."

"Glad you liked it. I know I did."

"Somewhere up in Heaven, good ole Dale Earnhardt is smiling down on us," said Gatch.

"And speaking of Heaven, I want to offer up a little prayer," Deac said. "Lord Jesus, y'all know that what we've done here tonight we've done for your glory."

"Praise you, Jesus!" Gatch cried, hamming it up.

"Shuddup, Gatch," snapped Deac. "Lord, we thank you for allowing us to blow the shit out of the enemy. And we thank you in advance for letting us be Top Tank."

"All right, amen, amen," Hansen said. "Deac? You'd best

forget that career as a minister. Gatch? Well, I'm not a deeply religious man, but you make fun of God, and someday he'll make fun of you."

"LT? I'm five foot six, standing on my toes. God already beat me to the punch."

WEBBER GLANCED OVER at Keyman, who had been listening to Hansen's run over the aux-a radio monitor. "What do you think?"

"I think he's got us. I think he smoked that engagement."

"No way."

Keyman sighed heavily in disgust. "You'll see. We lost Top Tank to fucking Biff, the butterbar from West Point."

"He's good."

"No, he's not. Not really. Do you know anything about how assignments get picked at West Point?"

Webber shook his head.

"Well, I do. The guys with the best GPAs get to pick first, and nobody wants Korea. So by the time they got down to Hansen, all the good places were already gone, and he got stuck coming here. He might've gone to West Point, but he was probably near the bottom of his graduating class."

"But he still went to West Point. So, you going over there?"

"You kidding?"

"You want me to check the reticle again?"

"Fuck you, Webber."

"Hey, if the shit ever hits the fan, we'll be kicking ass and taking names. Not those guys. Us."

Keyman's expression widened in surprise. "What are you trying to do? Cheer me up?"

Webber grinned crookedly. "Nah. Just softening you for the blow."

"I thought so. Asshole."

* * *

AT THE DEBRIEF, Hansen's eyes burned and his heart was in his throat. He had barely heard Sergeant First Class Zorn announce that the crew of Red One, operating aboard the tank *Crimson Death,* had just scored a perfect 1,000 points. Perhaps the lack of sleep, the countless hours of preparation, and the adrenaline rush had taken their toll, because Hansen found himself strangely removed from the moment, as though it were happening to someone else.

Captain Van Buren and First Sergeant Westman were there to congratulate him. Better still, the First Tank Battalion commander, Lieutenant Colonel Michael Thomas Burroway, and battalion Command Sergeant Major Willard Alton were also present to offer their congratulations to the newest Top Tank in the battalion. For Hansen, it was a rare occasion to speak one on one with them.

Alton, a rugged-faced black man with a sharp jaw and an aversion to long sentences, was nearing forty and had left his sense of humor back in Kuwait, according to those who knew him well. "Good job, Lieutenant." The Command Sergeant Major's handshake was rock solid.

"So, you're the famous Lieutenant Jack Hansen." Lieutenant Colonel Burroway stepped over and gave Hansen the once-over as he stood at attention. The commander had a stare that, like Superman's, could light a candle, and his graying crew cut did nothing to hide his missing left earlobe, which, according to legend, was still buried in the sands of Iraq. "They said you were a good-looking kid."

Hansen blushed.

Burroway smiled. "They lied." Suddenly, he slapped Hansen on the back. "Congratulations, Lieutenant. You've earned it." Then he took Hansen's hand and gave him the hardest handshake he had ever felt.

Moments later, Hansen stood outside the tent, being jabbed and slapped by so many people that he thought he might tumble into the snow. But he didn't. And he thanked the well-wishers, shook hands, smiled, and didn't even feel the cold. At one point, Deac and Gatch tried to hoist him onto their shoulders, but he shoved them away.

Lee suggested that they return to Ajima's for some "munchies" (Gatch had taught him the word) and celebratory drinks of coffee, though they all wished they could have some real booze, but drinking in the field was a big, bozo no-no.

Inside Ajima's drafty tent, Deac told the old woman that they had won Top Tank. Ajima bared her remaining teeth and cried, "Fuckin' A!"

After they received their cups of steaming lifer juice, Deac raised his Styrofoam cup in a toast. "To the best god-damned tank crew in the world—us!"

Hansen was still in his blur as he took a tentative sip on his mud and let the warmth spread through his icy chest.

Keyman ducked abruptly into the tent, and Hansen realized only then that his wingman had not attended the review. Webber, Morbid, and Smiley brought up the rear.

Without a word, the staff sergeant marched right up to Hansen, thrust out his hand, and said tersely, "Congratulations, sir."

"Thank you." Hansen winced under Keyman's grip, though it still wasn't as powerful as Burroway's.

"You're lucky to have a gunner like Sergeant Lee."

"Yes, I am."

Although he hadn't said it, the implication was clear: Keyman thought Lee's quick thinking had won them Top Tank—not Hansen's.

"Well, I guess our platoon is in good shape," Keyman said, releasing his hand. "Providing our enemy is an independent force of plywood tanks and plastic troops who don't shoot back."

There he was again, trying to downplay the gunnery.

"You're definitely right," Hansen answered. "We are in good shape."

"Hey, Keyman, our coffee was supposed to be on you," said Gatch. "But you can buy us our refills."

Keyman cocked a brow, made Gatch shrink a little with his gaze.

"No, refills are on me," Hansen said, then dropped his voice to pose a challenge to Keyman. "Sergeant, get yourself a cup of joe and some for your men. My treat."

Keyman's gaze tightened, as though deciding if the peace offering was genuine or not. "Thank you, sir. But we have a lot of work to do. Good evening." With that, he waved his people out of the tent.

But no one followed, and the second Keyman was gone, Webber glanced to Smiley and Morbid, then shook his head. "We're off duty. And we're staying for coffee."

Hansen nodded at Webber. "Consider that an order."

"I think we're making a big mistake," groaned Morbid. Smiley smiled.

"I'll go back and get him," Webber said, cocking a thumb over his shoulder. "Keyman's a sore loser, but he'll get over it. And the getting should start now. I'll be right back."

A few minutes later, Webber returned sans the staff sergeant.

"What happened?" Hansen asked.

"I couldn't find him. Went all the way up the trail. It was like he just disappeared."

AFTER COMPLETING HIS own four night engagements and earning a grand total of 992 points for the gunnery, Sergeant First Class Matthew Abbot had attended Hansen's, Keyman's, and Neech's reviews. All four crews had scored over 900 points, garnering them distinguished ratings, or in the lieutenant's case, the highly coveted Top Tank. Although he had not checked the scores from the other companies, Abbot felt comfortable that no other platoon in First Tank would outshoot his. The Top Tank Platoon award was almost as highly regarded as the Top Tank award, at least for a platoon leader and platoon sergeant. With Red's gunnery complete, Abbot intended to spend a few more hours in the tower, watching Blue and White Platoons make their runs. Often referred to as a tanker's tanker, Abbot loved armor so much that he sometimes felt like eating a tank for breakfast. Was he nuts? Nuts enough to be doing the job for nearly two decades. He had seen the good, the bad, and the ugly, and nothing had made him quit.

But he had come close. During the first Gulf War he had been a tank driver, and his platoon had been part of an operation to assault an Iraqi stronghold held by a battalion. The attack had unfolded brilliantly, with howitzers sending almost three hundred 155 mm high-explosive shells to soften up the target before they went in. That kind of firepower could've leveled an entire city block. Every time Abbot remembered that night, the artillery and the radio transmissions still rang in his ears:

"Driver, orient the tank west to cover the exposed flank until the other two platoons arrive."

"Roger that."

"I see dismounts. Maybe twenty. One thousand meters."

"Aim the coax forty-five left. Fire in the air."

"Roger. Firing!"

"They're returning fire! Possible shoulder-launched weapon coming to bear!"

"Gunner, coax troops!"

Staring grimly at his night sight display, Abbot had borne witness to the massacre of "enemy" troops.

Damn, he still found the incident hard to comprehend, even after so many years had passed. Their intelligence regarding the stronghold had been completely inaccurate. The target had already been captured by American forces. And not only had he and his crew attacked American forces, but the CO had actually forgotten about an entire platoon, whom he had left sitting in the rear, doing nothing. Among the dead was Charles "Chuck" Hamilton, Abbot's childhood friend, his very best friend, the kid who had persuaded him to join the Army in the first place.

Nowadays, Abbot always kept one hand on the TC override at his station. No gunner under his command would ever have a chance to get trigger happy while calling his own targets. And while Abbot had not literally pulled the trigger ending his buddy's life, he felt no less responsible. He spoke of the incident to no one save for his wife, but even then it had taken over a decade of marriage before she had pried open his heart and had helped him deal with the guilt and the nightmares.

On his way to the tower, Abbot saw a lone man seated in the meager grandstand that had been erected for visiting VIPs who, of course, only observed gunneries during the more pleasant summer months. Tugging up his collar against the frigid wind, Abbot broke off the path and headed over, realizing as he drew closer that the idiot freezing his ass off in the bleachers was none other than Keyman. The staff sergeant was leaning forward, his hands tucked firmly under his arms. He craned his head at Abbot's approach, then averted his gaze and spat a milky brown ball of saliva.

After booting off some snow from the bench, Abbot took a seat beside the long-faced tank commander. Together, they watched the first track from White Platoon roll out onto the range. "See old Swindle out there? That son of a bitch has been doing it a lot longer than you, and he won't get no nine ninety-six."

Keyman spat again and started rocking himself against the cold.

"You're going to get sick out here. *I'm* going to get sick out here."

"Then leave."

"Where's your crew?"

"Sippin' java with the enemy."

"The enemy? Look out there, buddy. Out past the range, past those hills. There's your enemy."

"If you say so."

"I don't get you, man. I really don't. Hansen's still got a lot to learn, but he's got the right attitude."

"You saying I don't? Look, I just lost fuckin' Top Tank, all right? I came out here to just—"

"What?"

"Nothing." Keyman rose, brushed off his snow-covered ass, then shuddered. "Fuckin' cold . . ." He took a step forward, hesitated. "Look, pops, I'm . . . sorry. Okay? I appreciate your concern."

"No, you don't. But maybe someday you will."

LATER ON, AFTER Abbot had received his fill of watching main battle tanks breathe fire and glowing lead across the landscape, he decided to hump back to his own beast to put the remainder of his gear away and ensure the vehicle was secured in the motor pool. He would then head over to the barracks to rack out. Along the way, he met up with Keyman's gunner, Sergeant Webber, who was seated on a can of some sort and watching Lieutenant Colonel Burroway's tank, *Hedda Hopper 2,* head off to the range. The commander's tank name always started with an *H* for Headquarters Company and was named *Hedda Hopper* in the 1950s after the then-famous gossip columnist/actress paid a visit to the members of First Tank during a USO tour. Through the years, the tradition was carried on by many commanders, with the M1 dubbed the *Hedda Hopper 2.*

Usually, the battalion commander was first during gunnery, but there had been a malfunction during the colonel's qualification run, and he was off now to fire an alibi engagement. It was obvious to the unbiased evaluators that, though all crews were equal when it came to Tank Table VIII evaluations, some were more equal than others, and there was no way the battalion commander, Crusader Six, could bolo an engagement. It just wouldn't look right, and Zorn would make sure that didn't happen.

Abbot watched the tank a moment more, then shifted closer to Webber. "Hey, why aren't you back in the barracks, sleeping? Is Keyman farting again?"

"I'm sure he is. And you know something? I was a little surprised that he just took off for a while, came back, then went right to sleep. I thought he'd scream at us some more. Kind of weird, if you ask me."

"Yeah, he's a weird guy. And let me tell you, he gets away with a lot of shit around here because he's so damned good. Word to the wise: don't ever be like him."

"Fuck no, Sergeant."

"So what're you doing out here? Don't tell me you came to watch the colonel's run?"

"Matter of fact I did. The gunner on that track, Brophy? That fuck owes me a hundred bucks."

"So?"

Before Webber could answer, a round boomed from *Hedda Hopper 2,* echoing across the hills.

As Abbot flicked his gaze in the tank's direction, an eighteen-foot-long sheet of flame erupted from the end of the gun tube. "Ho-lee shit . . ."

Webber nodded approvingly as the flames died and smoke rose from the colonel's gun tube. "See that, Sergeant? I just collected my debt—with interest." The gunner rose from his seat, a now-empty can of lube grease. "Have a good night."

Abbot's jaw fell open. It was bad enough that a man

from his own platoon had just pulled off a stunt like that. And it was even worse that the prank had been perpetrated against the battalion commander's track.

But what made Abbot feel absolutely horrible was that he, the platoon's mentor, the man who was supposed to set an example, had taught Webber the trick of packing the main gun tube with lube grease and watching the fireworks show.

"Yup," Abbot muttered to himself as he shuffled off. "I'm going straight to hell."

A COUPLE OF days later, after completing the drill of clearing the range and cleaning all of the facilities, Hansen and the rest of the 1st Battalion, 72nd Armor left the training center. They headed south about eighteen kilometers to their home in Dragon Valley, located on the west side of Camp Casey and at the base of Mount Soyo. Technically, they lived apart from the rest of the camp, and that seclusion afforded them a strong sense of community and esprit de corps. Hansen had heard that First Tank was a close-knit bunch that worked hard and played hard, and he had felt humbled and honored to become a part of their family.

While the camp was among the forty-two whose soldiers received Hardship Duty Pay, Hansen considered life in the valley to be pretty decent, taking into account the hellish weather and terrain. They had their own full-service laundry, barbershop, and shoppette, as well as the requisite PX, a chapel, and the famous Chaplain's Coffee House, where soldiers from all five companies watched movies, admired the collection of signed sports memorabilia, or drank coffee and just hung out. At the First Tank KATUSA Canteen, U.S. and KATUSA soldiers alike could purchase freshly made Korean food. For a taste of home, they could trek across the camp and get Burger King, Taco Bell, Baskin-Robbins, or some Popeye's Chicken, which they

usually did on Sundays. Neech's loader, Private First Class
Choi Sang-ku, was a fried chicken maniac whom everyone
called Popeye Choi. He joked that colonels were only good
at making war, not chicken.

The old Quonset hut hooches where soldiers used to
live had been replaced years ago by three- and four-story
barracks. The billets within were split three enlisted to a
room, two sergeants or staff sergeants to a room, and one
E-7 sergeant first class to a room. No hooch would be complete without a day room, where guys played pool or
sacked out in front of the big-screen TV to watch DVDs or
AFKN for English-language programming. They could
also drop a few bucks at the snack bar to buy microwav-
ables if they were sick of mess hall food or too tired to go
downrange to the strip in Tongduch'on to get something
different. For the barracks rats who rarely left their rooms,
the KATUSA Canteen delivered OB beer with just one
phone call. The limit of alcohol in a room stood at one six-
pack per man—a rule that was *severely* ignored by tankers.

If Hansen could change anything about the living
arrangements, he would have preferred to billet with his
men, instead of living in The Lieutenants' Hooch on the
other side of the valley. It had nothing to do with the fact
that battalion lieutenants were paired together in rooms the
size of average American master bedrooms. His fellow officers would call him insane, but he hated the separation
because it undermined his mission to be considered a regular tanker by his men.

Then again, he imagined that Deac and Gatch must live
like total slobs, and being near those party animals might
prove annoying, if not disgusting. Hansen's own roommate, Second Lieutenant Gary Gutterson, twenty-three,
freshly commissioned, and in country just one month, was
about the most obsessive-compulsive individual Hansen
had ever encountered. Gutterson, a lean, dark-haired bird
of a man, not only had to have everything in its place, but

every time he returned to the room, he made an inspection. Hansen caught on to that pretty quickly and began fucking with the guy by moving Gutterson's toothbrush, shifting his boots, hiding a pair of socks, and so on. The green lieutenant always asked, "Did you move this?" And Hansen kept his poker face. "Nope."

Two days had passed since the gunnery, and Hansen was finally going to Tongduch'on to meet up with his girlfriend, Karen Berlin, a woman who taught English to Koreans in the travel and tourism industries. He was seated on his rack, tying his shoes, while Gutterson lay in his rack, reading one of two Army manuals, TM 9-2350-264-10-1 and -2, nicknamed the dash tens. All maintenance on the Abrams was done in accordance with them, and, barring serious malfunction, all maintenance was performed by tank crews. For every hour they spent running the tank, they probably spent eight hours on maintenance.

Surely Gutterson had read the manuals many times before and was just scanning to satisfy yet another compulsion. "Come on, Gary. There are some pretty good clubs in TDC. You can meet up with the guys and have a good time."

"Jack, the war may be tomorrow. Are you going to be ready?"

"If the war is tomorrow, I'll be glad I went out tonight!"

"You really like it here?"

"All right, the weather sucks. But come on. It's not that bad."

"For you. Because you're Top Tank and have a girlfriend."

"Well, that helps, but I'm not one of those guys who starts counting the days until his tour's up."

"I'm not counting the days."

"I saw your planner."

"Hey, a little privacy, okay?"

"All right. But you can't keep putting up this wall between yourself and your men. You have to party with them. They'll respect you for it. So, are you coming?"

Gutterson consulted his watch. "It's twenty-one ten."

"Right. The party hasn't even started."

"I'm sorry, Jack."

Hansen shrugged, crossed to the door. "Don't wait up."

Gutterson forced a grin, then returned to his manual.

As he left, Hansen couldn't help but feel badly for Gutterson. The guy was trying to live up to some fantasy of a tank commander, and in doing so, might alienate his crew. Hansen thought he would have a word with Abbot, who in turn might speak with Gutterson's platoon sergeant.

For the time being, though, Gutterson wasn't Hansen's problem. He needed to focus on his present mission: deploying his ass to the Flower House, a local hotel, where he and Ms. Karen Berlin would advance breathlessly past Phase Line Foreplay and into the trigger zone.

Like Korea? Hell, he loved it.

CHAPTER
FOUR

SPECIALIST RICK GATCH had been in country for eighteen months. When Lieutenant Hansen had asked why he had volunteered for a second year in hell, Gatch replied, "This ain't hell, sir. Hell's when you run out of liquor, or when the condom breaks. This? Shit . . ."

Still, two years in Korea was a serious commitment. Was Gatch trying to earn more scars to compensate for his height and criminal record? Leave that question to the shrinks. He just wanted bragging rights, liked roaring around in tanks, and couldn't see himself wearing a tie and sitting in some cubicle like a zombie while listening to some self-important asshole in a cheap suit talk about monthly sales goals like they were as important as brain surgery or childbirth. Or war.

Gatch had issues with the uncivilized civilian world.

So he was a lifer. Some guys were born to shovel shit, and some guys were destined to blow it up. You had to listen to fate. You didn't want to break fate's balls by wasting time with other crap. If you knew you were a tanker or a

NASCAR driver, then do it. Just like Gatch had. Just like Dale Earnhardt had. You don't fuck around.

Presently, fate was telling Gatch that he needed to get downrange, get drunk, and get to bumping uglies with some bar girl, but the evening's plans weren't working out as expected.

"You believe that shit? We're supposed to be a tank platoon. Leave it to Keyman to be an asshole about everything." Gatch leaned back on his rack, pillowing his head in his hands. "I'm telling you, Deac, I wouldn't last more than five minutes on his track."

"I don't know why you're surprised," said a shirtless Deac, who was splashing Brut cologne over his gargantuan shoulders and thick neck.

"Dude, you smell like a three-dollar whore."

Deac tossed the green bottle at Gatch, who caught it, but not before getting doused on the cheek. "Hey, if she's three bucks, I can put up with a little cheap perfume."

Gatch tossed back the bottle. "It won't be the same without Smiley."

"No, it won't."

Deac and Gatch shared a room with Keyman's loader, who usually partied with them. But Keyman had warned Smiley to stick with his crew, and a few minutes ago, the South Korean had left the billet to go downrange with Webber, Morbid, and Mr. Asshole himself, saying he was sorry that he couldn't join Deac and Gatch because "Keyman hates Lieutenant."

"I just love watching that little shit get drunk," said Deac. "He's so proper. But you get a kettle or two in him, and it's all over."

"Kettles" were a mixture of punch or juice and a bitter-tasting Korean liquor called *soju*, which had no smell and was distilled from rice, barley, and sweet potatoes. When he had first come to Korea, Gatch had gone for the cheap drunk, only to discover that in the morning, there was a midget inside his skull, trying to carve his way out with a butter knife. Gatch had never felt a headache as severe. During his next trip downrange, he went back to the vendor and hollered at the guy, who just flashed his yellow teeth and chuckled.

With his watch now reading twenty-one twenty, Gatch sat up and groaned, "Lee won't show."

"I think he will," said Deac, buttoning up his shirt. "He's feeling pretty pumped up over that gunnery. And who wouldn't want to party?"

"But what do we do with him when we're . . . you know . . . He won't sleep with any of those girls."

"Well, then, the boy's on his own."

Sergeant Lee arrived at the their open door and rapped a knuckle on the wood. "Sorry I am late. Some things to do first."

Gatch sprang from his bed and slapped Lee on the shoulder. "Better things to do now. Let's rock 'n' roll."

"Before we go, I want to thank you for the invitation."

"Just glad you're coming. Now you're going to see what you've been missing!"

As always, Gatch led the party crew outside, where it was oftentimes difficult to remember how close they were to their enemy. Prior to the terrorist attacks of September 11, 2001, they had been allowed off post until curfew, at which time they had to be back inside their camp. However, the coveted 2ID Warrior Pass would allow them to remain off post partying until either the alcohol took control and forced them back to the barracks or they met that night's love of their life who took them back to a hotel. It seemed that all the officers and senior noncommissioned officers had a Warrior Pass, but on rare occasions the junior enlisted soldiers could obtain one from the company first sergeant for a night of uninhibited release.

After the terrorist attacks, the Warrior Pass was essentially eliminated, and all soldiers were required to return to post prior to curfew. Guys like Gatch understood that at first, but soon it seemed like another way for the division's leadership to limit their ability to raise hell like true warriors. Booze and women were a natural component of the Warrior Ethos, but the leadership hardly agreed. Fortunately, when the FPCON, or Force Protection Condition, was low, everyone except screwups would be allowed to travel off post as long as they were with a battle buddy.

Once Gatch, Deac, and Lee were clear of the MPs at the main gate, they crossed a railroad spur and entered TDC's bar district, a narrow, three-block-long row of mostly ramshackle buildings. According to the locals, the number of clubs had fluctuated over the years, with as many as twenty-five operating at one time.

For tankers who had never been to Korea, the nightlife of TDC offered an experience like no other. The incessant buzz of the neon lights merged with the throngs of hooting, half-drunken men staggering from club to club, seeking out a moment of passion in whatever form. Most clubs were owned and run by Koreans, but they typically employed girls from the Philippines or southern Russia to mingle with the soldiers. These drinky girls would sit and visit with the soldiers for the price of a single drink, a price typically ten times that of the soldier's round. At some clubs, the services offered were much more than mere conversation. Though soliciting prostitution was illegal, it was not uncommon. Many girls were looking for the opportunity to meet a young man to provide for their future. Others wanted money to help support a family back home. Some had no idea what they wanted.

The first bar they passed was Cheers, often referred to as the First Tank Officers' Club because of its popularity with the battalion's leadership. Bar girls there were more interested in friendly conversation than in soliciting their personal goods. Sometimes Deac and Gatch would stop to get a warm-up round before taking on the whole strip.

One of the more notable establishments was the Silver Star, a country bar owned by a soldier who had retired in TDC after 'Nam. One foot inside, and you swore you were back in Austin or Albuquerque. The bar was home of the Silver Star Outlaws, a tight group of regulars who wore denim vests with their crest on the back. To join, a member in good standing sponsored you, plus you had to survive the club's hazing rituals designed to prove your worth. Some of the city boys like Keyman thought the whole place was a bit hokey, and some black soldiers like Sparrow, Abbot's driver, were offended by the Confederate flag hanging in the bar, but the Silver Star was a piece of home taken quite seriously by its patrons.

Bars, of course, weren't the only businesses in TDC. Tailors and leatherworkers made an okay living. You could show them a photo in a catalog, and they could design for you a high-quality knockoff suit or jacket. Costume jewelry shops sold sterling silver necklaces and ankle bracelets that you could ship to your wife or girlfriend (or both!) back home.

If you were hungry and didn't want a sit-down deal, food stands jammed many of the streets, their operators offering everything from friend chicken to Korean fried dumplings called *yakimondu*. The *soju* tents were set up on the corners, and Gatch always laughed when he saw an unsuspecting soldier decide to buy a kettle.

Two blocks later, after bumping into a few buddies and trading a few gunnery tales, Gatch and the others reached their destination: the Together Club. They walked in, and their ears were immediately assaulted by Golden Earring's "When the Bullet Hits the Bone" thrumming from ceiling loudspeakers as a big-screen TV flashed a homemade video of helicopter gunships unloading rockets and machine gun fire.

Deac waved a fist in the air, "Hooah, motherfuckers!"

"You ever been here?" Gatch shouted in Lee's ear.

The gunner shook his head and crinkled his nose. A cloud of cigarette and cigar smoke hung so thickly over the long bar that Gatch couldn't see the opposite wall. Judging from Lee's pained expression, he wasn't a big fan of American hard rock or heavy metal, but if he hung around with Gatch and Deac long enough, they would turn him into a dedicated head banger. Since he usually declined their offers to party, they would have to seize the opportunity for Lee's education.

After a brief recon, Gatch deliberately steered them to a small table near three guys he had run into before: crunchies from the 1st Battalion, 503rd Infantry Regiment.

While infantrymen called tankers *DATs* (dumb-ass tankers), Gatch and his brothers from First Tank were proud to uphold the armor tradition of calling ground pounders *grunts* (ground recon unit, nontrainable), *track grease,* and *crunchies,* the latter referring to the sound soldiers make when a sixty-eight-ton tank is rolling over them. However, in the field, it was all business, and most tankers and infantrymen had a mutual respect for each other—not that they ever voiced those sentiments.

Two more guys arrived at the crunchie table, and Lee found himself jammed up behind Sergeant Shiffas, a husky guy with the hairless face of a newborn. A lit stogie jutted from the corner of the sergeant's mouth, suggesting a cartoon character instead of ass-kicker. A couple of months back, Gatch and Shiffas had nearly come to blows over a comment the crunchie had made about Gatch's height, but Gatch had decided to let the remark pass. Deep down, though, he was hoping the sergeant would now give him an excuse.

After they ordered and were served their first round of beers, Gatch traced a finger over the tattoo of a Celtic cross that spanned most of his right forearm. "See this?"

Deac rolled his eyes. "I heard this one already."

"But good old Lee hasn't. See this, buddy? I got this because of a college girl I met. Name was Debbie. She came down to Daytona for spring break. Think she was from Ohio, somewhere Midwest, who gives a shit, right? Point is, this girl had the most perfect body. Lean. Natural. Nothing fake about her. And she wore a cross just like this. When she got on top, she rode me like a wild stallion, and the whole time this cross is just dangling in my face, dangling in my face, and she's moaning and groaning, and the cross is dangling . . ." Gatch blinked hard, breathed hard, was getting hard just thinking about it. "Whew! Brother! I found my religion!"

Lee grimaced.

"So the asshole gets a tattoo to remember some one-night stand he had with a college girl," said Deac.

"Not a college girl," Gatch said, still lost in the memory. "*The* girl. The future Mrs. Gatch. And someday I'm going to find her."

Deac rolled his eyes again, then faced Lee. "So what made y'all change your mind about coming out?"

"Tonight is anniversary of my parents' death."

"Oh, man," Deac groaned.

"Wait a minute, now," said Gatch. "You never told us about that."

The Korean shrugged. "You never ask."

"Hey, buddy, can you move in a little?" asked Sergeant Shiffas, one eye narrowed as cigar smoke billowed into his face.

Lee jammed himself into the table. "Okay?"

Shiffas gave an ugly grin, then turned away, removed his stogie, and took a long pull on his beer.

"So when did your parents die?" Gatch asked.

"Oh, come on, do we have to talk about it?" asked Deac. "I can't get depressed before getting laid."

"What're you bitching about? That happens to you anyway when Little Deac won't come out to play."

"I'm just saying it kills the mood."

"Just shut up," Gatch told the muscle head. "Okay, Lee . . ."

"When I was eight years old, my father and mother try to smuggle me to the south. I remember my father's face when soldiers came. I saw him cry."

"Oh, Jesus Christ," moaned Deac.

"I want to hear this," Gatch snapped, then regarded the gunner. "So what happened? They get shot or what?"

"I did not see them. But I heard my mother cry. And then a shot. She cried more. And then another shot. I was in a wagon, under a blanket."

"Whoa, whoa, whoa," growled Shiffas, his cigar wobbling between his lips as he shifted in his chair to face them. "Just what in the fuck are you DATs talking about?"

Gatch frowned. "None of your business."

"Hey, I remember you. . . ."

"Surprise, surprise. Brain check positive. Now, if you don't mind, this is our conversation, not yours. If you can't squeeze your fat, fucking ass into that chair and have to crowd my gunner, well, I guess you'll have to listen." Gatch widened his eyes. "And that's too fucking bad, ain't it?"

"Whoa, the little man's got a big voice," said Shiffas.

"Yeah, and he's got big friends, too," said Deac, rising dramatically from the table like King Kong in a khaki dress shirt.

"No, no, I am sorry for offending you," Lee said, craning his head toward Shiffas. "I am sorry. We just came for drink. No trouble, please. No trouble."

"You'd best accept his apology," said Gatch. "This motherfucker is a Tae Kwon Do instructor. He will polish the ice with your ass."

"No trouble, please," said Lee.

Shiffas burst from his seat, the rest of his crunchie cronies following suit. "You got trouble of the worst kind."

Gatch puffed up his cheeks and mimicked Shiffas.

"Okay, boys," began Deac. "Y'all ready for this? Because we're going outside. . . ."

IN ROOM SIX of the Flower House on the other side of town, Hansen and Karen had already reached the trigger zone and had paused for resupply. They lay on the Western-style bed, she on her back and taking long drags on her cigarette while he remained on his side, tracing sweat circles between her small, round breasts.

"I'm going to miss this," she said.

Hansen caught a flash of green before she closed her eyes, her face draped in shadows as the candle burning on the nightstand caught a draft from the old window, flickered, and nearly went out. He kept staring, kept admiring, her shoulder-length brown hair taking on a rich warmth of red tints.

Ever since his first kiss in kindergarten, Hansen had preferred brunettes with mousy features, petite girls who were meticulous about their clothes, their hair, and their nails. While many of his past girlfriends were serious babes, more often than not there was nothing upstairs but a desire to shop and watch soap operas.

But then during his first week in country, Hansen had been in Itaewon, the club district in Seoul. He was drinking alone in some little club way off the beaten path when he spotted Karen sitting with this paunchy, balding, American guy whose skin bore enough craters to intrigue NASA scientists. For a few seconds, Hansen locked gazes with her, but then she looked away, only to look again and offer a coy smile.

Gulping down the rest of his drink, Hansen rose and

began to navigate toward Karen's seat, but a crowd of GIs had just shouldered up to the bar, and by the time he made it past them, he found her table empty. Even as he muttered, "Shit," a tap came on his shoulder. He turned. Lost his breath.

"I told him I was going to the bathroom," she said, as though they were already old friends. "And he said he was going, too. Let's get out of here before he gets back. Come on." She grabbed his wrist and led him out.

Hansen was a good soldier. He knew how to take orders.

"What're you thinking about?" she asked, drawing him back to the hotel room.

"That night in Itaewon."

Her expression brightened. "When I rescued you from your loneliness?"

"Rescued? I think I was the one who—"

"Hey, come on. Tim was the only American guy I knew."

"Are all English teachers as hot as him?"

"You're cruel, you know that?"

He put a finger on her lips. "I didn't mean it. You just look all sexy when you get mad."

She tapped out her cigarette, then grabbed his shoulders. "And you look all sexy when you get on top. Consider that an order, Lieutenant."

"Roger that, ma'am. We are resupplied and ready to move out!"

GATCH, DEAC, AND Lee stood in the street outside the Together Club. Sergeant Shiffas and his fellow crunchies had them surrounded.

Another group of infantrymen from the 503rd who had been heading inside had taken notice of the "disagreement" and were hanging around, egging on Shiffas and waiting to see how far things would escalate. For all the stress built up in the field, there were seldom any brawls in TDC, which made the incident all the more intriguing for everyone.

Gatch didn't like the numbers, didn't like them at all. He looked around, cleared his throat, then screamed at the top of his lungs, "FIRST TANK! FIRST TANK!"

While the crunchies glanced around, confused, Gatch watched and listened as the call echoed up the street, carried on the lips of other tankers. Within seconds guys started pouring out of the nearby clubs, all up them tankers come to herd up and help out their buddies.

Raising his chin a little higher, Gatch said, "All right, you crunchies. You want to settle this?" He directed his gaze to Shiffas. "Tell you what? Maybe I'll cut you that slack. You apologize to Sergeant Lee, and we'll walk away before you get too busted up to get laid. Sound good? Because you do not want to pull our punk cards."

"You believe this?" Shiffas asked his men. "This motherfucker's been breathing fumes for too long! And grasshopper over here, who's supposed to be some fucking Tae Kwon fag instructor is pissing in his skivvies right now, just like his mom and dad did when the time came."

In one fluid motion, Lee drew back and executed the most perfect, most beautiful wheel kick Gatch had ever seen. And for a slo-mo second, Gatch thought he was watching the whole goddamned thing on pay-per-view. Shiffas hit the ice and snow hard, his head rebounding, his still-burning cigar arcing in the air like a tracer until it came to a skittering halt in the middle of the road.

The thing about Gatch was that he didn't care if he needed to fight dirty to get the job done.

Which was why the spilt second after Sergeant Shiffas hit the deck, Gatch charged forward and kicked a field goal with the nearest guy's nuts. As the second crunchie doubled over, Deac did a number on the third guy, blocking a roundhouse while sending a right jab into the idiot's jaw.

Though he could not be certain, Gatch figured that at least eight, maybe nine fights broke out at once, with someone striking a direct blow to his back, sending him onto his gut like he was dropping to give twenty to some dickhead drill sergeant. Then someone fell on top of him, and a shower of snow and dirt blasted into his eyes. He rolled over, tried to get up, blinked hard through the dirt, and saw Deac falling straight for him. "Look out!" hollered the loader.

Gatch held up his hands, and Deac crashed on top of him, their faces coming within inches of each other before the loader could roll off. Gatch was about to puke up his beer over the experience when, from the corner of his eye, beyond the still-fighting tankers and crunchies, he saw a swarm of military police and courtesy patrol making their way toward the melee.

"Deac? Lee? Let's go," he shouted.

"They're going to tear this place apart for us," said Deac, as he clambered to his feet.

"I am sorry," said Lee, as he hustled over and dragged Gatch to his feet.

Deac shot a look over the crowd. "Oh, man. Here they come. We're screwed."

"Not yet," corrected Gatch. "Run!"

HANSEN ALREADY HAD a feeling that Karen was the one, and he already believed that barriers of time and distance could not affect them. He was a hopeless romantic, no doubt, a fool who could fall in love with a woman after knowing her for only three months.

He should have known it couldn't last.

As they lay there in one of their heavenly postcoital moments, he on top and still inside her, they still catching their breaths, she whispered in his ear, "It can't end. It shouldn't end."

"What are you talking about?"

She tensed. "Nothing."

He gave her the same stern look he used on his men when he wanted to draw out information, one brow cocked.

She gave in. "My contract with the institute is up. I'm going home at the end of the month."

"So that's what you meant before."

"What?"

"When you said you'll miss this."

She nodded, held his face in her hands. "But maybe it shouldn't end, right?"

Hansen pulled slowly away from her, letting himself drop onto his side. He felt hollow and suddenly relived his first day in Korea. "I don't want this to end."

"We can make a promise to each other."

"No."

She looked at him, confused.

"You picked your life, I picked my mine. Then this happened. You don't want it to end, and neither do I. But that's life, right?"

"I don't really want to, but I could sign on for another year. The money is pretty good. It's just . . . I miss home, you know? I really miss it."

"If going is right for you, then do it."

She rolled onto her side to face him. "You sound cold."

"Nah, just, I don't know. When we started this, I never thought about you having to leave. That was pretty stupid."

"I did the same thing. If I stayed, you'd only be here for another nine months, then after that? Who knows. I'd have to keep following you around everywhere."

"Then maybe we should just end it—"

She put her hand over his mouth. "We'll have Christmas together. And then we'll see what happens."

He was about to nod when alert sirens blared from Camp Casey.

CHAPTER
FIVE

THE WAR MAY be tomorrow. Are you going to be ready?

As Hansen jogged carefully over the packed snow toward his tank parked in the motor pool, two questions consumed his thoughts: What was the exact nature of the alert? And if war had truly begun, why hadn't it been able to wait until tomorrow (as in late morning), just like Gutterson had said?

The answers would come soon, perhaps punctuated by artillery fire. . . .

Hansen neared the Charlie Company line, noting that Keyman, Abbot, and Neech were already at their tracks, with Keyman spouting orders into his mike and looking about a half second away from a major coronary. Abbot offered a quick wave, and Neech followed as he tugged on his CVC helmet. In short order the entire platoon would be ready to shoot, move, and communicate—a holy trinity and operational mantra meant to keep them alive.

His heart racing, Hansen approached *Crimson Death*

from the rear and climbed onto the tank's hull. He picked his way gingerly across the turret, skirted the open hatch, and settled down into his commander's station. As he dropped fully into the tank, he fastened his chin strap and adjusted his mike. "Some night for an alert, eh guys?"

"Lieutenant, y'all have no idea," said Deac, his voice shivery.

"Red One, this is Red Four," Abbot called over the platoon net.

"Go ahead, Four."

"Division called the alert."

"Roger that," said Hansen.

"Holidays are coming up soon. Terror alert is high. What did we expect?" asked Abbot.

"I hear that."

First Tank alerts were carried out several ways: crews would assemble aboard their tanks but would not deploy; crews would assemble and deploy to an LTA (local training area); and crews would engage in a real rollout that could mean the obvious: fight's on!

"Driver? Fire in the hole," ordered Hansen.

"Clear," Gatch responded, providing warning to anyone standing behind the tank. Fifteen hundred horses woke beneath them, and a steady clicking from inside the turret indicated that the heater was thrumming to life. "Sir, we are ready to rumble!"

"Gatch, don't fuck around," Hansen said, much too sharply.

"Sir?"

"You heard me."

While Hansen had grown used to the driver's commentary, he wasn't in the mood for it. He could thank Karen for that. Shit. Why couldn't he just be a dog like some of the other guys? Why did he have to grow attached? "Crew report."

"Driver ready!"

"Loader ready!"

"Gunner ready!"

Hansen reached up, shut and locked his hatch. "Red, this is Red One. Report when REDCON-1."

"Red One, this is Red Two. We are REDCON-1, over."

Hansen responded to Keyman's report, then did likewise as Neech and Abbot checked in. With the platoon set, Hansen called over the company net. "Cobra Six, this is Red One. Red is REDCON-1, over."

"Red One, this is Cobra Six," responded Captain Van Buren. "Remain at REDCON-1 and stand by."

Heaving a sigh, Hansen rubbed his palms and reminded himself that even though Charlie Company's motto was "Strike Fast, Kick Ass," sometimes you needed to sit on your ass first. Hurry up and wait. Welcome to the Army.

More readiness reports sounded over the radio; then, abruptly, Gary Gutterson's terse voice cut in: "Cobra Six, this is Blue One. Blue is REDCON-1, over."

Tomorrow had come for Gutterson, all right. He had probably driven his platoon insane with his nit-picking. If the young Jedi wasn't careful, he could easily turn to the dark side and become a Keyman.

"Crusader Six, this is Cobra Six," Captain Van Buren began, calling Lieutenant Colonel Burroway. "Cobra is REDCON-1."

And there it was: Red, Blue, White, and the HQ platoons of the Charlie Company Cobras were ready to move and fight.

Hooah . . .

As the alert sequence continued, the one-hour mark approached, at which time the battalion commanders would report their current combat status and convey any issues they might have to the brigade commander, who would then relay any requirements from division as well as any of his own.

As they continued waiting for the order to stand down,

Hansen's thoughts drifted back to the Flower House. He raised his hand to his face. He could still smell her perfume on his fingers, still hear her. "I'm going to miss this," he said with a snort.

"Miss what?" asked Deac.

"Nothing."

"You mean waiting around?"

"No, it's just . . . forget about it."

"You okay, sir? I got a Snickers in my CVC bag. You want one?"

"Nah, it's okay, Deac. It's too bad they called the alert before we had our drink, huh?"

"Yeah. You said you were buying."

"I was. I could use a drink about now."

Van Buren suddenly announced, "ENDEX, ENDEX, ENDEX. Stand down."

Hansen passed the word to the rest of the platoon. He was about to order his crew to switch off all systems when the captain called again, passing down word that Lieutenant Colonel Burroway had ordered a battalion formation in the motor pool, where all such formations were held.

"What's happening?" Lee asked Hansen as they prepared to dismount.

"I'm not sure. But it can't be good. Call me a pessimist tonight."

"Yeah, I'm with you," said Deac, opening his hatch. "This here's one of them nights that God can have back. I'm going to customer service for a refund."

"Me, too," said Hansen. "Me, too."

The other tankers from Ace Company, Black Night Company, and Demon Company had dismounted their tracks and were falling in to their company formations. The Aces and Black Knights stood one side of the U-shaped group of men, while the Cobras and Demons took up the other. The base of the formation was established by the

Headquarters and Headquarters Company, the Head-hunters, who were comprised of mechanics, cooks, clerks, medics, staff personnel, supply specialists, ammunition handlers, fuel handlers, scouts, mortar men, intelligence analysts, and all the other individuals whose sole purpose was to support the combat power of the battalion. Though often underappreciated, they were critical to the 1-72's success.

The battalion command sergeant major's HMMWV pulled up, followed closely by the battalion commander's. Just as the Headhunters finished forming up, Command Sergeant Major Alton made his way to the front of the formation, instructing the battalion to fall in. After receiving an accountability report from the company first sergeants, he conducted a parade-perfect about-face and strolled to the front of the assembly. Once he reported to Lieutenant Colonel Burroway and took his post, the colonel instructed the battalion to fall out and fall in on him.

Within ten seconds over six hundred soldiers transitioned from a formation of military precision to a group of warriors rallied around the leader of the mightiest tank battalion on the Korean peninsula.

"Gentlemen, I wanted to take this opportunity to congratulate you on an outstanding gunnery. Hooah!"

As the hooahs echoed, Deac said, "Maybe this night ain't so bad after all."

Just then two Heavy Expanded Mobility Tactical Trucks (HEMTTs) rolled up to the formation, pulling to a halt near Burroway's HMMWV. The trucks were piled high with transit cases marked MILES 2000, an acronym for Multiple Integrated Laser Engagement System. When a tank and its personnel were fitted with the MILES gear, coded laser beams would simulate the firing of every weapon on board. Laser detector systems would sense opposing fire and register a near miss, hit, or kill. MILES 2000 was latest version of laser tag gone government, relatively new to the tankers of Korea, and very bad news on a cold, December night.

Hansen adopted a lame Southern accent and whispered sadly, "Nope, Deac. We ain't getting no refund."

Burroway went on, his tone suddenly hard, "Men, as part of the division's readiness exercise, we have been tasked to roll out one company to Twin Bridges to conduct extended MILES training. I have selected the Cobras to execute this mission. First Platoon will provide OPFOR against Second and Third Platoons. Remember to be safe but aggressive. Now, fall back in."

Immediately, the men transitioned back to the parade field formation in less than ten seconds. As with all formations, Burroway ended with the First Tank rally cry, responded to by Hansen and every other solider.

"Who you with?"

"FIRST TANK!"

"Who you with?"

"FIRST TANK!"

"Who you with?"

"FIRST TANK!"

With all the motivation and enthusiasm they could muster, Hansen and the rest then added, "Everybody fights. Nobody quits. Hooah!"

Burroway turned the formation back to Command Sergeant Major Alton, who put out some quick administrative notes before finishing off with his traditional cry, "If you ain't First Tank—"

Everyone thundered back in response, "you ain't shit!"

"See, I told you, Deac," Gatch said after they were instructed to fall out. "You jinxed us. You jinxed us good. Now we have to hook up all this laser crap and play war games all night when we could've been downrange and—"

"Quiet," Hansen ordered as he started back to the track. "Now, boys, is there anything you want to tell me?"

"'Bout what?" asked Gatch, rushing up to Hansen's side.

"About why we're being punished."

"Well, everybody knows that someone played pyro with Burroway's track. Maybe he thinks it was one of us," said Deac as they all reached the tank.

"I hope to God it wasn't one of us," Hansen said in his most threatening tone.

"Fess up, Lee. We all know you did it," said Deac.

Lee threw up his hands. "Maybe it is my fault, Lieutenant. There was a fight earlier this evening—"

"Okay, Lee, that's enough," said Gatch.

"A fight, eh?" asked Hansen. "I thought I heard some guys talking about that on the way back."

"And we should talk about it later," said Gatch. "We have a lot of crap to hook up."

Hansen gave the driver a dubious stare. "All right, guys. Let's get our gear."

WEBBER WAS HELPING Keyman tape one of the MILES's detector belts to *Cold Steel*'s turret when Command Sergeant Major Willard Alton rolled up in his HMMWV. "How you doing, Keyman?"

"I'm doing well, Sergeant Major."

"Good. You feel bad, Webber?"

"Excuse me, Sergeant Major?"

"I say, you feel bad?"

Webber frowned. "I'm not sure what you mean, Sergeant Major."

The command sergeant major tossed something to Webber, who abruptly caught it: a roll of twenty-dollar bills.

"That's a hundred bucks," explained the command sergeant major.

"For what?"

"From Brophy."

After a sudden loss of air, Webber held back his surprise and tried to act mildly confused. "I'm not sure what this is, Sergeant Major. I mean I know it's money, but—"

"You tried to rip off Brophy. He didn't go for it. You took revenge."

"What is this, Webber?" Keyman demanded.

Webber's gaze flicked to Keyman, then back to the command sergeant major. "Sergeant Major, whatever Brophy told you is a lie."

Keyman's jaw fell open. "What's going on here?"

Alton aimed an index finger at Webber. "Here's the grease monkey motherfucker who packed the colonel's barrel."

Keyman's eyes switched on like a pair of warning lights, and he suddenly began to hyperventilate. "Webber . . . Webber . . . what did you do? WHAT DID YOU DO?"

"This is a joke. Some idiot's trying to get back at me for a little personal loan problem, that's all it is," Webber said quickly.

"Shut your hole!" Keyman hollered. "Sergeant Major, whatever the problem is, do not worry. I will take care of it."

"So will I," Alton said slowly, ominously. "I can't prove anything. But I know. I'll be waiting . . . and watching."

With that, the command sergeant major ordered his driver to move off, and as the truck rolled away, Keyman nodded slowly at Webber and said, "Okay, Sergeant. Now, it's my turn. . . ."

Webber grimaced. It was just too damned late and too cold to get torn a new asshole. But it was inevitable. At least he would become a legend for lighting up the old man's track, for getting his hundred bucks back, and for surviving Keyman's wrath. (Could he assume the latter already?) He tried not to smile as the bald maniac shouted and spat in his face. "I'm going to put you on every shit detail I can find! Do you hear me, Webber?"

"Yes, Sergeant."

"Do you hear me, Webber?"

"Yes, Sergeant!"

PREVENTIVE MAINTENANCE CHECKS and Services (PMCS) were performed by all Abrams crews prior to operating their tanks. Likewise, conducting PMCS of the MILES system was mandatory before Hansen and his crew could get under way. Thus, with checklist in hand, he began his walk-around inspection of *Crimson Death*, making sure everything was properly and securely installed. He would also search for cracks, dirt, or any other anomalies that might pose a problem with the gear. Indeed, they had adorned the old girl with some pretty fancy jewelry that needed to do a lot more than just shine.

Bands of detectors wrapped around the turret, and Small Arms Transmitters (SATs) were bolted to the barrels of the M2 and M240 machine guns to register their fire.

The gas tube under the barrel of the coax now sported a clip-on coax microphone assembly to pick up the sound of blank fire, which would then cause the main gun to fire.

A Universal Laser Transmitter (ULT) was mounted to an adapter that was bolted inside the main gun's breech. The ULT would fire the laser, simulating a round on the way.

The Main Gun Signature Simulator (MGSS) was comprised of two parts: a Fire Control Unit (FCU) and a Firing Unit (FU). The MGSS FU was loaded and clung like a box-shaped barnacle to the forward left side of the turret, while the FCU was mounted inside the tank, on the right wall of the gunner's station. The MGSS FU produced a flash and bang to simulate main gun firing.

Farther back, near the rear of the turret, jutted a Direct/Indirect Fire Cue (DIFCUE) that was also loaded and would flash, make noise, and produce smoke to simulate the old girl being hit by direct or indirect fire.

After marking his checklist, Hansen crossed to the rear of the tank to inspect the dome-shaped Optical Turret Positioning device (OTP), also located on the left side but affixed to the hull. The unit provided an optical reference signal to the turret detector belts to determine the turret position with reference to the hull. They were good to go there.

Above the OTP was the Kill Status Indicator (KSI), which sat atop a mast U-bolted to the bustle rack in back of the turret. The whoopee light would flash to indicate a hit, near miss, or kill. Deac called the beacon a "big, ole taillight that told no lies." No, it didn't, and hopefully Hansen's would only flash to indicate near misses.

Satisfied with his external inspection, Hansen mounted the tank, reached Deac's open hatch, and glanced down at the main gun's open breech, where the loader was tightening the last bolt on the ULT assembly. "How's it going?"

Deac beat a knuckle on his loader unit, a small computer panel with display and eight push buttons taped near the ammo door. "Got my LU hooked up and in place." He tossed a glance to the right side of his seat, where on the shelf stood the eight-pound power controller equipped with a rechargeable battery pack and glowing LED indicator lights. "As you can see, power's up." He waved his wrench at the breech. "And the ULT here is good to go, sir."

"That's what I want to hear."

Hansen shifted around to his open hatch, lowered himself into the tank. Lee had already taped the MILES control unit to the wall of Hansen's station. The CU featured a small display window and, like Deac's loader unit, touch buttons for scrolling up and down, as well as those marked Weapon Effect, Ammo Effect, Reload, Ammo Status, Range, BIT (Built-in Test), User Info, CTR S Volume, and Power On/Off.

Now it was time for them to don their Individual

Weapons Systems (IWSs) that included helmet and torso harnesses in addition to SATs. The harness sets had detectors to receive coded transmissions from lasers, amplifiers for amplifying and forwarding those messages to the IWS consoles for decoding, infrared transmitters to link the torso harness with the weapons' SATs, audio alarms to indicate that laser signals were received, helmet inductive loops to transfer data from the helmet harness to the torso harness IWS console, and IWS consoles to serve as Data Process Control Units for the entire system.

While the gear and its various functions were as complex as they sounded, the system was designed to work using the very same firing procedures Hansen and his men used during training and real combat—though beeps hardly simulated rounds exploding over their hull.

Hansen slipped on his torso harness and fastened the pair of vest clips. He made sure to wipe clean all detectors and the IWS console. That done, he installed a nine-volt battery in the console and made sure the system was functioning. The elastic helmet harness slid right over his CVC helmet and contained four laser detectors and an amplifier in the back. He lined up the fastener tape patches until the unit was secure. Meanwhile, Lee and Deac did the same. Gatch didn't get to play with the harnesses, and that was just fine by him.

After calling for a crew check, Hansen got on the platoon net and learned that Keyman, Neech, and Abbott were set. Time to call the commanding officer. "Cobra Six, this is Red One. Red is REDCON-1, over."

"Roger that," answered Van Buren. "Guidons, Cobra Six. SP time now. Order of march is Red, C66, White, C65, Blue, then company trains. Let's roll."

WEBBER WAS IN his gunner's seat, glancing over at Keyman's station. The staff sergeant stood tall, his hatch open, his goggles on. He boomed the occasional course correction to Morbid when he wasn't muttering the words "Bullshit," which was what he thought of the whole exercise, and "Asshole," which was what he thought of Webber.

Smiley, who also stood at his station, had earlier looked petrified and had told Webber that he was "bad man" for getting their tank commander angry. Morbid had agreed and had added that Webber was going to get them all sent to hell by way of Leavenworth.

Where was the love?

Webber closed his eyes and yawned deeply. He had thought it was going to be a long night of partying. He tugged angrily at the MILES torso harness on his shoulders and heard Keyman's voice ring out in his thoughts: *This is all your fucking fault! All your fault, Webber! Do you understand?"*

Some party.

ABBOT HAD SEEN the command sergeant major's HMMWV roll up to Keyman's tank, and Abbot was pretty good at reading lips. The command sergeant major must have figured out that Webber had pulled the prank, and now Burroway was making them all pay for it. Abbot bet that he felt more guilty than even Webber did, and the least he could do was make sure that he and the crew of Red Four did a top-notch job of kicking ass.

As they followed the snow-covered path toward Twin Bridges, Abbot wondered if he should tell Hansen what was going on; the guy seemed nice enough and could probably handle it without dropping a nut like Keyman had.

"So whose fault is this?" asked Abbot's loader, Specialist Jeff Paskowsky, a big-eared blond with downcast eyes who stood rigidly before his M240.

"I don't like lying, Paz. So don't ask."

"I knew you knew."

"Who's your daddy? Me. Of course I know everything."

"And the guy's from our platoon, isn't he."

"I told you, don't ask."

"It's Webber, isn't it. The guy's got bad juju. Every time I get near him, I can feel the old Paskowsky curse coming up through my blood, coming up to curse us all."

Paz had caught his wife of just six months sleeping with one of his best friends. When he wasn't obsessing on that or buying all kinds of talismans to ward off the evil spirits, he was telling stories about how his ancestors had been killed in famous disasters, including fires, earthquakes, plane crashes, and floods. He even claimed to have a relative who had gone down with the *Titanic*.

Funny. Every crew had its pessimist, but Paz was just too damned young to be so negative. "Listen, kid. Just stop worrying about why we're out here and concentrate on what we have to do: kill eight tanks and get back home."

"Okay, Sergeant. But I think this is a win-win for us. If we don't take out the tanks, we can blame it on the MILES. If they kill us, we can blame it on the MILES."

"Paz, the Army ain't looking for excuses. They're looking for killers."

The loader nodded, grabbed his machine gun, and pretended to lay down fire, his teeth bared.

"Sparrow? Watch out for that ditch on the right," Abbot said, spying a slight drop-off that seemed to encroach on the road.

"I see it," said the driver, veering left to evade.

Specialist Dwight Sparrow was a soft-spoken African-American who hailed from south central Los Angeles—but you would never know that unless you got into a fight with him. He spoke as though he had already obtained that college diploma he dreamed of and quite seriously reported that he was going to become the first black president of the

United States. He was a good kid, hardened by the hood but highly motivated to succeed. Abbot had been so impressed by Sparrow that he had even let him change the name of the tank to *Compton Posse*. Paz thought the name suggested that they were all gang bangers ready to do drive bys in an Abrams. "No, no, no," Sparrow had corrected. "It's much deeper than that. It's an homage to all those brothers from the hood who made the ultimate sacrifice."

Sparrow had had some trouble explaining that to the tank's twenty-two-year-old gunner, Sergeant Park Konsang, who understood Compton as a place but could not fathom why they were called a posse, since Abbot was not a sheriff and they were not wearing cowboy hats. That was Park, all right. He was one of the most literal but most curious and risk-taking KATUSAs that Abbot had ever met. He would go downrange to TDC, then return to proudly try out all the new English he had learned: "I met a most charming woman, then I received my game on and turned into a player with goods to acquire booty."

Okay, so a few guys downrange had been pulling his chain, but Park didn't care. He wanted to soak up as much American culture and language as he could, and he ignored those guys who picked on him. He saw his two years of service as a once-in-a-lifetime experience, and he had busted his ass to become a gunner, which was quite rare among KATUSAs. In fact, he and Sergeant Lee were the only South Koreans in the company who sat in that seat.

With Park's eagerness to learn in mind, Abbot decided to teach the gunner much more than just tank operations. As the husband of a Korean woman, he understood where the gunner was coming from, and Park was one of the few Koreans who, when he discovered that Abbot had taken a Korean wife, had been much more accepting than some of the other KATUSAs who often claimed that Americans were stealing their women.

"Getting colder," Paz announced as the tank hit a shallow pothole and jostled them.

"Yeah, it is," replied Abbot. "I want to say I'm too old and too cold for this shit."

"But you won't. Because you love it."

"Aw, hell. You're right. Driver? Let's pick it up a little. Come on!"

STAFF SERGEANT RICHARD "Neech" Nelson had had a weight problem before joining the Army, which was to say that he'd had a gut from the second grade. In his senior year of high school, he wound up taking a fat girl to the prom because that's what fat geeks did. During a slow dance she lowered one of her colossal heels on his foot and broke his toe. And then, when she had leaned over to have a look at his wound, she had split her dress. Ah, a night to remember.

Sixty-three and a half pounds later, Neech was a shadow of his former self. It was funny, though. He still thought like a fat guy, still wanted to pig out every chance he got, still wanted to stuff some pogie bait into his face as he stood at his station, watching his loader, Private First Class Choi Sang-ku, absolutely devour an Almond Joy.

"It ain't chicken, Popeye," Neech hollered over the hum of *C U Later*'s engine and the clanking of her tracks.

Popeye Choi smiled and raised an index finger. "Chicken and chocolate. Numba one!"

Neech shook his head in envy and disgust. The kid ate everything in sight, bribed guys for their chicken, and never gained an ounce.

"Hey, Popeye?" cried Sergeant Romeo Rodriguez from his gunner's station. "Pussy numba one!"

Neech grimaced. "Which is why you don't get any, Romeo. You numba ten! Because you are lewd. You are crude. You have no manners!"

"Come on, Sarge. We all know who's the stud on this track."

Rail thin, basically an ugly little runt who considered himself a "tuner" of imported sports cars, Romeo claimed that what he lacked in height God had made up for between his legs. He also claimed to have "the best line of shit anywhere," one that the ladies would fall for every time. However, when pressed, he wouldn't share the line with you, saying that if he gave it away, there wouldn't be any women left for him. He was a real character, all right.

"Romeo, your mama gave you the wrong name. The wrong name."

"Say what you want, but I got a witness. You ask Batman what happened a few hours ago downrange."

"Uh, don't get the caped crusader involved in your seedy dealings," said the tank's driver, Private First Class William "Bruce" Wayne. "Batman don't play that."

"Yo, don't make me pull rank on you," Romeo sang.

"Don't make me pull rank on you!" Neech reminded the gunner.

"All right, *Staff* Sergeant."

"Ah, whenever I climb," Neech began through a sigh. "I am followed by a dog called Romeo."

"There he goes again," said the gunner. "Spouting off more quotes from his god Nietzsche. So what's the dog's real name?"

"Ego."

"Whoa. That's deep."

"Here's another one for you, Romeo. He who fights monsters must take care lest he thereby become a monster."

"Why do read that junk, Sarge?"

Neech ducked down to face the gunner. "I read it to avoid becoming a monster like you!"

"Yeah, but I like what I am! Stud monster, keeping it real for the ladies."

With a quick roll of his eyes, Neech resumed his position, then jerked forward as the road descended in about a thirty-degree grade. His tank was the only one in the platoon fitted with a mine plow, which made driving the beast much more difficult. "Driver? Slow down! What're you doing down there? Reading comics?"

"No, Sergeant."

"Building models? Playing with your action figures?"

"Yeah, he's playing with his action figure, all right."

"Shut up, Romeo. Now driver? Watch the damned road!"

"Yes, Sergeant."

Sometimes Neech felt like a baby-sitter, but he reminded himself that the other guys were all under twenty-one. Though he was only twenty-four, Neech felt like the old man. And the truth was, he didn't read Nietzsche to avoid becoming a monster. He wanted to avoid becoming an ignoramus who was unable to carry on an intelligent conversation with his father, a humanities professor at a little community college in northern California. Neech had figured he would join the Army to lose the weight. Along the way, he would educate himself so that when he got out, he could prove to his father that he hadn't wasted his time and was ready for college. He could even pay for his education without taking out loans or borrowing from Dad. Mom, were she still alive, would have approved. Damned cancer.

So, despite his father's reservations, Neech had enlisted. And then . . . something had happened. He had grown up in the Army. He had become a man in the Army. Become a tanker, a tank commander. And suddenly he knew what he wanted to do with the rest of his life. And maybe he read Nietzsche because he felt guilty for that choice, for breaking his father's heart. Maybe he was just trying to make his father feel that he had not raised an idiot.

Consequently, Neech fancied himself an armchair scholar and philosopher. He wanted everyone to consider his M1A1 Abrams and its crew as "the think tank."

However, with winners like Popeye Choi, Batman, and Romeo on board, well, his work was cut out for him.

CHAPTER
SIX

SLIGHT HILLS BROKEN occasionally by patches of woods stretched across the terrain outside of Camp Casey. Choke points wove through snowy trails beside windswept rice paddies that had yet to freeze over and remained bogs that ate tanks for breakfast, lunch, and dinner. Hansen observed one such bog as he and his men rolled closer to the training area. He shivered at the thought of sinking up to the gun tube in muck and imagined Keyman standing atop his own tank and shouting, "Hey, Lieutenant? Tanks don't float."

Asshole.

Word came down from Van Buren that the exercise wasn't taking place until dawn and that the entire company would be making a serpentine road march to Twin Bridges. It was not uncommon for units to travel fifty kilometers to reach an assembly area that was only twelve kilometers away, because most roads and culverts had not been designed to support the weight of tanks. Consequently, there were only a limited number of routes available. And worse, any number of maintenance problems could occur during such a march, adding more time and headaches to the movement.

"Damn, and I thought we'd be finished by dawn," Deac crooned. "What a night."

They forged on, stitching their way over the hills, working dangerously close to the paddies, weaving along dilapidated roads through small towns and villages, the earth shaking as they rode by. Hansen must have rubbed his eyes and smacked his cheeks a dozen times, trying to stay awake. The rest of the crew was just like him: tired, cold, and bored.

What felt like a lifetime later, they approached Soju Alley, a strange little town where many Koreans staggered around in a twenty-four-hour drunken state. If nothing else, the place indicated that they were close to Twin Bridges.

About fifteen minutes later, Hansen and his platoon, along with the rest of Charlie Company, stopped and dismounted in a clearing referred to as the Southern Bowl. There, in the grainy light of dawn, they met with the Observer/Controller team, tankers who had been tasked from Second Tank, 2nd Battalion, 72nd Armor also known as Deuce Tank. "Second Place is good enough only if you're Second Tank," said many First Tank crews. Needless to say, as the only other U.S. tank battalion in Korea, there was no love lost between the two battalions.

Each of Charlie Company's platoons was assigned an O/C lieutenant or sergeant first class who operated from a HMMWV and who monitored the platoon's activities, resetting and troubleshooting equipment as necessary. The O/Cs were known as the Keepers of the God Guns, since their controller guns were capable of "killing" everyone on the battlefield. Captain James Loudermilk, Second Tank's Apache Company commander, oversaw the entire exercise and would remain with the company's HQ platoon, evaluating Cobra Six.

After going over a few details with Captain Van Buren, the red-faced Loudermilk finished blowing his nose and addressed the company: "All right, gentlemen. Like you, I'm still a bit ragged from the alert and road march, and I've contracted a terrible cold. But we are going to conduct this training as we've been directed to, and hopefully we will all come away better prepared to fight those bastards to the north if we're called to do so. That said, here's your mission: Red Platoon? You are a recon element of an NKPA brigade. Your vehicles will be marked with red star placards on the front and rear of your turrets. Blue, White, and command tracks? You will conduct a movement to contact and destroy enemy reconnaissance forces, preventing the penetration of Phase Line HOME. Make no mistake, if even one Red tank makes it across PL HOME and is still able to shoot, move, and communicate, the company loses. Also, per the lieutenant colonel's orders, Red's thermal sights will be covered with tape to more accurately simulate the enemy's equipment."

Hansen's crew did a fair job of hiding their cynicism, as did Keyman's, but a few groans came from Neech's and Abbot's crews.

Of course they all knew that Loudermilk's explanation for covering the thermals was less than sincere. Burroway was just trying to screw them a little more and had found a convenient and justifiable way to do so. The absence of thermal capabilities would make it that much harder for Hansen's platoon to locate their opponents; however, Burroway had cut them slack by having the exercise take place at dawn—never mind the fact that they had just spent most of the night engaged in an exhaustive road march.

"After the O/Cs reset and run their checks, Red will hold while the rest of the company occupies an attack position in the Northern Bowl," Loudermilk added. "Good to go?"

"Hooah!" the group cried, some more enthusiastically than others.

As they fell out, Sergeant First Class Mike Stone, a friendly looking man with big ears and a harelip, introduced himself to Hansen. "I'll be your O/C tonight, Lieutenant. If you'll have your men stand by their tanks, I'll get started."

Hansen lifted his voice, gave the order, then returned to his own track with Stone.

While Deac and Gatch began attaching the red star placards and Lee started taping up the thermal sights, Hansen crawled down into the commander's station while Stone waited outside. Hansen keyed on the Control Unit, which displayed vehicle status as Cheat Kill just as the whoopee light began to flash continuously. Stone reset the vehicle by setting his God gun for Reset and firing at the detector belts. The KSI flashed once, then stopped flashing, and the vehicle intercom sounded with "Reset." Hansen's tank could then be made mission ready in one of two ways: Stone could set up information for the vehicle and weapons type on the MARS computer in his HMMWV and upload the data to his God gun, which he would then upload to the tank via the optical port on the KSI. Or he could set the vehicle status to Control Mode On, and the required info could be set from Hansen's CU.

After switching places with Hansen, Stone plugged in the data, then emerged from the commander's station. "All right, Lieutenant, you're good to go here."

"Thanks."

"And sir? I heard you guys ran away with everything at gunnery. Top Tank, the whole nine. That's awesome, sir."

Hansen hardened his voice. "Yeah, but now we eat humble pie. It's going to be an interesting day."

As the NCO headed to Keyman's track, Hansen glanced over and gave the hardass a tentative thumbs-up. Keyman's lip twisted, then he turned away and helped Stone onto his tank. Hansen sighed.

Once he was back down at his station, he asked, "How we doing, guys?"

Deac hollered in a bad North Korean accent, "*So-wi,* we ready to kill American scum!"

"I wish that were funny, Deac."

"Sorry, sir. Just trying to keep up some morale. Y'all look like we're about to get whacked by ten tanks."

Lee turned away from his gunner's sight. "For once, Deac, you speak truth. No thermals? No good."

"See, what'd I tell you, sir?" Deac shook his head.

"What about you, Gatch?" Hansen asked over the intercom. "You don't think we can win this?"

"We can win it. But Burroway don't want us to win. So we're going to lose. There it is."

"Burroway wants us to lose?" Hansen thought aloud. "So why don't you guys tell me who pulled that prank? And by the way, that's not a suggestion."

"I swear, sir, I don't know," answered Deac. "And if I don't know, then Gatch don't know. And if Gatch don't know—"

"All right, I get it. Lee? What about that fight you wanted to tell me about?"

"Sir, that has nothing to do with this, trust me," said Deac. "Just a couple of knuckleheads from the 503rd is all. Nothing to do with this."

Hansen lifted his chin at Lee. "Let him talk."

"Yesterday was anniversary of my parents' death," the gunner said quietly. "One solider offended me. I am sorry, sir."

"I take it none of you got caught," Hansen concluded.

"No, sir, but it got pretty hairy on the street," Deac explained, going breathless as he seemingly relived the moment. "You should've seen—"

"Okay, that's enough. Let's forget about everything else for now and think about what we're supposed to do out here. We're going to take on ten tanks. And we're going to win!"

The men gave a halfhearted "Hooah!"

Hansen did not like what he was hearing. Didn't like it one bit. He was about to ride off into a simulated battle with a bunch of defeatists. "Come on, guys. We're Top Tank. Don't forget that. Being outnumbered and outgunned is what we're about. We'll just focus. And we'll kill them all!"

Another less-than-enthusiastic "Hooah!" barely filled the turret.

And then, for a dangerous few seconds, Hansen's thoughts turned to Karen, and suddenly he felt as defeated and miserable as the crew did. Damn it. He'd better start practicing what he had preached, otherwise he would be the first one to choke and bolo. He pulled out his 1:25,000 map of the training area and narrowed his gaze in thought.

TEN MINUTES AND one minor headache later, Hansen dismounted to discuss a battle plan with his tank commanders. He and his men all understood that there were four characteristics of offense: surprise, concentration, tempo, and audacity. They should use speed as well as covered and concealed routes to surprise their enemy. They should mass the effects of their weapons systems while still dispersing vehicles. They should attempt to maintain a fast tempo during operations. They should take advantage of battlefield opportunities by using violent initiative.

In addition, they needed to analyze the terrain using factors of OCOKA: observation and fields of fire, cover and concealment, obstacles, key terrain, and avenues of approach. Hansen had done so, noting the choke points and rice paddies on his map. He had decided upon an avenue of approach that was not the most obvious. He had noted three key terrain features on his map: a triangular pattern of wooded zones that would present gaps or "dead space" in the platoon's battle space. He had realized that he might need to reposition Abbot and Neech to cover that gap and, perhaps, charge them with providing overwatch while he and Keyman moved through one of two nearby choke points. He had picked out a few observation points from where he believed the enemy could observe and engage the platoon: the highest hills shown on the map. He had marked possible Battle Positions (BPs) the enemy might use as well as noting a few possibilities for his tanks. He also considered a few areas along the forest perimeters from where Van Buren could stage an ambush.

Now Hansen and his tank commanders hunkered down before his tank, and in the growing light, he went over the map. As he spoke, his excitement began to return. They were hunters, primeval hunters about to go out and feel more alive than most people will ever feel in their entire lives. The hunting of people was, in truth, fun and exhilarating and satisfied a deep, dark, powerful desire for challenges and thrills. Back at West Point, Hansen had read the words of Ernest Hemingway: "Certainly there is no hunting like the hunting of man and those who have hunted armed men long enough and liked it, never really care for anything else thereafter."

Hemingway was right. And the greatest exhilaration of all was turning from the hunted to the hunter. Winning against long odds was every soldier's dream, and Hansen knew he needed to remind his men of that.

So when he was finished with the map, he said, "Gentlemen, forget the hour, forget this is punishment, forget that we're supposed to lose. Remember that we're the hunters. We carry the fire. Hooah!"

"HOOAH!" the men responded.

"So what do you think of this plan?" he asked them.

"Sounds good," said Neech. "I'm ready to kick some ass."

Keyman folded his arms over his chest and sighed deeply in disgust. "Sir, we might be the hunters, but we're still being set up for a fall, so if you ask me, it doesn't really matter. Just tell me where and when I have to be. That's all."

"Not exactly the answer I was looking for," Hansen snapped.

"Uh, sir, providing overwatch through that chokepoint is a good idea," said Abbot, trying to distract Hansen. "One thing we can do is play this more like a game instead of the usual rogue platoon scenario, where on contact we use one of the old seven battle drills."

"It is a game," said Keyman. "That's all it is."

Abbot raised his voice. "What I mean by *game* is that we need to get one tank across PL HOME. Just one tank. Not the whole platoon. Once we make contact, why don't we put one section, Alpha or Bravo, out front. They go in, guns blazing, drawing their fire, while the other section feints left, then charges right toward the end zone?"

"Yeah, while an entire platoon fires upon us," Keyman said with a snicker.

"Look at this," Abbot said, tracing a finger over the map. "If our guy with the ball follows this trail, which runs parallel to our primary approach, he can use these woods here and here for cover, plus the rice paddy over there will keep them from getting too close. Also, there's a pretty big hill over here that ain't on the map. Our guy comes around this side, then roars right on through with his wingman covering, and he's only exposed while crossing this leg, right here. If he's moving fast enough, he can cross the line before they do too much damage."

"Yeah, but that's providing they stick to the BPs we think they'll be in," said Keyman. "What if they use the woods you're talking about using for cover? I know I would."

"Maybe they will," Abbot agreed. "But our guy with the

ball will have the pedal to the metal. If they're in the tree line and we blow by them, maybe they'll get off a few minor hits and near misses, but there won't be enough time for a knife fight."

"And what doesn't kill us makes us stronger," said Neech.

"All right, I want to go with this," Hansen said. "But who runs with the ball?"

"The track with the best driver in the platoon," said Abbot. "Your track, Lieutenant."

Hansen cocked a brow. "You think Gatch is the best we have?"

"He's the most experienced and the only guy driving with Dale Earnhardt's blessing. So my money's on him."

"I agree," said Neech.

"What about you?" Hansen asked Keyman.

The staff sergeant drew back his head, a little dumbfounded. "I didn't know we had a say. Whatever . . ."

"All right, so we're set," Hansen said. "If it goes down otherwise, I might hand off the ball, and then we play it by ear. Good to go?"

"Good to go," all three answered.

Five minutes after they were back aboard their tanks, the call came in from Captain Loudermilk: "Red One, this is Apache Six. The remainder of Cobra elements are in place. Conduct your attack to PL HOME."

"Roger that, Apache Six," Hansen replied. "Red is LD at this time!" He had just given the cue that his platoon was crossing the line of departure, a graphic control measure designated to coordinate the departure of attack elements.

It was game on!

Standing proudly at his station, Hansen gazed across the line of tanks as they advanced, waves of exhaust warping the air, antennas swinging in the early morning wind.

Within minutes they were out of the attack position, bounding and bouncing across the hills toward their first choke point. The exhaustion, the cold, and the boredom were gone.

Second Lieutenant Jack Hansen was totally alive, his every sense screaming to reach out farther into his environment. Gooseflesh rippled across his neck as he scanned the terrain ahead, looking for smoke, antenna masts, even the occasional glimmer along the crests of hills that might betray a tank hiding along the reverse slope. Other than the stands of trees, there weren't many good reference points, and Hansen had assumed the enemy would exploit that advantage by picking initial BPs along those nondescript slopes.

He kept scanning, his mouth going dry, his view stolen by the damned snow booted up near the peaks. Where were they? As his frustration mounted, he reminded himself that if he cleared his mind and let his training and instincts take over, he would be all right.

Back in the early days at Knox, he had learned that there were four actions on contact with the enemy: deploy and report, evaluate/develop the situation, choose a course of action, and recommend/execute a course of action. However, when the battle began, it was hard to think straight—and most steps you executed simultaneously while people were screaming their lungs out. Bottom line: the platoon needed to react instinctively and instantly to the contact in order to survive it. And it was Hansen's job to make sure of that.

"Red Four, this is Red One. No joy here, over."

"Red One, this is Red Four. Same here."

"All right, Bravo section, set in overwatch while Alpha advances through Checkpoint Two," ordered Hansen.

Abbot and Neech peeled away from the group, heading for the tree line to the east so that they could cover the gap created by the narrow stand of trees lying ahead. A section of two tanks or even an entire platoon could come tear-assing around those trees to stage a quick and deadly ambush.

Meanwhile, Hansen and Keyman veered left, running parallel to the western woods. Snow and ice clung to the boughs, painting the zone an eerie bone white.

Hansen steadied his breathing as he and Keyman rolled on through the choke point, putting that stand of trees at the tip of the pyramid behind them. "Bravo, this is Alpha section. We've reached Checkpoint Two."

"Red, this is Red Three! Contact! Three tanks moving southwest from Checkpoint Three toward your position!" Neech cried into the platoon net.

"Bravo, bound forward! Alpha, set overwatch for Bravo's move!" Hansen ordered, spotting the three shadowy tracks rumbling over the slope about eighteen hundred meters away. He ducked down into the tank, placing his hatch in the open protected position. "Driver, get us the hell out of here!"

"I'm gettin', sir!"

At that instant the DIFCUE attached to the rear of the turret boomed to simulate incoming fire, then the CU beeped.

"Shit," Hansen muttered, glancing at the CU display, which read Hit. "Gunner, get us a target!"

"Searching," said Lee. "Targets obscured."

"Red One, this is Red Four," called Abbot. "Identified two M1s moving southeast toward my position."

ABBOT HAD SPENT all but about four years of his career on tanks. Of those four years, two had been spent in the numerous schools he was required to attend as he moved up in the enlisted ranks, and two had been spent on the trail as a drill sergeant at Fort Knox. He had seen time on the M60, the M1, the M1A1, the M1A2, and back on the M1A1. He knew tanking, which was why his vehicle scurried along the low ground, almost invisible to the less experienced tank commanders moving on the high ground toward his position.

Within seconds the flashing lights atop the enemy turrets indicated once again why Abbot was the platoon sergeant. He had scored Red's first two kills with the quiet precision of experience. Two down. Eight to go.

"**RED ONE, THIS** is Red Two," reported Keyman. "Contact. Two tanks rolling out of the tree line we just passed. They're firing!"

Hansen grabbed the TC override, slewed the turret around to the targets.

The DIFCUE boomed again, and his CU registered another hit. He knew he had to seize control of the situation. "Alpha section, orient south to destroy those two tanks. Bravo, set an attack by fire position to destroy the three tanks up north."

"Hang on!" Gatch yelled over the intercom.

A heartbeat later the tank barreled up a hill and was suddenly airborne like the *General Lee* from the old *Dukes of Hazard* TV show.

Hansen was about to mutter "Holy shit" when they crashed once, twice, a third time onto the snow, threatening to break the tank's torsion bars and knock molars from all of their mouths.

"The eagle has landed!" Gatch shouted.

"Shit, dude, that was awesome!" cried Deac.

Gatch quickly pulled back on the right side of his T-bar, making a hard right turn, orienting the thick protective armor of the front hull back toward the tanks set in ambush. The M1's stabilization system kept the main gun oriented on the enemy tank section as the entire hull turned 180 degrees.

"I have a target," Lee announced, and with that Hansen

released control back to the gunner. "The XO's tank! I want to kill his ass right now!"

"Up!" Deac reported.

Hansen bit his lip, then yelled, "Kill his ass!"

"On the way!"

Hansen's CU flashed. "Catastrophic kill, yeah!"

"Who the men? We the men!" screamed Gatch.

"*Crimson Death* strikes back!" added Deac.

Lee's face split open in a shit-eating grin. "I like killing ass!"

"Boys, are we having fun yet?" Hansen asked.

All three knew the answer: "HOOAH!"

For his part, Hansen was panting, drooling, and grinding his teeth while his pulse raged in his ears. He felt swollen with power. He wanted to rip off his Nomex coveralls, beat his fists on his bare chest, and let the world hear his war cry. But he had to contain himself and concentrate. Taking one great breath, he peered out of the hatch. "Whoa, slow down a second, Gatch. Let Keyman get between us and those other tanks ahead. Here he comes . . ."

ALL WEBBER NEEDED from Keyman was the order to fire, and the remaining tank assaulting them from the rear would be toast. "I say again, target identified! It's Van Buren's track!"

"Wait!" the staff sergeant ordered.

A sharp bang came from the DIFCUE out back. "He's firing at us!"

"Gunner, do you have a target?" Keyman asked.

"I've been saying I have! Target identified."

"Up!" hollered Smiley.

"Fire!"

"On the way!"

But it was too late. Even as they fired, the captain's tank answered.

"Aw, God damn it," Keyman shouted over the beeping. "Mobility kill! We got twenty seconds to stop this tank! Driver stop!"

While a hit from the other tank had taken out their ability to move, they could still shoot and communicate.

"Target identified!" Webber said. "Are you going to let me shoot his ass? Or do you want to think about it?"

"Shut up, Webber!"

"Up!"

"Fire!"

"On the fuckin' way!"

Once again, they traded fire with Van Buren's track, and while they scored a catastrophic kill, so did the captain.

"We shot the sheriff and his deputy, but now we're done," groaned Webber. "Hey, Sergeant? Any reason why we waited to fire?"

"You're dead, Webber," Keyman said, collapsing into his seat. "Make me happy and stay that way."

"I seem to be dying a lot these days. . . ."

"THEY GOT KEYMAN," Lee reported.

"Don't worry about it," Hansen said quickly. "We'll take them all on ourselves!"

"That's right, Lieutenant! We'll kill 'em all!" added Deac.

Still, Hansen bit back a curse and banged a fist on his TC's armrest. One of his tanks was already gone, and now Abbot and Neech weren't faring very well with the three tanks moving southwest. Both of them had taken hits, and Neech had sustained a firepower kill that had disabled his main gun. Abbot managed to take out one of the three before sustaining a commo kill that disabled his communications. Still, the score was five to one in their favor.

Hansen knew he had to get moving again. "Gatch, turn us around and get us back in this fight. Let's go!"

While the two remaining M1s closed to most assuredly finish off Neech and raise hell with the platoon sergeant, Hansen urged Gatch on while screaming at Lee to target at least one of the two tanks closing left.

"Identified," the gunner finally said.

"Up!"

"Fire!"

"On the way!"

The MGSS issued its flash and bang, then Hansen's CU registered a firepower kill just as they took another hit. But just a hit. "Okay, we're not dead yet," Hansen said. "But neither is he. Gatch!"

"Go faster, I know!"

They were leaving the three wooded zones behind, racing up onto higher ground, the surface growing so rough that Hansen could barely keep a steady eye through his extension. Nevertheless, he was having a ball. Despite the tense situation, he couldn't wipe the grin from his face. He was in an elite gun club whose members fired some very big guns and tear-assed around Korea like gods and monsters. Yet in their hearts they were just boys, loving the rush as they pushed their incredible toys to their limits.

He panned his scope a few degrees, and there they were: the last three tanks chewing their way up and over a hill to his eleven o'clock and about twelve hundred meters out. Distance to PL HOME? About fifteen hundred meters.

"Three moving tanks! Left tank first. You want a piece of us, you bastards? I don't thinks so! Come on, Lee! We're almost there!"

"I have a target."

"Up!"

"Fire!"

"On the way!"

Flash. Bang. Catastrophic kill. "Target! We got him!"

The crew whooped and hollered. Seven down, three to go.

"Driver, go right," Hansen said, spying a broad gully that appeared navigable and would get their turret down.

"Big bump," Gatch announced as they rode up over a hump, then suddenly plummeted at a forty-five degree angle for exactly three seconds and were momentarily swallowed by a huge cloud of dirt and snow as they hit bottom and leveled out.

"Fucking roller coaster," grunted a stunned Deac.

Hansen was gasping now. "Go! Go! Go!"

The tank fishtailed for a second, then Gatch regained control. The engine wailed in protest as Mr. NASCAR did his thing the way only he could. "Sir, I don't know if I can get us out of here. The next hump looks too steep!"

"We can do it!"

"Here goes nothing!"

A mottled wall of snow and sand grew before them, and Hansen wanted to call off the rocket ride, but Gatch suddenly jerked the T-bar left, toward a less steep bank that appeared from the shadows. The tracks dug in, grinding hard, carrying them up . . . and over the top.

"Thank you, Dale," Gatch whispered into the intercom. "Thank you . . . thank you . . ."

"Two moving tanks," Lee yelled. "Eight hundred meters. Wait. There's three now. I have a target."

"Up!"

"Fire!"

"On the way!"

Before Hansen's CU could register whether or not they had killed the tank, the unit registered a near miss on his track, then glowed great news: a catastrophic kill. Eight down, two to go.

"Target! He's dead!"

"I have another target!" Lee announced.

"Up!"

"Fire!"

"On the way!"

Even as they "destroyed" the next tank, Hansen realized they were just five hundred meters away from the PL HOME, with the last tank closing from seven hundred. And that last tank was commanded by his roommate, Gary Gutterson.

"This is it, boys! Just one more and we got this!" Hansen told them, never more emphatic. "The Phase Line is right there! Right there! Gunner, do you have a target?"

"Not yet."

"Come on!"

"Wait. Target still obscured."

"Gatch, can you level us out?"

"If we had wings I could!"

"Then grow us some wings!"

"Target identified."

"Up!"

Hansen's CU beeped, and his heart dropped to the bottom of the turret. "Son of a bitch!"

Catastrophic kill. Second Lieutenant Gary Gutterson had just waxed their asses.

"Red One, this is Apache Six. You are dead. I say again. You are dead. All of your vehicles have been destroyed. Clear all weapons systems and advise when clear, over."

"God damn it," Gatch said from his hole. "Couple seconds more was all I needed to get our turret down. Shit."

"Driver, stop," Hansen moaned. "Game over."

"Lieutenant, although we were killed, we fought valiantly," said Lee. "I did not believe we would get this far."

"He's right," said Deac. "We came pretty damned close. I mean, look at Keyman back there. That baldy bean got killed right away."

"Yeah, he did, didn't he," Hansen said. "Like he just rolled over."

* * *

THEY RETURNED TO the assembly area for a painful after-action review during which they suffered from the residual effects of the adrenaline rush. Being so high—even for a short time—made Hansen feel as though he had been wrapped in a sheet and dragged around Twin Bridges for a few hours. When the meeting was over, Gutterson came up to him and thrust out his hand. "That was a good run."

"Yeah, did okay." Hansen shook hands, then tugged up the zipper of his coveralls.

"And you came pretty far for a guy who spent most of his night partying with his girlfriend."

Hansen gave a faint snort. "What're you saying? I would've done better if I had stayed home and read the dash tens like you?"

"I'm just saying the war could be tomorrow. That's all."

"Yeah, well, you keep saying that, Gary." Hansen offered a lopsided grin, then turned to leave.

"Hey, just wondering . . . I saw the CSM talking to Keyman and Abbot back in the motor pool. What was that about?"

"I must've been in the turret. I didn't see that."

"Yeah, well, rumor has it that we got dragged out here because of something those guys did, like grease Burroway's gun tube?"

"You're going to believe that?" Hansen forced his crooked grin again, then marched back to his tank.

There, he found Abbot waiting for him. "Win some, lose some, huh?"

Hansen flicked his gaze to Keyman's track, where the staff sergeant was just mounting the turret. "He doesn't look too upset about losing. . . ."

"Maybe he's getting used to it."

"Or maybe he threw it."

"I'm not sure about that. Yeah, he thought this was all bullshit, but he's still pretty damned competitive."

"I'm going to ask you something, and you don't have to answer if you don't want to, but it's pretty obvious that Burroway singled us out for this. And it's obvious that he thinks one of us pulled that prank."

"You want a name."

"Yeah, I do."

Abbot sniffled, tugged at his red nose, then sighed loudly. "It was me."

"What?"

"I did it."

"Bullshit."

"I'm serious, LT."

"I don't believe you."

"Believe it. Burroway's been busting my balls for a long time now. I just wanted to see him get his for once. That's all. My mistake. And I'll accept the consequences."

"Did you see the CSM talking to Keyman and Webber?"

Abbot tightened his lips, then finally answered, "Yeah, I did."

"Do you know what it was about? Or should I get it from Keyman himself?"

"Lieutenant, we're all good people here, you know that. And you've told me how you want to be known as a real tanker, not just a butterbar. I respect that. Everyone respects that. And you proved yourself by winning Top Tank. With the exception of Keyman, morale's pretty high."

"Where are you going with this?"

"What I'm saying is that I do have a name for you, but I can't give it up. An investigation would ruin the platoon's morale, tarnish our reputation, and undermine everything you've done so far. But I'll do this. I'll go to the man, see if he's willing to talk. But he won't talk unless he's sure you'll keep it on the QT. We can settle this in house. Trust me. It's the best way."

"Sergeant Abbot, you've been a straight shooter since I

got here, and that's why we get along. But frankly, if some-one in my platoon has fucked up, I want to know who it is, and I want to know now. Then, and only then, will I decide whether I'm booting his ass out or not."

"Yes, sir."

"Give me a name."

Abbot opened his mouth.

BACK AT THE motor pool in Dragon Valley, Webber couldn't stop squinting and yawning as he helped the oth-ers strip the MILES gear from the tank and return it to the transit cases. When they were finished, he dragged himself up the hill leading from the motor pool to Cobra Com-pany's barracks.

When he pushed open his door, he found Lieutenant Hansen seated on the bunk and waiting for him.

"Hey, Webber."

"What's going on, Lieutenant?"

"I sent your bunkmate on a little errand so you and I can talk."

Webber took a seat on Keyman's bunk. "You don't have to say anything, Lieutenant. It was my fault. Keyman was giving me the order to fire, but I delayed. I didn't think I had the target. But then I did. It was too late, though. We shouldn't have died so quick. But we did. And like I said, it was my fault."

"Sergeant Webber, I didn't come here to talk about that. I understand that you like to help guys in need. I under-stand that you're quite the businessman. . . ."

Holy shit, Webber thought. *He fucking knows!* "Are you talking about loan-sharking, sir?"

"Exactly. And you know something, Webber? I like you. You're a nice guy. And a damned good gunner. Don't fuck it all up, man. You know what I'm saying?"

"Yes, I do, sir."

"Just one warning. That's all you get. You cease and desist. And you know what? Years down the line, you'll thank me for this little talk—because we both know that going to jail really sucks."

"Sir, you're right. Thank you, sir."

Hansen stood. "Oh, and just one more thing; you didn't delay firing, Keyman did, didn't he . . ."

Webber lowered his gaze and gave the slightest of nods.

"I thought so. All right, are we clear on all this?"

"Perfectly clear, sir."

"Good. Get some sleep."

"Yes, sir."

Two seconds after the lieutenant left, Webber fell back on his bunk and gasped. Jesus, he had finally pushed it too far. And thank God he had a lieutenant who was giving him another chance. Some other maniac would not have been as generous.

Okay. The holidays were coming. So was the new year. He would turn over a new leaf. Change his ways. Go honest. Somehow. Even though loan-sharking gave him a rush almost equal to being an Abrams gunner, Webber would quit cold turkey.

CHAPTER
SEVEN

SPIRITS WERE RUNNING high in Hansen's platoon. They had already licked their wounds from the MILES exercise, and now, at 0800 on Christmas Eve, they looked forward to an easy day of routine maintenance and recovery operations. Better still, they would be getting off duty by 1200 hours because the Army worked on a half-day schedule beginning around December 20 and continuing through the first part of the new year. While midtour leaves during the holidays weakened First Tank by about 10 percent, with some soldiers having gone stateside to be with their loved ones, Charlie Company was almost fully staffed, as were Alpha, Bravo, and Delta Companies.

Unfortunately, one of the disadvantages of the standard one-year tour in Korea was that soldiers were always coming and going, so it was difficult for a unit to maintain 100 percent of its authorized strength. The average monthly personnel turnover was almost 20 percent.

Despite all of that, the men of First Tank managed to bond with each other, even more so during holidays. You could feel it in the air. The only dark clouds hanging over the day were the persistent rumors filtering down from 1st "Iron" Brigade. Word had it that the North Koreans were reinforcing their first echelon along the DMZ as well as transferring elements of their mechanized corps northwest of Kaesong to more southern positions. Hansen was well aware that the intelligence folks in Maryland and around D.C. kept a very close eye and ear on the DPRK forces, and those folks were never starved for information. Still, too much data sometimes resulted in misinterpretation or in something being overlooked. Hansen hoped those people doing the analysis would lay off the spiked eggnog and stay sharp.

Like the other tankers, Hansen had his own ideas about why the North was shifting forces, and like the others, he assumed that whatever they were doing was meant to ruin American morale during Christmastime. When you knew your enemy was celebrating, why not piss him off by shifting forces and playing psychological games?

"I'm telling you, sir, they're going to call another alert tonight—because that's the kind of luck we have," said Deac.

Hansen and the loader were on the turret, having just returned from field-stripping and cleaning the machine guns in the supply room. Gatch was tightening a couple of Wedge-Bolts, and Lee was lending a hand.

"Just try to stay positive, Deac, all right?" Hansen asked. "No CO in his right mind would call an alert on Christmas Eve."

"Well, there it is, then. Brigade has gone insane."

Second Lieutenant Gary Gutterson came strutting down the tank line, headed toward his own track.

Hansen got an idea that he knew would lift the loader's spirits. "Hey, Deac? Time for a boom check, huh?"

Deac looked surprised for a second, then he grinned broadly. "Yes, sir!"

"Hey, Gary," Hansen called. "Can you give us a hand?"

"Come on, Jack, I'm busy right now."

"No, come on. This'll take a second."

The lieutenant swore through a sigh, then ambled over as Hansen crawled down from the tank and dropped onto the snow. "We need to see if the bore evacuator needs to be cleaned," he began. "But we don't want to pull the damned thing off and relube the threads if it's still good."

Gutterson frowned. "So why do you need me?"

Deac and Lee had already depressed the gun off to one side of the tank, about even with Gutterson's head.

"Just go ahead, lean in there, and yell boom a few times, as loud as you can," Hansen instructed.

"Hey, I don't have time for this."

But Hansen was already mounting the tank. "Come on, Gary. I thought you were a team player."

The unsuspecting lieutenant glanced around impatiently, then, as Hansen dropped into his station, Gutterson said, "Boom."

"Louder, Gary. We still can't tell."

Gutterson wrapped his hands around the gun tube, pressed his face forward, and yelled, "BOOM! BOOM! BOOM!"

Gatch and Deac lost it, and as Gutterson removed his face from the tube, Hansen lost it, too.

"What the hell is this?" Gutterson demanded.

"Boom check complete," Hansen said through his laughter. "You're dismissed now, Lieutenant!"

Replacement cost of the M1A1 Abrams?

Over four million dollars.

The look that came over Gutterson's face?

Priceless.

"Fuck you, Hansen! Payback's a bitch! Just remember that!" The lieutenant flitted off.

"Sir, the boom check's a little hazing thing we usually do to new officers," said Gatch.

"Yeah, I know, and I was surprised you didn't pull one on me. But I would've been ready for it. Lieutenant Gutterson on the other hand . . . well, I just had a feeling we'd get him good. We owed him anyway for killing us."

"That was pretty cool, sir," said Deac.

"It *was* pretty cool, wasn't it. But he's going to whine for weeks. Mark my words." Hansen took in a long, cold breath. "All right, let's get this done before we freeze our balls off."

"Frozen balls . . . not good," said Lee.

SECOND LIEUTENANT SUH Jae Sung took great pride in the antiquity and continuity of his society, which dated back to pre-Christian times. His descendants had been part of migratory groups that had entered the Korean peninsula from Siberia, Manchuria, and inner Asia. They had founded a society that had lived harmoniously for thousands of years. They believed, as most North Koreans still did, that the emphasis should be placed on the group's harmony and happiness.

Contrarily, the Americans were selfish individualists about to celebrate a holiday whose focus was on attaining goods. They were so wrapped up in themselves, so preoccupied by their purchases, that they had forgotten the true meaning of their holiday. They had succumbed to an evil force that had turned them into obsessed consumers who taught others, like the South Koreans, that happiness was measured by material wealth.

With a populace as corrupt as that, Suh did not understand why his American and South Korean counterparts were willing to mount their tanks, fight, and die so that others could continue to lead shallow lives of greed. He could not reconcile that. However, his lack of understanding did not change the fact that those American and South Korean fools would fight bitterly to the death.

As would Suh and his men. Moreover, they would do so in a Soviet-made tank that the Americans considered obsolete and somewhat easy to kill.

Given the opportunity, Suh would surprise them.

Never mind the tank's cramped crew compartment, its thin armor, its crude fire control system, and how its fuel and ammunition storage areas were vulnerable to enemy fire.

Never mind how dangerous levels of carbon monoxide could accumulate inside the turret from a malfunction in the automatic spent cartridge ejection system.

And never mind that rapid-fire and second-hit capabilities were limited and that Suh could not fire the main gun from his position.

Consider that their 115 mm smoothbore main gun fired sabot rounds whose penetrators flew in very flat trajectories, making them extremely accurate to a maximum effective range of 1,600 meters.

Consider that their tank had been retrofitted with full NBC collective protection systems, including air filtration and overpressure.

And consider that they now had improved night vision, a basic stabilization system, and a laser range finder that had replaced the stadiametric reticle range finder.

They were not so obsolete after all—and soon they would prove that.

Suh's company commander had just informed him that two infantry regiments reinforced with tanks and artillery would, under the veil of an approaching blizzard, launch a major offensive sometime during the night. Those regiments would be accompanied by special forces troops whose numbers could reach 100,000. Once those initial elements breached the DMZ, Suh's brigade would move in to envelop and destroy all forward deployed enemy forces, paving the way for the third echelon to rumble down toward Seoul. The dear leader in Pyongyang had envisioned reunifying the peninsula within thirty days and planned to fight a two-front war: the first front consisted of forces breaching the DMZ to allow others to head down toward Seoul; the second comprised of special operations forces that would penetrate the enemy's rear to launch disruptive attacks on his infrastructure.

Indeed, Suh had predicted that the dear leader would seize the opportunity to act, and Suh had already taken great pride in telling the skeptical Sergeant Yoon Jeong-Seop that "You were wrong," and that the North would liberate the South.

All afternoon Suh and his crew, along with the crews of the other two tanks in his platoon, made sure that every component of their tracks was fully functional and battle ready. They had never been more serious.

Now, as the sun began to vanish behind the mountains, Corporal Kang slid out of his driver's hole, then climbed down onto the snow to stand beside Suh. "*So-wi,* our tank is full, and all fluid levels are in order."

"Excellent, driver." Suh glanced at the man, saw a question in the corporal's gaze. "What is it, *Sambyong?*"

"Are we really going to war?"

"Yes. Are you afraid?"

"No, *So-wi.* I am angry."

"Angry?"

"Yes, because I am a new driver. I wanted more time to become more proficient."

"*Sambyong,* we are on a noble mission to liberate the people of the South. Our revolutionary spirit will assure our victory, not your driving skills."

"Yes, *So-wi.*"

"If you are still angry, then you can take out that anger on the enemy, when we meet him on the battlefield."

"Yes, *So-wi.*"

Suh caught a last glimpse of the sun, just as it shied away and cast a pink halo over the peaks. He might not live to see such beauty again. He closed his eyes and tried to remember.

A LIGHT SNOW was beginning to fall as Hansen finished wrapping the simple gold necklace he had bought for Karen. While they had only spoken once on the phone since that night at the Flower House, they had confirmed their plans to attend a party at the Warrior Club, a facility on Camp Casey that had a decent restaurant and a room that would be decorated for the holiday. Hansen had already made arrangements with his chain of command and the provost marshal's office to get her into Camp Casey. With the present wrapped, he just sat there at his desk, staring out the window, watching the snow come down. He called back to Gutterson, who was lying on his bunk, reading the most recent copy of *Armor* magazine. "Hey, you hear that?"

"Hear what?"

"Listen . . . boom. Boom. BOOM!"

"You're an asshole."

"Gary, you're just way too uptight. You're like one of those commissars from the Red Army."

The second lieutenant sat up. "How could you embarrass me like that in front of your men? How could you show such utter disrespect for a fellow officer?"

"Utter disrespect? Gary, it was a fucking joke."

"No, you're the joke, man. You are. A real officer wouldn't have done something like that. Now the entire company will be talking about me, laughing behind my back. I didn't come here to be laughed at. I came here to expose the weaknesses of my platoon, eliminate them, and turn my men into the kind of tankers that First Tank deserves. I'm not kidding. I'm not making jokes. I'm here to do a job. Not be turned into a fool."

"Look, Gary, we're the only ones who know about it,

and my guys won't say anything, okay? Like I said, it was just a joke. I'm sorry if you can't understand that."

The slight young man thought a moment. "Do you have any idea what I went through with those fucking maniacs back at the Point? Do you have any clue? I'm not you, Hansen. I don't look like officer material. I'm lucky I made it out of there alive. Then I get here, and I got you."

"Gary, I didn't know. I'm sorry, all right? No more jokes. Maybe you just need, I don't know, a good shagging. Get rid of all that pent-up energy. Next time your men go downrange to TDC, you have to go. Really."

Gutterson lay back on his bunk, throwing an arm over his forehead. "Right now, back home in Ohio, my mom's baking cookies. Every Christmas Eve she bakes cookies. That's what I need. Not some skanky bitch. Just one of those cookies."

Hansen closed his eyes, took a breath through his nose. "Yeah, man. I can smell them. Chocolate chips with raisins and walnuts . . ."

"What kind of heathen are you? They're butter cookies, man. Butter cookies . . ."

THE CHARLIE COMPANY Christmas party was in full swing as Webber, Smiley, and Morbid swaggered into the day room like they owned the place. Festoons of silvery garland draped down from the ceiling, along with multicolored lights that winked like one of Ajima's cheap whores. A Merry Christmas banner that someone had printed out on a computer hung lopsided from the back wall, near which stood a folding table weighed down by bowls of punch, coolers full of beer, and a whole assortment of pretzels, chips, and dips. There were even a half-dozen fruitcakes guys had received from their grandmas or old aunts living in West Palm Beach, along with boxes of chocolates from every confectionary company on the planet. A boom box lying somewhere behind a knot of guys from Blue Platoon blasted a golden oldie: Ozzy Osborne's "Crazy Train"—appropriate holiday music to be sure.

A few of the Korea lifers had told Webber about the time Ozzy had paid a visit to First Tank. While touring military installations throughout Asia, the rock star had stopped in at Camp Casey to tour First Tank's facilities, get a ride on an M1A1, and perform for the soldiers of the 2nd Infantry Division. His trip was forever memorialized on the inside cover of his album *Live at Budokan*.

"Ozzy," Webber said, grinning and nodding to the powerful beat.

"I knew it," began a dour-faced Morbid. "Chips and beer. That's all we rate, even on Christmas Eve. Chips and beer."

"Shut up, you depressing piece of shit," Webber snapped. "It's time to party! And when Keyman gets here, we're going to get him silly drunk and have some fun!"

"What about our famous platoon leader?" Morbid asked. "I bet he ain't coming. He'll be over there with the rest of the officers, eating all kinds of hors d'oeuvres and drinking expensive champagne."

"Maybe, but the lieutenant's a stand-up guy," said Webber. "Trust me on that one."

"Now who are you guys trying to impersonate?" said Abbot, shouldering his way around a few other guys. "Oh, I get it now. You're Moe," he told Webber. "You're Larry," he told Morbid. "And you're, well, you're just Smiley. You all know my wife, Kim?"

Abbot's wife was quite the looker for a middle-aged Korean babe—slim, with a surprisingly angular face and long, shiny hair. But Webber just hated it when she opened her mouth and spoiled the illusion. "Y'all ready to have a good time tonight?" she asked in her Texas cowgirl twang.

Webber nodded, then pretended he saw someone he knew. "If you'll excuse me . . ."

"Hey, where you going?" Morbid called. "Don't you know misery loves company?"

"Dude, look around. Most of the company is right here."

Webber wove his way to the punch bowl, where he found Keyman, open beer in hand, guzzling his first. "Didn't see you come in," he told his TC.

"Figured I'd target a beer first." Keyman reached into his breast pocket, produced something that he kept in a closed fist. "Webber, you are without question the biggest fuckup in this platoon. But as a gunner, you are second to none—which is why I want you to have this." He pushed the object into Webber's hand.

When Webber opened his palm, there sat a long, brass shell casing. "What's this?"

"Just something that means a lot to me. Don't lose it. Merry Christmas." And with that, the tank commander drifted off, swaying to the beat as the music segued into another ironic Osborne classic: "Mama I'm Coming Home."

Webber stood there, holding the shell casing, his jaw going slack as he muttered, "What the hell was that?"

"Well, well, well, what do we have here?" said Neech as he and his crew moseyed on up to the drink table. "Is it man or beast? I tell you, Popeye, I just don't know."

The KATUSA who loved chicken grinned. "Webber, I want beer. You move."

"Yeah, come on, Webber," added Romeo. "Get your white boy ass out of the way, otherwise I'm calling for backup."

"And Batman's right here," said Wayne, his voice deep but hardly threatening.

"Jesus, go back to the Land of Misfit Toys, all of you!" Webber cried as he shifted aside. "And where's my Christmas present? Come on, you cheap bastards!"

"We got you something," said Sparrow, who was chatting

with fellow crew members Paz and Park from Abbot's tank. "It's a candy cane. Now bend over, and we'll show you how it works."

"Yeah, you'll make some politician, Sparrow," Webber said. "You already know the drill."

HANSEN WAS EXCITED about meeting Karen at the gate, but he also worried that there might be an awkward moment in which he let down his guard and revealed his lingering disappointment over her decision to leave South Korea. However, when the time came, she rushed to him, gave him a bear hug, drew back, then dove back in for an open mouthed kiss that sent a chill straight down his spine. When the kiss finally ended, she looked at him and whispered, "I missed you."

"I missed you, too," he said, pulling her bright red scarf away from her face. "Look at you, with your fancy wool jacket and this scarf. . . ."

"I'm all wrapped up—because I'm your present."

"Let's get out of here before this conversation gets too cute—"

"No, wait. I just want to tell you something." She moved in close, held him by the shoulders, batted her lashes, then widened those terribly beautiful eyes. "I'm home."

"What?"

"I'm home. Right here." She squeezed his shoulders. "I'm going to take a chance on you."

"What does that mean?"

"It means that I'm not letting you go. It just took me a few days to realize that."

"So you're staying?"

"I already talked to my boss. They'll renew my contract in a heartbeat." She smiled like a naïve schoolgirl. "I'm Numba One English Teacher."

"I don't know what to say."

"You could just jump up and down and act happy if you want. . . ."

"Oh, I'm happy. It's just . . . I don't want you to resent me for the sacrifices you'll make."

"That's why I needed to think about this alone and make my own decision."

"Yeah, but I come with sixty-eight tons of baggage, and that's only the tank I'm talking about. There's the people I'm responsible for, the moves, the deployments. . . ."

"So you've said. I've thought about everything. And I've made up my mind. So now, can we get out of this cold?"

He slid an arm around her back, then led her to officers' country, where a quite civilized party was in progress at the Warrior Club, a party they would only attend for a half hour or so before Hansen took her to Dragon Valley, where they would spend the remainder of the evening partying with his men. Originally, they were going to spend the better part of their night at the club because Hansen didn't want the boys to meet the woman who was about to dump him. But lo and behold, she had changed her mind, and so had he. And damn, if that didn't feel good.

After greeting Captain Van Buren and company executive officer First Lieutenant Chase, whose eyes told Hansen that they thought his date was as stunning as she was articulate, he and Karen drifted over to the bar, where a lone Gary Gutterson sat, nursing his drink. Hansen kept the introductions short, then said, "Gary, it's Christmas Eve, and you and I are going to party with our men. We expect them to die for us, so this is the least we can do."

"Yeah, come on," Karen teased. "I heard you're a good dancer." She winked at Hansen, who had never said a word about Gutterson's rug-cutting abilities.

The dour-faced lieutenant glanced up. "Well, all right. But I'm not staying long."

* * *

WEBBER WAS FEELING a decent buzz as he returned to the drink table. Keyman leaned on the nearby wall, beer in hand, gaze panning over the crowd as Romeo and Sparrow joined forces to teach the others how to hip-hop with the best of them. Webber, like Deac and Gatch, was more a metal head, so he had taken the opportunity to refuel. "Hey, you going to lean on that wall all night?"

Keyman just looked at him, taking a sip of his beer.

Webber reached into his pocket, pulled out the casing, held it up. "So what is this?"

Something caught Keyman's attention. "Aw, shit. You have to be kidding me."

A crowd of tankers was gathering at the door, where Hansen, a beautiful dark-haired woman, and Lieutenant Gary Gutterson stood, shaking hands, banging fists, and saying "Merry Christmas" to all who approached. It was quite an entrance, and while it wasn't unusual for a couple of officers to crash a party thrown by NCOs and enlisted, no one really expected them to show up.

Especially Keyman.

"What's the matter?" Webber asked the TC. "The room's not big enough for the both of you?"

Keyman was already seething. "He doesn't belong here."

"I think it's cool," Webber argued. "He's showing us he's not too good for us. Give the guy a chance."

With his gaze riveted on Hansen, Keyman finished his beer, then crushed the can in his fist.

"Whoa, tough guy in house," Webber said in a bad Korean accent. "He crush can like Terminator!"

Keyman pushed himself off the wall and staggered into the crowd, homing in on Hansen.

"That's my cue," Webber muttered to himself as he fell in behind the TC, fearing the worst. When Staff Sergeant Timothy Key got drunk, club owners and *ajimas* up and down the TDC strip locked their doors, moved their children into the cellars, and waited for the storm to pass.

"Hey! Hey! Hey!" Keyman yelled. "Well, if it isn't Mr. Top Fucking Tank himself, Lieutenant Jack Hansen, straight from New Yawk. City slicker comes here to the snow-white mountains of Korea to teach all us number-two guys how to be good, obedient soldiers." Keyman staggered up to Hansen, gave a shaky salute, then shouted, "STAFF SERGEANT TIMOTHY KEY, REPORTING FOR DUTY, SIR!"

Webber shrugged at Hansen, who widened his gaze in a plea for Webber to do something. "All right, all right," Webber said, driving himself in front of Keyman. "The staff sergeant just wanted to say hello."

"Tell me, Lieutenant. How'd it feel out there, all alone with all them tanks breathing down your neck?" asked Keyman. "Sucks losing, don't it? Feels shitty, don't it?"

Hansen pulled away from his girlfriend and started toward Keyman, but Deac and Gatch, who had been standing nearby, jumped in to grab the lieutenant's arms. "You rolled over out there!" Hansen cried, trying to rip himself free. "You gave up! Not me! Maybe we could've won. But now we'll never know."

Webber had already seized one of Keyman's arms, and Abbot had come in to wrap both of his arms around Keyman's chest. As the platoon sergeant began hauling Keyman away, the drunken idiot hollered, "Merry Christmas, Lieutenant! Merry Christmas!"

SHOVING OFF DEAC and Gatch, Hansen smoothed out his sleeves and tried to compose himself.

"Sorry, Lieutenant," said Gatch. "That's not Keyman. Just the beer talking."

"No, that was him."

"Well, shit, we ain't going to let that ruin our Christmas Eve," Deac said.

"Nice work, Jack. You've obviously won the hearts and minds of your men," said Gutterson.

"Shut up, Gary."

"You all right?" Karen asked him.

"Yeah, let's get a drink and try to let that roll right off our shoulders. It's Christmas Eve!"

One of Gutterson's men, a loader from his wingman's tank, came up and started a conversation with the lieutenant.

"Looks like he'll be all right," said Karen as they headed for the drink table.

"Weird. I didn't think I'd need saving," said Hansen.

"What's his problem with you, anyway?"

As they reached the table and Hansen grabbed a couple of beers, he faced her, shoved a beer in her hand, and said, "Forget about him. Let's get a little drunk. Then we're going to dance."

"Jack, I've seen you dance. It's not pretty."

He winked. "Which is why you're getting drunk."

WEBBER AND ABBOT steered Keyman toward his bunk, then plopped him down. "I don't want you back in there if you're going to be like this," Abbot told Keyman.

"You just tell me when he leaves," Keyman said, slurring his words. "Then I'll come back and play nice."

"Stay with him?" Abbot asked Webber.

"Aw, come on, Sarge. It's Christmas Eve. I don't want to be a baby-sitter!"

"What the fuck are you talking about?" Keyman asked, his head now wobbling. "Gunner, you sit down and find me a fucking target right now!"

"You heard the man," Abbot said, heading for the door. "And don't worry, Webber. He'll pass out in a minute."

"Two tanks! Stationary tank first," babbled Keyman, his

eyes now closed. "Up! Fire! On the way! Target! Cease fire! Cease fire!"

Webber pulled up a chair beside Keyman's bunk. "You know, Sergeant, I wanted to get you drunk and have some fun. But you got yourself drunk and ruined my fun. What's wrong with that fucking picture?"

"Where's that shell casing I gave you?"

"I got it right here in my pocket."

"Give it back, you ungrateful bastard."

With a sigh, Webber pulled out the casing, looked at it, then said, "No. I'm keeping it. It's my Christmas present. Don't be an Indian giver, you asshole."

Keyman's eyes opened wide. "Give it to me now."

"Okay. You tell me what it means to you, and I'll give it back."

"My father gave it to me. Now give me the fucking thing."

"What's the story behind it?"

Keyman leaned forward, propped his elbows on his thighs, but one slipped and he nearly fell onto the floor. Webber stood and drove the staff sergeant back, onto the bunk, where he lay his head on his pillow. "When I was a kid, my dad and I went out hunting. I shot my first white-tail. And that's the casing."

"Here . . ." Webber shoved the piece of brass into Keyman's hand.

"No, it's okay. I want you to have it." Keyman forced the casing back into Webber's palm.

"Why?"

"Because you're the only one here who's ever had the balls to stand up to me."

"Because you're an overbearing prick who always has to be number one."

"It's not my fault," Keyman snapped. "It's his fault. His fucking fault!"

"Whose? Hansen's?"

"No, my father's. That day we went hunting . . . that's the only day I can remember that I didn't fuck up. That day, I was number one, and he got to see it."

"Sounds like Dad was a real winner."

"He did not tolerate losers. And my older brother, that motherfucker, he was always the winner. Not me."

"So you're an overbearing dysfunctional prick. I can deal with that—so long as you're willing to stay here and let me go have some fun."

"You're dismissed, Webber."

"Thanks. And by the way, you're taking me off all the shit details, right?"

"Yeah, whatever you say. . . ."

Webber took a last look at the staff sergeant. Suddenly, Keyman was no longer the imposing bald man who breathed fire and spat chew. He was just a fucked up little kid whose dad probably had no idea of the scars he had inflicted. Webber had to catch himself, though. In his schemer's head, he was already plotting ways to use the staff sergeant's confession against him. To the old Webber, blackmail was a Victoria's Secret model whispering in his ear. But he was the new and improved Webber, the extreme Webber, the Webber who . . . cared. But hadn't he already used the moment to get himself off the shit details? Damn, old habits die hard.

HANSEN COULD HARDLY believe what he was seeing. Gutterson was seated in a corner, surrounded by his men, and telling a story that had them captivated.

"Look at that," he told Karen as they swayed to some bluesy ballad whose title he had forgotten. "Geek boy makes friends."

"He's just shy, that's all."

"Let's drift over there. I just have to hear what he's talking about."

He led her toward the edge of the crowd, but before they could get close enough, they bumped into Abbot, who was dancing with his wife. "Lieutenant, I don't believe I've introduced my wife to your lovely date. This is Kim."

"Hi, I'm Karen."

"Y'all make a beautiful couple," said the Korean woman, shaking hands.

Karen grinned in surprise. "Wow, I assumed you were—"

"Most people do. But I've spent so many years in Texas that I guess it's rubbed off. Now I have fun with it—especially here."

"That's cool. The first time I went to England and heard a black person speak with an English accent, I was taken aback because as Americans we have these biases associated with language and race. It's a really interesting topic to study."

"Karen's an English teacher," Hansen explained. "Can you tell?"

"Oh, I'd better watch what I say," said Abbot. "My grammar sucks."

"Don't worry, I never correct people—unless they're paying, of course."

"A businesswoman, too?" Abbot noted with a broad grin. "All right, Lieutenant. You hit the jackpot."

Hansen smiled at Karen, nodded. "Well, we're going to keep making the rounds."

"Us, too," said Abbot. "Catch up with you later."

Karen and Kim exchanged the requisite "Nice to meet you"s, then Hansen took Karen's hand and led her over toward Gutterson. However, the group was breaking up and making a beeline for the food. "Hey, Gary? Merry Christmas, man."

"You, too. And hey, this was a good idea."

* * *

IN THE HALLWAY outside the day room, Gatch met up with Deac. While they each had four beers on board, they were still sober enough to accomplish the mission.

"You get it?" Deac asked.

"Yeah, man. We're good to go."

"I don't know, man. I'm a little worried."

Gatch made a face. "Dude, are you kidding?"

"Yeah, I am. This is going to be a fucking blast!"

"Cool. The recon unit has already issued their report. The target is in place."

Deac gave a furtive glance toward the door. "Then what are we waiting for, buddy? Let's roll!"

Gatch began humming that classical music from the movie *Apocalypse Now* as he and Deac strode down the hall, ready to attack. The big, hillbilly loader joined in, and they had some serious humming going on by the time they reached their destination.

CHAPTER
EIGHT

A HALF-DOZEN STRAGGLERS remained in the day room, nibbling on busted chips and broken pretzels from the bottoms of bowls and ladling out the last dregs of punch. The beer was long gone. A bad bulb in one string of blinking lights had left half the set dark, and the Scotch tape holding up the computer banner had finally failed. Even so, the room still felt festive to Hansen, probably because the mixture of heavy metal and hip-hop music had given way to someone's CD collection of traditional Christmas songs.

The division leadership had seen fit to slightly extend the curfew hours for the evening, but it was quickly approaching the time when Karen would have to leave the camp. Since she was not a Department of Defense employee or a military dependent, she could only remain on post for a certain amount of time. It was just another challenge to their challenged relationship.

While "Silent Night" played faintly from the boom box,

they sat on the sofa, and he gave her his present. "It's just something little. Merry Christmas."

She reached into her purse and handed him a gift wrapped package slightly larger than his. "Go ahead. Open yours first."

He did. Inside, lying on a bed of cotton, was a solid-looking pocket watch, mostly silver but trimmed in gold. He pressed a small button, and the watch opened to reveal a clock face on one side and a picture of her on the other. It was a damned good picture, too, one of those Glamour Shots deals. She looked hot, all made up and glowing.

"I told you my grandfather fought here back in the day, and my grandmother said she had given him a pocket watch with her picture in it. She wanted to be sure that even though they were apart, they'd still be spending *time* together."

"That's a good pun. And this is really cool. Thank you." He gave her a soft, passionate kiss.

Then she opened her present, gasped a little at the elegant gold necklace, and asked that he help her put it on.

"I'm not real good with jewelry," he said. "I mean picking it out."

"You did fine. It's beautiful. Thank you."

"To be honest, I wasn't sure I should get you something. I didn't want to put any pressure on you. But I figured I'd give you this just to say thanks for making my time here so . . . so great."

"Well, you're welcome. And the feeling's mutual. But now do I really have to go?"

He sighed. "Yeah, the snow's coming down pretty hard. But it'd be nice if you could sleep over."

"I'll have to write the president about that."

AFTER MAKING SURE that Karen got home safely, Hansen returned to the camp, and, as he lay on his bunk, staring at his new watch and at her picture, he felt good about, well, life. He was Top Tank. He had a terrific girl-friend. He had even helped his roommate come out of his shell. And even though the situation with Keyman had taken a turn for the worse, he still maintained hope that one day they would reach some kind of an agreement, tacit or otherwise.

Gutterson, who still hadn't fallen asleep, was listening to the Elvis Presley Christmas album via his clock radio/CD player.

"Hey, Gary? At the party, what where you talking about with your men?"

"I was telling them this story about my uncle Jack. He was a tanker, a platoon leader, just like us. It was back in the winter of 1980, in some shit hole in Germany, where he took part in this really intense exercise. Long story short, eight guys and two tanks made monkeys out of a hundred and fifty of America's best, guys who were equipped with something like twenty-five vehicles."

"You're kidding me."

"Nope."

"What happened, man? Come on."

"I'm tired. I'll tell you in the morning. Merry Christmas."

"All right. You, too."

NINETEEN-YEAR-OLD PRIVATE JANG Se Yong was assigned to the Reconnaissance Battalion, 7th Infantry Division, II ROK Corps, First ROK Army, and he had just returned from a patrol through the DMZ along the Chorwon Approach. They had driven through predesignated sectors of the border, and they never made the same route twice. It was impossible for every patrol to cover their entire sector effectively; moreover, doing so would require a certain level of regularity that the enemy could exploit. Thus, Jang and his comrades had patrolled those multiple sectors and had returned to their debriefing shack.

At the moment, he stood on the far side of the shack, out of visual range of possible snipers. He hadn't been able to smoke during the patrol, so he was taking deep pulls on his 88 Brand, his gaze always fixed north, toward the danger he still had not grown used to, even after serving for nearly a year along the border. The darkness and the falling snow obscured everything, and Jang couldn't wait to get out of the cold.

Not halfway through his smoke, Jang was interrupted by a flurry of activity. He learned that a group of North Korean special forces commandos had just launched a mistimed attack on an ROK command post about a kilometer east of their position. ROK forces were putting down the raid and had learned that a regiment was attempting to break through the DMZ via a tunnel. Seismic monitoring had confirmed that NKPA infantry forces were on the move. ROK intelligence still believed that it would take the enemy at least forty-eight hours to fully mobilize for an assault. But that didn't matter. Jang would not be racking out. He would be on alert all night.

As he sighed loudly in anger, NKPA artillery fire suddenly slashed across and lit up the stormy sky. He craned his neck and just stood there for a second, watching the glistening streaks in utter disbelief. As the explosions echoed behind him and his commanding officer broke into a fit of hollering, Jang snapped out of his trance and sprang forward toward his gun position. Automatic weapons fire reverberated in the distance, then drew closer, closer still.

"**JACK! HOLY SHIT**, man!"

Alert sirens blared.

Hansen's eyes snapped open. Darkness. The wind was rattling the windows—but a more significant sound reverberated even louder: multiple explosions. Dozens of them.

"They've opened up," said Gutterson. "They're hitting the reverse slope! Come on!"

For a few seconds, Hansen's senses were overloaded. Was this someone's poor idea of a practical joke? He sat up and squinted as Gutterson put on the light. Attack? Were they really under artillery attack? More muffled sounds of explosions and the incessant warbling of the siren seemed to provide the unbelievable answer. He went to the window, wiped off the condensation. The northern sky flickered with light as though it were wired to a faulty circuit.

"Jack!"

In his mind's eye, Hansen saw himself standing at the window as a shell struck, tearing apart the building as effortlessly as it tore apart his flesh. He shuddered and caught his breath, reminding himself that for the moment, they should be all right. Most of the NKPA's hardened artillery sites (HARTS) were not in position to make direct strikes on Camp Casey because the base lay in a valley running from west to east and was protected by Mount Soyo to the north. Long-range fires required low trajectories and could not be accomplished with Soyo towering in the way.

Still, there was speculation that the NKPA could somehow move their 122 mm guns or even the big 130 mm Koksan guns to points about five kilometers west of the DMZ and fire upon Casey from a west-to-east axis. Although the terrain in that area was not suitable for artillery because of its steep slopes, and the direction of the mountains made orienting HARTS even more difficult, the NKPA could have an unlikely but deadly surprise up their sleeves.

Or they could simply choose an easier and much more deadly route: unleash one of their long-range NODONG-1s, a SCUD-like, surface-to-surface guided ballistic missile whose range included not only the entire Korean peninsula but Japan as well. Though not terribly accurate, the missile could carry high explosives as well as chemical and biological agents. The slang term for getting hit with such agents was getting slimed, and that fear produced a mindset of confusion that could easily unravel Hansen and his men. If in doubt, they would protect themselves, but getting into all that chemical protective gear would kill their peripheral vision and reduce their overall efficiency by 25 percent or more.

After rushing into his Nomex coveralls, Hansen grabbed the CVC bag he kept loaded with the essentials like socks, underwear, extra boots, and personal hygiene items. He and Gutterson bolted out of their room and into the chaos of the hallway as half-dressed, half-asleep, and half-hungover officers shuffled, staggered, or jogged toward the exit. Most looked well enough for duty, but Hansen suspected that there might be a few whose spirits were willing but whose bodies would not function. In some cases, men would need to be removed, their tracks riding out with crews of three instead of four. Gunners would serve as loaders while tank commanders identified their own targets and fired the main gun. Crews might even be shuffled around to make up for the missing personnel. Hansen could only hope that his platoon was good to go, and he worried most about Keyman.

"It's tomorrow, Hansen!" Gutterson called back. "Do you hear me? It's tomorrow!"

"I hear you."

Was it all-out war? What else could it be? And while Hansen could say he was mentally prepared to fight—even on Christmas Day—he still feared that if the NKPA was launching a major assault and was able to breach the DMZ, then First Tank and Second Tank would be mere speed bumps in the enemy's attack to Seoul.

Sure, that possibility scared the hell out of him, but he had been taught that the guy without fear was the guy who got whacked first. Fear, if kept in check, would keep him sharp. Someone at West Point had once told him that courage is the art of being the only one who knows he's scared to death. Likewise, he could deal with all of the emotions if he focused on being a warrior. Within that word lay the purpose for his existence: war. No matter how realistic the gunneries, MILES exercises, and EXEVALs were, they could not replace the real thing. While he knew in his heart of hearts that good men would die, that innocent civilians would die, he could not temper his excitement.

That's right. His excitement. He and his men might very well prove their mettle on the battlefield. Those who did not understand the warrior's spirit, those who lacked the mean gene for war, would simply label them warmongers or sadists. But Hansen and his fellow tankers were just young men trained to do a job most men could not stomach. They would die willingly for their country because words like duty, honor, and valor defined who they were. Of course, not all were idealists, but even those who were cynical still wondered and grew anxious over how courageous they would be on the real field of battle.

And some, whether they tried to or not, would become heroes. The very best would not seek glory, medals, or admiration. If you tried to foist those upon them, they would dismiss you, saying they were just doing their jobs. However, those who understood the enormity of their occupation also recognized their incredible humility.

Admittedly, Hansen wanted to be one of those guys who went through hell and said he was "just doing his job." While he wasn't outwardly seeking glory, he wouldn't turn it down, either. Like so many other kids who had stood in their tree forts and had raised their fists in victory, he wanted to feel the rush, the power. It was undeniable. He figured humility would come in time.

As he jogged out of the lieutenants' hooch, right on Gutterson's heels, he realized what a presumptuous idiot he was being. He was not Abrams or Patton, standing on his tank with a pipe in his mouth as he surveyed the smoking ruins of a hundred enemy tracks. He was just a butterbar from New York, a young man who would never fully understand the sheer scale of a second Korean War. Nevertheless, he understood that he had a job to do—and he had better get to it.

WEBBER AND A seriously groggy Keyman hauled hungover ass toward their tank, drawing stares from guys at the motor pool guard shack and from everyone else they passed. Keyman had rolled out of bed, wriggled into his coveralls, grabbed his CVC bag, and had made his way down the hill from their barracks to the motor pool with Webber, who had failed to mention something new about the man's appearance besides his bloodshot eyes.

However, once they reached the tank, Smiley and Morbid could not stop staring at the TC.

"What's your fuckin' problem?" Keyman screamed at them.

Morbid gestured with his finger toward his own lips. Keyman frowned a second, then got it. He dragged fingers across his mouth, the fingers coming up red.

"Merry fuckin' Christmas to me! All right, which one of you dumb asses wants a size twelve enema? Which one?"

GATCH GAVE DEAC a high five as they watched Keyman freaking out over the lipstick. "What shade was that again?" Gatch asked the loader.

"Hearts Afire."

They shared a grin, but the artillery fire increased, and the sky to the north was printed negative by all the flashing. "Hey, man. It looks really bad out there," Gatch said, quickly sobering as Deac mounted the tank. "I think this is it. Fuckin' war."

"That crazy bastard finally went through with it."

"Yeah, but now what? Is he crazy enough to go nuclear?"

"Some say the boy is. He dresses just like Dr. No from that James Bond movie, and that guy was all about the bomb, if I remember. . . ." Deac lowered himself into his position to begin the long, arduous process of pulling each sabot from the semiready rack behind the tank commander's position, removing the protective foam cover from its tip, then inserting the round into the easily accessible ready rack behind the ammo doors at his station.

While Deac started on that, Gatch inspected the Wedge-Bolts and center guides, though he was positive the tank was in tip-top shape. Lee was no doubt putting the firing pin into the breach block. He would also put the recoil springs and back plates into the crew-served machine guns. Soon he would begin his prep-to-fire checks, doing computer and laser range finder self-tests to ensure all systems were operational. He would do that while Deac and Gatch broke their backs loading 10,000 rounds of 7.62 mm ammunition for the coax into the huge ammo bin and 1,400 rounds of 7.62 mm for the loader's M240 into the bustle rack. They would also upload almost 1,000 rounds of .50 caliber ammunition for the TC's weapons system. The company maintained small arms ammunition in the motor pool in unit basic load ammunition holding areas, or BLA-HAs. The company would receive additional ammo once the support platoon transported it from the First Brigade ammunition holding area to a designated resupply point.

All three men could ready the tank in their sleep, but Gatch knew damned well that the other two were as wide awake as he was, if not also shaking in their boots. It wasn't the enemy that scared him so much as the unknown.

The shouting continued around the motor pool, and the snow thickened as Gatch finished his inspection. He took an icy breath that stung his lungs before he climbed into his hole and swung the hatch closed. He glanced up at his Dale Earnhardt bumper sticker and rapped a knuckle on the lucky number three.

BACK IN HER second-floor room at the American Language Institute, Karen Berlin frantically packed her knapsack as the shelling continued. She had already declined several offers from her fellow teachers to get her out of TDC and back to Seoul. "No, it's okay," she had told them. "My boyfriend's with First Tank. They're getting me out."

About a month after they had been dating, she and Jack had had a conversation about the growing tensions between the United States and North Korea and how the Second Infantry Division ran semiannual NEO exercises. Although the noncombatant evacuation operations were reserved for military dependents, Jack had told her that if anything ever happened, she should stay put and wait for a phone call. She needed to trust him. She would.

Dressed and with her bag packed, she went to the window and watched people flee from the buildings and into the storm. Little Daewoo cars worked their way haphazardly up and down the icy street, and one had actually crashed into the corner of the building next door, its horn wailing out of tune with Camp Casey's sirens. She pressed fingers on the cold glass, closed her eyes, and prayed for the phone to ring.

A knock came at the door, startling her, and for a second, she turned reflexively toward the phone.

"Karen?"

She went to the door, opened it. Her boss, Michael Martinez, a middle-aged businessman with bright red cheeks and a woolen cap pulled down over his ears, stood in the hall. "Come on. I have a car waiting."

"No."

"Are you sure?"

She took his hands in her own. "Michael, thank you. But I'm sure. He told me to wait—"

The phone rang. She darted for it. "Hello?"

"Is this Karen Berlin?"

"Yes."

"Ma'am, this is Staff Sergeant Owens from 1st Battalion, 72nd Armor. I'm the battalion NEO Warden. Lieutenant Hansen asked me to take care of you. Pack light, and I'll meet you outside the institute in five minutes."

"I'm ready to go."

"Outstanding. Just look for my Hummer, ma'am."

"I will. Thank you."

Karen regarded her boss, then crossed the room and gave him a hug. "Get going, Michael. And please, be careful."

"You, too, Karen. God, I hope this isn't as bad as we think."

She nodded, wiped a tear from her cheek, and waved as he headed toward the staircase. As a particularly loud group of explosions echoed off the buildings, she rushed back into the room, slid into her heavy coat, and grabbed her knapsack. She would be evacuated by the military, even though she wasn't officially a dependent. Jack had clearly pulled some strings or had called in a favor. Now she no longer worried about herself. What was happening to him? Was he out there, getting ready for war?

HANSEN, GUTTERSON, AND Second Lieutenant Dariel "DT" Thomas, leader of Second or White Platoon, met up with Captain Van Buren next to the CO's track. The battalion S2 intelligence officer and S3 assistant operations officer were just rolling off toward Delta Company's line. Van Buren passed out overlays for their maps that covered the battalion's movement and intended deployment area. "All right, gentlemen. First, let me pass on some words from the colonel. He says we're not being punished. He's giving us a specific mission because he needs his strongest company in a critical blocking position. It looks like we will be working with the ROKs on this, but I don't have any of the specifics yet. The S3 is at Brigade now, trying to get more details."

DT, a somewhat beefy black man from Chicago with a weak chin but a penetrating stare, frowned deeply at the acetate overlay. "Sir?"

"Yeah, I know, hold on," said Van Buren. "Let's back up some. North Korean forces breached the DMZ along all three templated approaches, but the one that concerns us most is the Chorwon. They've opened up about a klick there. The ROKs took out most of the breaching force, but a lot of special ops still got through, plus there's more armor and infantry rolling in behind them. This storm has grounded our air support, but hopefully that'll change soon. In the meantime, the armor brigade of the ROKA V Corps, which has been sitting in defensive positions about ten klicks south-southwest of Chorwon, has been taking a serious beating. They've already seen forty percent attrition, but our counterbattery fire has eliminated most of the artillery threat."

"Sir, you said more armor and infantry are on the way," Hansen began. "What exactly are we looking at?"

"Intelligence reports confirm that there's at least one reinforced mechanized brigade heading toward V Corp's position, possibly attempting to bypass the zone defense at Chorwon and muscle down to Seoul or establish blocking positions to cut off withdrawing or reinforcing units. The ROKs are already hitting them with artillery and planning an ambush, but you can count on fifty, maybe seventy percent of those forces making it through. And those are the guys we're after."

Hansen eyed DT and Gutterson, their grave expressions matching his own.

Van Buren glanced down at some notes. "So here's what I'm seeing: we'll be released to the 5th Special Brigade, V Corps, Third ROK Army, where we will support their defense and counterattack as ordered by V Corps TROKA." Van Buren faced them. "We need to buy time for CFC reinforcements to arrive from the west and for the civilians to clear the route through the TDC area and down toward Seoul."

"Sir, what about the rest of the battalion?" Gutterson asked.

"They're heading off to establish a defensive perimeter along the TDC corridor to catch any elements that slip by. We'll join the road march up MSR 3, then halt to refuel and rearm at R3P 1, following which we'll head north to our engagement area." They would be stopping at Rearm, Resupply, and Refuel Point 3. There they would get the fuel necessary to continue north as well as the remainder of their basic load of ammunition. The support platoon and elements from the 302nd Forward Support Battalion (FSB) would run the site.

"Any word if they've slimed us?" asked Hansen.

"None yet. Brigade always expects they'll throw some nerve gas and the rest of it at us to deny movement, create a panic, and make fighting just a real pain in the ass. At least the weather's on our side. Persistent agents last twenty-four hours, nonpersistent two. So it's not really worth it to them. But you never know." Van Buren was referring to the fact that most chemical weapons did not work well in the cold, and the storm would further weaken their effects. He added, "You take the good with the bad. I'd still like to have air support right now. Anyway, a FRAGO will follow. You have authorization to battlecarry main gun and load small arms. Let's finish our prep and get ready to roll."

* * *

"SIR?" DEAC ASKED as Hansen thumped down into his station, then brushed the snow off his shoulders.

Hansen glanced at the loader, who obviously wanted the skinny. "Not now, Deac. Battlecarry HEAT."

The crew had heard that command over and over at gunnery, but that was on a training range with training ammunition. Ironically, the indirect artillery fire exploding in the distance did not convey the realization that they were going to war nearly as much as that one command. Deac slowly and deliberately transferred a service HEAT round from the ready rack to the breech of the main gun. Once the round was loaded, Hansen asked for a crew report.

"Driver ready."

"Weapon safe, HEAT loaded, loader ready!"

"HEAT indexed. Gunner ready!"

He looked at the men. Each one represented selfless service, courage, loyalty, dedication . . . the list went on and on. They were his crew. Though they were from different walks of life, they were one color: camouflage. "All right guys, this is it. Time to earn our pay."

On the radio, Hansen instructed the platoon to battlecarry main gun and load small arms ammunition, then send up their REDCON status.

"Red One, this is Red Two, we are REDCON-1, over."

"Roger, Red Two."

Abbot and Neech followed, then Hansen sent word: "Cobra Six, this is Red One. Red is REDCON-1, over."

"Roger that, Red One. Stand by."

Hansen reached into his pocket, withdrew his watch. *She got out,* he told himself. Owens was a good man. He wouldn't go back on his word. Karen was probably scared sick now, and he wished he could call to say he was all right. •

They continued to idle, waiting for the order to move out. Hansen got on the platoon net and relayed the OPORD to his men. Indeed, the balloon had really gone up, and command had received their code word, letting them know that the real fight was on. Codes such as *fog rain* or *red snow* were sent and authenticated before war plans were ever pulled from safes and opened. But Hansen, like everyone else, suspected that those plans had been compromised even before the ink had dried. And he wondered, like everyone else, if the enemy was already waiting to ambush them.

Knowing that they lacked technological superiority, the North Koreans would instead rely upon surprise, shock, speed, and overwhelming numbers of troops, coupled with their well-trained special operations force that may have already perpetrated acts such as contaminating the local water supply with cholera. The North Korean military doctrine was based upon a combination of Russian operational art, Chinese light infantry fighting tactics, and lessons they had learned during the Korean War. The national goal of *chuche* (self-reliance) influenced the way they adapted those imported strategies to the geography and the social and economic conditions found in their country. They knew the resolve of the ROK border units and would throw wave after wave at them, seeking force ratios of five to one in armor, eight to one in artillery, and six to one in infantry, though breaching forces could be expected to seek even higher ratios.

Van Buren finally gave the word: "Cobra elements, this is Cobra Six. SP, time now."

Hansen stood at his station, helmet and goggles fitted tightly to his head. Oblivious to the heavily falling snow, he looked over at Deac as the tank kicked into gear. "Loader, where are my tunes?"

"Coming up. I got a CD I've been saving." Deac reached down into the turret, where Gatch had hot-wired his Walkman to the 1780 commo amplifier. The music could be cut off by either their voices or the platoon net. Every tank in the company had some kind of Walkman or MP3 player patched into the 1780; it was a common practice to listen to tunes, especially during long road marches—or when taking off for battle. With the touch of a button they were rolling out of the motor pool, the cutting guitar of George Thorogood's "Bad to the Bone" thrumming in their ears.

TRACES OF LIPSTICK still clung to Keyman's lips, but Webber would not dare mention that to the staff sergeant. He and Smiley were standing at their stations, the snow coming in through the open hatches and melting on their boots. If Keyman was hungover, he was doing a damned good job of concealing that fact, save for his eyes.

The heater was running full blast, and while Webber might ordinarily become sleepy from the warmth and engine fumes, he was anything but, just sitting in his seat, his leg twitching. He had asked Keyman if they could kick out some jams to get them pumped up, but the asshole had snapped, "I don't want to hear a fucking thing but this track's engine!"

The engine whined, all right, but it couldn't silence the voice in Webber's head: *You can't talk your way out of this one, buddy.*

Damn, they were going to war. The folks back home were probably watching it on CNN. Meanwhile, Webber's life was now in a dysfunctional prick's hands—and that sucked. He wanted to remind the staff sergeant that now that the shit had hit the fan, they were the ones who would kick some ass. Oh, well, Webber had to believe that Keyman was all about the job—because second best now meant death.

ON BOARD ABBOT'S track, Sparrow had insisted that they listen to a recording he had made of George C. Scott's speech from the movie *Patton*. Abbot was okay with that.

He always loved the part about how it was his job to make the other poor bastard die for his country. When the speech was over and they all hooahed, the intercom fell silent.

They all knew the odds were against them returning to Dragon Valley. Their personal effects, which included keepsake jewelry, family pictures, and drawings done by their children were irreplaceable memories they had been forced to leave behind. Though the Second Infantry Division was supposed to be "Ready to Fight Tonight," it had been ready for over fifty years. At some point the waiting always wore on soldiers, as it had on Abbot, and he had begun to consider Camp Casey as just another duty station. The prospect of war had been the last thing on his mind and on the minds of his men. More important things ran through their younger heads, like when they could get their next shot of ass downrange.

Thousands of soldiers had come before Abbot and his crew. They had walked on the same ground upon which he and the others were preparing to fight. How many others had sat in Dragon Valley, waiting for this day? And now, how many would return?

"Hey, does any one mind if I say a prayer?" Sparrow asked.

"Go ahead," said Abbot.

"Lord, today is the birthday of your only begotten son, and on this day we ask that you guide us and protect us. We ask that you keep us strong and get us all home to our families. Amen."

"Amen," said Abbot. Short and sweet. Abbot was certain Jesus liked it that way. He and the almighty had become old buds during the Gulf War.

NEECH AND HIS men were listening to a song that would never get old: AC/DC's "Thunder Struck." Popeye Choi liked to bob his head to the music, and you couldn't help but smile at the KATUSA turned head banger, thanks to Neech. Romeo and Batman wanted to hear something more contemporary, and their CVC bags were loaded with choices, but they knew Neech had to have his way, given the circumstances. By the time the guitar solo broke in, the crew was fully charged. They were knights riding upon a metal steed.

And they were ready to face the monsters.

CHAPTER
NINE

KAREN BERLIN STOOD near the curb outside the language institute. She tugged nervously on the necklace Jack had given her and wished to God she had not forgotten her gloves. The tips of her fingers were already numb, yet she was the only one out there acknowledging the cold. The street had grown even more crowded with fleeing locals, some now on mopeds, some in the notorious Bongo Truck, and many on foot attempting to avoid the vehicular traffic quickly stacking up. Merchants tugging on rolling carts ran alongside the mess, while bicycle riders struggled to find traction in the snow. The knapsack on Karen's shoulder began to slip, and she tugged it up, reminding herself of a vacation she had already planned, a vacation she had yet to mention to Jack. In the spring, they could go hiking on the island of Cheju-Do. It was supposed to be the Hawaii for Koreans. She would take the knapsack. They would have a great time together. It would be romantic as hell.

An overweight Korean ran into her, causing the knapsack

to fall from her shoulder and hit the snow. She cursed. Wanted to kick it. Wanted to scream at the people in the street but more so at the bastards in North Korea who were ruining her life.

At the corner, the crowd began to part, admitting a slow-rolling HMMWV that reached her and squeaked to a halt. A grim-faced solider hopped out of the passenger seat, carrying an M16 rifle. Seeing her, he shouted, "Karen Berlin?"

"Yeah!"

"I'm Staff Sergeant Owens. Let's get back to Casey while I can still get through this mess!"

She hustled into the backseat, tossing her knapsack onto the deep floorboard. She had barely shut the door when they roared into the street, with Owens yelling in Korean and English for people to get the hell out of the way.

A CONVOY OF civilians moved south down Main Supply Route 3, the only passable escape route for an improbable collection of cars, limos, bicycle riders, and even those fixtures of Korean farmers, the one-eyed buffalos—tractors with only one headlight and two wheels balanced by a hitch to a wagon.

Part of the war planning process for such displaced persons was to provide control points with food, first aid, fuel, and recovery capability to keep the DPs moving to where they wanted to go. Rear-area security was the concern of the Second Korean Army, and Hansen had heard that they devoted something like twenty or more divisions to it. Their organization was already geared up for security concerns and DP control.

Riding tall in his station, Hansen waved to a farmer whose wagon buckled under the weight of personal belongings and cages filled with roosters and hens. The man's weathered face betrayed neither defeat nor faith. He was simply there, battling through the snow, trying to preserve the meager life he had made. He did not return the wave as they passed.

All along the route were a mix of ROK and U.S. MPs, who were helping to clear a path for the combat forces moving up and down the main supply route to get to their respective assembly areas.

Leading First Tank was the battalion quartering party consisting of one Nuclear, Biological, Chemical (NBC) tank per company and each company executive officer who would move to a probable new site of operations in advance of the main body to secure, reconnoiter, and organize an area prior to the main body's arrival and occupation. No one from Charlie Company was moving with the battalion quartering party this time, which indicated to Hansen that something else was in store for them.

At the head of the battalion's main body were the Alpha Company Aces, followed by the Bravo Company Black Knights, and the Delta Company Demons. Like Charlie Company, each tank company was typically comprised of fourteen tanks divided into four tank platoons and the headquarters platoon. The latter consisted of the company commander's tank, the executive officer's tank, and the company trains controlled by the first sergeant who traveled in his blunt-nosed M113A2 Armored Personnel Carrier, his war wagon.

The company master gunners and NBC noncommissioned officers each rode in an M998 HMMWV with drivers who typically worked in the company training room. The supply sergeant and armorer manned a cargo truck with attached 400-gallon water trailer, while each company's two assigned medics had an M113A2 APC of their own, modified to serve as an armored ambulance.

The fire support officer, an artillery liaison able to call in dedicated tubes, rode aboard the BFIST (Bradley Fire Support Team) track: a heavily modified M2 Bradley that had a ground laser identifier used to paint targets for smart munitions. Each company also had Linebackers, Air Defense Artillery vehicles that were, in effect, Bradleys modified to fire Stinger missiles.

Finally, the maintenance team chiefs, along with their turret and hull mechanics, operated their own M113A2 and LMTV tool truck, plus they had an M88A1 recovery vehicle. Affectionately called the Eighty-eight, it was the equivalent of a tank tow truck used to evacuate vehicles that could not be repaired on site within two hours. The PLL clerk would travel with the battalion field trains and set up in the brigade support area where they would receive and process all new parts before they were put onto company supply trucks for movement to each company with daily LOGPACs.

The logistics package was a grouping of multiple classes of supplies and supply vehicles under the control of a single convoy commander, typically the support platoon leader or platoon sergeant. Daily LOGPACs contained a standardized allocation of supplies and were organized in the BSA under the supervision of the S4 NCOIC.

Following the first three companies was the remainder of the battalion's headquarters company, the Headhunters, led by the senior company commander and first sergeant in the battalion. They controlled the battalion's logistical assets. Without them, First Tank could not fight. They oversaw the movement of the remainder of the support platoon, dining facility, and the battalion maintenance assets. The battalion maintenance officer and executive officer would supervise the recovery of any vehicles that went down due to maintenance or battle damage.

Since Hansen's platoon and the rest of the company were going to fight with the ROKs, Captain Van Buren broke ranks from the convoy about twenty minutes after they rolled out. He hopped in his HMMWV with the company's senior KATUSA, and they departed to receive the

operations order. Because Charlie Company was being released, they would receive an additional support package
consisting of fuelers, cargo trucks, and ammunition trucks
that would travel with them. The ROKA did not have the
people, equipment, and supplies to support attached U.S.
forces; thus the men of Charlie would have to provide their
own support. This was a logistical challenge not often in-
corporated into training or addressed during peacetime, so
it would become one of First Sergeant Westman's top priorities.

Though Hansen was not yet sure what their company
mission was, he did notice that a mechanized infantry platoon with Bradleys and dismounts had fallen in behind
their convoy. He suspected the platoon was from Alpha 2-9
IN (M). They would increase the company's combat power
and give Van Buren more flexibility on the battlefield.
Hansen just didn't know if they'd be losing a platoon of
tanks or not because sometimes infantry and armor units
traded platoons to form company teams.

For the moment, it appeared they would be Team Cobra, and they were in position to easily break off at the
rearm, refuel, and resupply point.

As they moved farther north, the tension increased dramatically. The darkness and falling snow made the convoy
that much more vulnerable to ambush and necessitated
that they move in a close column formation, with vehicles
just twenty to thirty meters apart because of the limited
visibility. Per their SOP, each tank had an assigned gun
tube orientation so that platoons could achieve a full 360
degrees of observation along the mountainous road, though
only the very last tank would orient its gun tube to the rear.
Loaders and TCs manned their machine guns, while the
gunners below were ready to retaliate via the main gun or
coax. Lastly, all headlights had, of course, been switched
off, and radio silence was observed as much as possible.
Though the Single-Channel Ground and Airborne Radio

Systems, or SINCGARS, provided a secure means of communications for the military, the normal chatter and cross talk was almost nonexistent. It was all business.

As they passed another group of DPs jammed into a small sedan, Hansen thought he had heard something and told Deac to switch off the tunes. Despite the muffle of his CVC helmet, a child's scream still managed to reach Hansen's ears. He looked over at the car, whose trunk was open. Piled inside were three women clutching their children, and one of the kids, a girl no more than five, wailed as though she had just received an inoculation. Or maybe she knew more than all of them. Hansen shook off the thought, blinked hard, and rubbed a gloved hand over his nose.

More headlights. Another trio of cars approached, all Daewoo limousines whose tinted windows were rolled down. Two young women dressed like bar girls and wearing flimsy, imitation fur coats were seated on the window jambs of the first limo and flipping the bird to the entire convoy.

"Aw, come on!" Deac cried. "I pay your salary!"

"Watch it, Deac," Hansen warned.

"Sorry, sir."

"They got a right to their opinion. Besides, you and Gatch probably know them—and they know you're bad tippers."

Deac grinned. "Probably."

When Hansen had first come to South Korea, he, as an American, did not expect to be loved. Over the years there had been several incidents between Korean civilians and U.S. military personnel that had resulted in civilian fatalities and had sparked the fires of resentment between the two.

Hansen wondered, though, if those girls truly understood what would happen to them were the North Koreans to take over their country. If they flipped the bird to North Korean soldiers, they would be cuffed and dragged away. Their relatives would share stories about how they had never been seen again. People had been arrested for far less, like just complaining over how long a food line was or for making a negative statement about the government. Those girls had no clue. No clue at all.

NEECH FELT HIS stomach drop, and before he could utter a word, his tank listed to the right like a boat that had just been torpedoed. The clanking tracks suddenly changed pitch, and the engine's rpms increased dramatically.

He had not realized it with all the snow on the ground, but they had been riding on a culvert. Beneath the road lay a massive but now crumbling concrete drainpipe that had been compromised by earlier elements of the convoy. Neech's tank had simply been the sixty-eight-ton piece of straw that had broken the concrete camel's back. The added weight of the mine plow had not helped, either. Their right track had dropped four feet before Batman had hit the brakes.

"Driver!"

"I know! I know!"

Neech called up on the platoon net that he had run into problems. He was the last in their platoon convoy, as they were traveling per their platoon SOP, with Keyman leading, followed by Hansen, Abbot, and Neech, who provided rear security.

As Batman tried to back them out of the hole, Neech realized that the left track was in the air and spinning free. Shit! They were high-centered, and the right track could do little more than spray mud and snow.

"Driver, stop!"

"Hey, Red Three!" Abbot called over the radio. "You're not high-centered, are you?"

Neech tried to sound optimistic but failed. "Not for long, right?"

Abbot muttered a curse, glanced down at Neech's track, then hollered, "Driver, back us up some." Abbot's tank roared in reverse, pulling up to Neech's track but keeping out of the line of traffic.

Neech grabbed a flashlight and joined Abbot on the ground. They carefully inspected both the front and rear undersides of the track.

"Man, you have to love this," Abbot grunted. "But don't worry, buddy, I think I can get you out."

Paz waved Abbot back to his tank to take a call from the lieutenant, who had already instructed Keyman to slow down and had informed the company commander about what was going on so they could adjust the company's speed appropriately. "Red Four, this is Red One. SITREP, over."

"Culvert collapsed," Abbot replied. "He's high-centered."

"I'll call for the Eighty-eight, over."

"Sir, I can do it quicker."

"You sure?"

The platoon sergeant gave Neech's tank another appraising glance. "Yeah."

"Then do it. Red Two and I'll provide security. I'll send word ahead, out."

"All right, I need some fucking elves down here with a tow cable," Abbot shouted to his men. "Come on, do you want to miss the goddamned war?"

Neech returned to his track, mounted the hull, then rapped on the driver's hatch, which quickly swung open. "Batman, I am not a happy camper, dude. Do you read me?"

"Loud and clear. I ain't making excuses."

"Don't. Just listen to me, and we'll get out of here. A lot of people are depending upon us. Do you understand?"

"Absolutely."

"Good to go?"

"Good to go."

Satisfied, Neech ascended the turret, resumed his station. He knew there was no way Batman could have known about the culvert. Neech had just needed to vent. At least he had shown some restraint. But if they didn't get the tank out within the next few minutes, he felt certain that his palpitating heart would finally explode.

STAFF SERGEANT OWENS dropped off Karen at the Hansen Field House on Camp Casey (an ironic and befitting name for the place), where military personnel and Red Cross folks were there helping to organize the evacuation. As Karen drifted through the crowd, a familiar face appeared from across the room. It was Kim Abbot, the Korean woman from Texas who spoke with a southern drawl. Their gazes met, and Karen wasn't sure what it was, some kind of kinship or something, but she felt immediately drawn to the woman. She reached Kim. Neither said a word. They just embraced. Then Karen took a long breath. "He pulled some strings to get me here."

"You're lucky to have him."

"I just . . . I just want to know that he'll be okay. But no one can tell us that, right?"

Slowly, Kim shook her head, then grabbed Karen's wrist. "Come on. They have hot chocolate over there. It's going to be a little while before we leave."

SECOND LIEUTENANT SUH Jae Sung and his platoon of three tanks rolled on toward the breach that had been opened up by the regiments and special operations forces. However, the brigade had already suffered a blistering attack from ROK Army and U.S. artillery fire and had been ambushed by ROK infantry and light armor that had allowed the recon company to pass and had been waiting for them as they came within a kilometer of the breach.

While the recon company was down only one BRDM-2, the rest of the brigade had lost just over 30 percent of its forces. Sixty-six vehicles remained in the mechanized infantry, and Suh's own tank battalion had been weakened by the loss of nine tracks, though his platoon and the company commander's track had survived unscathed. The artillery battalions had lost ten of their thirty-six guns, while two of the six multiple rocket launchers in that company had been destroyed. The antiaircraft artillery battalion was down to seventeen of their twenty-four guns, and both battalions of motorized infantry had taken heavy losses, especially to their thin-skinned trucks. Suh wasn't sure how many dismounted troops had survived, though he guessed slightly more than half, or about 500. The supply, engineer, and NBC companies had each lost about a third of their forces as well.

According to Suh's map, once they passed the breach, their route south would take them through a mountain pass approximately two kilometers wide and paralleled by fairly dense forest. Intelligence indicated that the ROK's V Corps was dug in along the south sector, about three kilometers behind a suspected minefield with accompanying double-strand concertina wire. The recon company would need to confirm the existence of that obstacle; then, if they determined that it could be breached, the brigade commander would order Suh's platoon and the rest of the brigade's first echelon forces to advance. Mine plows would clear a path while dismounts secured both sides of the obstacle. Suspected enemy defensive positions would be fired upon to neutralize any threat while the BM-21s launched rockets to create a smoke screen.

The forthcoming engagement played over and over in

Suh's thoughts as they rolled past the smoldering skeleton of a BTR-60, the ground scorched around it as the snow melted on the still-hot carcass. Two more BTRs lay in ruins about twenty meters east, with bodies strewn across the snow. Those troops had been attempting to dismount when they had been gunned down.

"Look at the heroes!" Suh shouted to his men. "There they are! The heroes! Is there a better way to die than in the service of our dear leader?"

IT'S CHRISTMAS MORNING, and I'm getting too old for this shit, but hell, something keeps me going. . . .

With his track now positioned behind Neech's paralyzed tank, Abbot turned his thoughts back to the job. He attached one end of the tow cable to the right front tow hook of Neech's tank; then he clipped the other end to the left rear tow hook of his tank. Neech traversed his gun tube slightly over the right side so that he wouldn't ram into the rear of Abbot's tank as they pulled free. Since Abbot's driver was unable to see the action, Abbot had instructed Neech to move forward of the tank and provide hand signals to Sparrow.

Abbot gestured for Neech to have Sparrow begin to pull slowly, very slowly straight forward.

The tow cable danced like a snake for a second until the slack pulled out and the line snapped taut.

As Neech's tank began to shift to the left with an uncomfortable creaking sound, Abbot cried, "Little more."

Sparrow moved the tank mere inches, when suddenly Neech's left track came down.

Abbot didn't need to say anything. Neech's driver had felt the tank level out and both tracks hitting solid ground. He gunned the engine.

With the force of two 1,500-horsepower engines driving

Neech's tank forward, the track pulled free of the collapsed culvert and arrived with a roar just a couple of meters from Abbot's tank.

"All right! Let's detach this cable and get moving," shouted Abbot, his shoulders slumping with relief.

Paz rushed in and began working on the cable, while Abbot and Neech used their flashlights to once again inspect the track's undersides. "You got lucky," Abbot told the man.

"And I'm going to stay lucky," Neech said.

Abbot switched off his flashlight, stood, and smacked Neech on the back. "Me, too."

CHAPTER
TEN

HANSEN STOLE A look back as all four tanks in his platoon raced up MSR 3, playing catch-up with the company. They had to be careful, though, because civilians were still fleeing south down the road, and one skid or slip of the wheel of someone's car could result in tragedy.

Thankfully, they reached R3P 1 without incident. They turned off the main road, rumbled down and onto the bumpy terrain, and were directed toward the 5,000-gallon fuel trucks from the 302nd FSB, waiting to top off their tanks. Fuel hoses were arrayed like tentacles, ready to pump the lifeblood into their armored beasts of war. Off in the distance, the support platoon had set up their ammunition HEMTTs to upload the tanks with the remainder of their main gun and additional small arms ammo, including some armor-piercing .50 caliber ammunition. A platoon of military police in up-armored HMMWVs created a perimeter around the site, providing local security for the operation.

While Gatch handled their refueling and rearming, Hansen and the other platoon leaders went to Van Buren's track to receive the FRAGO. Another lieutenant made his way over, as well, and he resembled the stereotypical infantryman, wearing a set of night-vision goggles mounted on his Kevlar, elbow pads, knee pads, camouflage paint smeared across his face, and a vest full of grenades. He carried a rifle with enough attachments to make it appear right at home in a sci-fi flick.

"Okay, gentlemen, here it is," said Van Buren, consulting his own notes, map, and overlay. "As you can tell, higher believes this mission is so important that they've beefed us up with a platoon of infantry from 2-Manchu. Their call sign will be Renegade."

First Lieutenant James Ryback, a senior platoon leader from the mechanized infantry company, was now going to fight alongside his armor brothers. Hansen, Gutterson, and Thomas quickly went around the horn making curt introductions, then the commander got back to business.

"We've been whored out by the brigade to provide armored support to the ROKs. We're fighting as a company team with three tank platoons and a mech platoon. The remainder of Alpha 2-9 IN will serve as a backstop for the defense and will provide dismounted support to secure key terrain throughout the defile.

"We've been given two GSR teams. One will be attached to Red Platoon during the defense, and one will remain under company control. We're supposed to have air support for this operation, but with this weather I doubt that'll pan out. Division has given up a full battery of artillery from 1-15 FA to support this fight and a liaison support team with SINCGARS capabilities to serve on the ROKA staff. Needless to say, this is an extremely important mission.

"Okay. Here's the enemy and friendly situation. In our

area of operations, an enemy mechanized brigade is attacking from north to south into an area defended by elements of V ROK Army Corps from grid PT960365 to PT030404. Their reconnaissance company should reach what I've labeled in the company graphics as Phase Line Ice in approximately two hours.

"To our east, the ROKs have established defensive positions with about a battalion worth of dismounted infantry whose task is to place antitank fires into the engagement area and to secure the key terrain. On the west we've got an ROK mech battalion whose task is to fix enemy forces to prevent the reinforcement of attrited elements. To our immediate south is the remainder of Alpha 2-9 IN who is the brigade's reserve.

"The brigade's mission is to defend in sector to destroy first echelon forces and to deny the enemy access to high-speed avenues of approach into Seoul.

"Our mission is as follows: On order, Team Cobra defends Battle Position Charlie to destroy enemy reconnaissance and lead elements of the mechanized brigade to prevent penetration of Phase Line Crush. I say again, on order, Team Cobra defends Battle Position Charlie to destroy enemy reconnaissance and lead elements of the mechanized brigade to prevent penetration of the Phase Line Crush.

"Intent. The purpose of our mission is to prevent the penetration of Phase Line Crush. Decisive to this operation is the destruction of his main body north of Phase Line Volcano.

"Concept of the Operation. White and Blue Platoons will occupy platoon battle positions in the southern sector of the mountain pass vicinity PT975371. White will occupy BP C2 to the west, and Blue will occupy BP C3 in the east. White, your task is to destroy the center task force to deny him the opportunity to establish adequate support by fire positions. You will tie in with Renegade Platoon, who is defending BP C GRUNT vicinity PT973377.

"Blue you will need to use your KATUSAs to coordinate with the ROK infantry on your eastern flank. Your task is to destroy any forces that make it past Phase Line Volcano to prevent the penetration of Phase Line Crush.

"Red, I need you to link up with Night Stalker Two at Checkpoint Four to escort the GSR assets into position. You will defend BP C1 vicinity PT973380 and destroy enemy reconnaissance forces and second echelon forces in EA Slam to protect GSR assets and secure the western flank of the company.

"The scheme of maneuver is as follows: once scouts or GSR indicate that the brigade's recon company has crossed Phase Line Ice, Red will use artillery to destroy enemy reconnaissance assets to deny him the opportunity to locate our main defensive belt. Artillery will continue as lead elements attempt to breach the obstacle at Phase Line Warm. We will use a combination of direct and indirect fires to destroy the remainder of his forces. When enemy armor reaches Phase Line Volcano, artillery will be shifted, and the focus of all fires will be on any enemy armor.

"We have three point targets and one linear target which the FSO will provide once we refine them. In addition, attached to your order is the current time line, my CCIR, the concept of support, and the command and control information. Get with me or the XO if you've got any issues. Questions?"

Hansen, Gutterson, Thomas, and Ryback finished making notations on their overlays and spent about five minutes going over their notes and their specific tasks. "No questions, sir," Hansen said, after a quick glance to the others.

The captain reached out, shook all of their hands. "Gentlemen, you're the best I've ever served with, and the pleasure has been all mine."

"Thank you, sir." Hansen's eyes burned.

Van Buren grinned, just staring at them for a moment more. Then he suddenly shouted, "Let's get some!"

Hansen exchanged more handshakes with Gutterson, Thomas, and Ryback, wished them luck, then walked away, his stomach beginning to knot. He wondered where the excitement had gone.

"Hey, Jack," Gutterson called, jogging after him.

"What do you need, Gary?"

"I just wanted to say . . ." He averted his gaze for a second. "I just wanted to say blow those motherfuckers to hell."

"You, too, man. You, too."

Gutterson squeezed him by the shoulders, then hustled away.

HANSEN FOLLOWED THE heavy stench of fuel back to his track, and once all four tanks were topped off and had received their full load of main gun and additional small arms ammunition, he led the platoon north to CP Four. There, near the perimeter of the forest, sat an idling M113 from the 102nd Military Intelligence Battalion. On board the APC was the GSR team, a sergeant, and two soldiers who would deploy and operate the AN/PPS-5B Ground Surveillance Radar Set. The unit resembled a mini–radar dish sitting atop a tripod and could detect and locate moving personnel at ranges of six kilometers and vehicles at ranges of ten kilometers, day or night, under virtually all weather conditions. Hansen signaled the track's driver, indicating their place in the column of tanks.

"Red Two, this is Red One. Night Stalker Two is in place. Continue to move. We'll follow the perimeter woods, moving into a hide position southwest of the BP to conduct a quick recon. Terrain looks really rough, so be careful."

"Roger," answered Keyman. "Moving out."

Hansen followed his wingman. Next came the GSR

team, then Abbot and Neech. So much snow had collected on the tracks that they blended in fairly well with the landscape; however, Mother Nature's camouflage, like tracers, worked both ways.

About two minutes into the trek, the woods grew so thick that Keyman began knocking down smaller trees with his track, paving the way for the rest of the platoon. Hansen estimated that they still had to move about another 1,500 meters before they reached the northern edge of Phase Line Volcano. Their bulling through the woods was eating up time that could cost them dearly.

Keyman's track suddenly veered right and stopped. Hansen could already see the problem: a pair of very thick trees blocked the path, and two more lay to the right, another three to the left. Keyman could try to slide between the ones to his right, but the tank could get wedged. He would have to back up and drive around to the right, but there the ground dropped away at a twenty-five-degree grade. With all of the ice and snow, their tanks could begin shifting out of control and even throw a track. Hansen looked for an alternate route to the left, but the trees gathered in tighter and tighter knots.

Keyman's tank backed up a few meters and stopped. He gestured to the slope on their right as he called Hansen on the net and suggested they move in that direction.

Seeing they had no other choice, Hansen gave him the go-ahead. Slowly, tentatively, Keyman's track turned and started around, grinding deeply into the snow and earth below. Hansen instructed Gatch to hold their position, then he held his breath.

With its engine revving, Keyman's track tipped slightly to the right, maneuvered around the trees, slipping only slightly as it did so. Abruptly, the track rumbled up onto more level ground. Down in the driver's hole, Morbid was probably celebrating.

Hansen breathed easy for a second, but then it was his turn. Gatch took them forward, steering them directly into the plowed-up path.

"She'll be comin' around the mountain when she comes," Gatch sang softly. "She'll be coming around the mountain when she comes. . . ."

While they drifted a bit wide as they hit the slope, Gatch compensated with a bit more acceleration and pulled them "around the mountain," not missing a beat with his song.

The M113 carrying the GSR team was able to dig a narrower path, closer to the trees, and rumbled swiftly around. Abbot's track came up behind them, made the crossing, and rolled on up. Neech, who had already been stuck once, was given the unenviable task of going last through the slushy snow. Hansen felt sure that the TC would be hard on his driver, and he was, getting them back on level ground perhaps a few seconds before his track might have begun sliding down the hill. If that would have happened, they would've had to call for sand, shovels, and recovery vehicles.

With one potential headache behind them, they pressed on, and Hansen switched his gaze between the pass ahead and the woods to his right, where somewhere out there, beyond the twisted, bony trees and gloom, lay the broad stretch of mountain pass designated Engagement Area Slam.

Were it not for their vehicles' engines and humming heaters, an almost devastating calm would have fallen upon the woods, a calm reinforced by the whisper of falling snow and the occasional clatter of limbs.

Keyman called for another short halt. Shit. What now? Was he stuck?

The staff sergeant explained that they were reaching the crest of a slope that would drop down rather steeply again.

Hansen passed the word back to be careful, and they advanced again, heading down the hill, trampling low-lying shrubs and a few skinny trees. Gatch applied just enough brake pressure to control their descent.

Once they reached bottom, Keyman swerved off to the right, moving toward a zone where the trees thinned out and the grade rose a few degrees, giving way to a sheet of snow-filled darkness. They continued for another five minutes until they reached the edge of the rising ground. Hansen checked his map. They should be near their intended BPs. "Red, this is Red One," he called over the platoon net. "Let's stop here. Tank commanders meet me at Red Two's location to move forward and recon the BPs. Red Two and Red Three, dismount your loaders with their M4s to provide security. Red Two Golf will take charge back here and set up local security and maintain radio contact." Hansen faced Lee. "Are you good?"

"Yes, sir," replied the gunner, though he swallowed deeply after he spoke.

Hansen tapped the M9 Beretta in his shoulder holster, then grabbed his map, overlay, and flashlight. He strapped his PVS-7B Night Vision Goggles (NVGs) around his neck.

"Sir, they could have scouts combing these hills," said Deac, who was at his station and manning his machine gun. "They could be watching us right now."

"Shouldn't be any problem for a coon hunter like you," Hansen said confidently.

"No, sir. Hurry back."

Hansen eased himself out onto the turret. He made the precarious climb across the icy armor until he reached the rear deck and lowered himself down. He turned to find Keyman already waiting for him, the staff sergeant appearing more bored than nervous or intense. At least some of the red had faded from Keyman's eyes, though he could've used drops to compensate. His lips, however, seemed more red than usual, probably from the cold.

"How you feeling?" Hansen asked.

Keyman seemed insulted by the question. He averted his gaze, then adjusted his grip on his M4 rifle. "What do you mean, sir?"

"Just that."

"I'm fine."

Hansen nodded, then looked away as Abbot and Neech came bounding up, armed with pistols, rifles, and grenades.

"Okay, quick sweep, then we regroup up there, near that tree," Hansen said. "Let's go."

They spent no more than five minutes on the sweep, and, confident that the area was, at least for the moment, secure, Hansen met up with them at the aforementioned tree.

With their heads low and weapons drawn, they picked their way carefully up the slope, snow crunching under their boots and coming up to their shins. Hansen kept them tight to the trees, and they dashed from one to the next until they neared the top and dropped to their bellies.

Silently, with only their breaths rising to betray them, they crawled the last two meters, propped themselves on their elbows, and squinted against a frigid wind that whipped snow in their eyes. Hansen estimated the temperature at below zero, not accounting for the windchill factor, but none of them complained. At the moment, there were more important discomforts, like an enemy mechanized brigade.

Hansen peered through his NVGs. "I got PL Volcano right there," he said, estimating where the ROK's trigger line might be. "About three hundred meters south of our position." He shifted, aiming the goggles north. After a careful search he spotted some of the concertina wire at PL

Warm. He imagined the minefield lying below, a band of death about 200 meters deep and stretching from one side of the mountain pass to the other. In October, the ROK Army dug holes for their mines, then they placed bags of rice into those holes and marked them with stakes. When the ground froze in winter, the ROKs could remove those rice bags and quickly replace them with mines, which was exactly what they had done at PL Warm.

"Okay, I see the obstacle. Two hundred and fifty meters north of here. Perfect. We're smack in the middle. Let's designate some target reference points real quick."

TRPs were easily recognizable points on the ground, either natural or man-made. The platoon would use them to designate sectors of fire and to refocus direct fires during the battle. Hansen designated TRP 1 on a hilltop to their immediate north, TRP 2 at the eastern edge of the obstacle, and TRP 3 on a hilltop to their immediate east.

Behind them, about a thousand meters back, lay the steeper slopes of the mountains, and to their left, a smaller, heavily forested hill with accompanying hillocks extended from the mountain base, providing an excellent shield for them as the enemy advanced into their field of fire.

"Sir, I suggest primary BPs along that little ridgeline. We can come up to them from the reverse slope," said Abbot, studying the area with his own goggles. "See how those will make good hide positions? They're just what? About ten meters back?"

"Yeah, about. Good. We can take alternate positions anywhere along the ridge." Those positions would allow the platoon to continue operations if their primary BPs became untenable. They would orient into the same engagement area and along the same avenue of approach.

Hansen recalled his time as a newly commissioned lieutenant at the Armor Officer Basic Course at Fort Knox, Kentucky. His small group instructor had been teaching

him about defensive preparation. Hansen had come up with
a drill to help him build a platoon defense. He thought of it
as the "three-two-one to defense building." Three: target
reference points, sectors of fire, and defining the engagement area. Two: battle positions (primary, alternate, successive, and supplemental) and routes into/out of the
engagement area. One: engagement/disengagement criteria. Those were the tools he would use to develop his
defense. Although the steps and principles were simple,
applying them in a combat situation was what the art of
war was all about.

"This all sounds okay," Keyman said, lowering his own
NVGs. "But this slope to our north is deceiving. The second we fire, their dismounts could hole up in there with
their RPGs or some PCs could cut through to flank us."

"They might," admitted Hansen. "And we have to consider indirect fire. Supplemental BPs?"

"Because of this defile, there really isn't any other way
he could come at us except straight down the middle," said
Abbot. "How about successive BPs?" Those were positions
located one after another on the battlefield. They would en-
able the platoon to conduct a delaying action or to fall
back.

"I say we're sitting on them," Keyman answered. "With
more behind us. And if we need to get the hell out of
Dodge fast, we've already plowed the path."

"I like it," said Neech. "We can run parallel to the enemy, then break back into the EA if needed. Plus we'll be
keeping that slope in our sector of fire."

Hansen studied the terrain once more, sweeping far left,
then slowly panning over the entire engagement area. "I
don't like pulling into the woods. Not enough room to
dance if we need to. The only secure ground is that which
you can fire at."

"The lieutenant's right," said Abbot. "Successive BPs

could be here, but better yet, we can shift directly south two hundred meters or so, following the ridgeline down toward the lower ground at PL Volcano, near Renegade's position."

"We don't know how much snow and ice are on that line or below it," said Keyman. "We run back there, who knows what we'll hit. This ain't the time to get stuck. But we *know* what we have behind us."

"We do, but we still don't know how easy it'll be to break through the woods and return to the engagement area," Hansen pointed out. "And resupply might be harder if we fall back to the original path. Sure, we can still use it if we need to, but I don't want to count on it."

Resupply was, in fact, a major consideration. Without food, fuel, and ammo (referred to as Class I, III, and V), no war could be fought. After moving into position, refueling was always a priority. After fighting the first battle, ammo would become a priority. And food was a priority no matter what you were doing. Hansen needed to be sure that they could move at least one terrain feature back for resupply if needed.

"We can't take ourselves out of the battle," he added. "And that could happen. And that's not what we're here to do."

After spending another minute to further inspect the engagement area, Hansen got down to the business of establishing his platoon defense. "So we've identified TRPs. I see Red Two covering from left of TRP 1 to TRP 2. I will cover left and right of TRP 2. Four will cover from left of TRP 2 to TRP 3. Neech, you've got TRP 3. Your primary focus is dismounts or antitank systems moving along the eastern flank. The engagement area is about centered on those TRPs in sectors of fire.

"The engagement criteria for indirect fires is one combat reconnaissance patrol south of PL Ice. Engagement criteria for direct fires is one battalion south of PL Ice or engineer assets at the obstacle. Disengagement criteria is a company or more south of PL Volcano."

Keyman snickered. "This plan is a joke. . . ."

Perhaps it was the lack of sleep, the stress, the moment, whatever, but Hansen finally surrendered to his anger. "Listen to me, you arrogant motherfucker. This is my fucking platoon, and you're going to play it my fucking way. No sarcastic remarks, no bullshit, no trying to embarrass me or undermine my command. I'm tired of it. Really tired. Truth is, I don't give a fuck what you think of me because that means jack right now. Those motherfuckers are coming through this defile, and we're going to blow them to fucking hell. Do you have a problem with that?"

Keyman's expression turned stony. "No, sir."

"Good. I appreciate your concerns. But do not fucking challenge me. Not now, motherfucker. *Not now*. Do you understand?"

"Yes, sir."

"Good. Primary BPs and hide positions are set. Alternates are good anywhere along the ridge. Successive BPs are two hundred meters south. Understood?"

The men nodded.

"Primary BPs will be fifty to seventy-five meters apart. That should give us maximum coverage. If anyone loses contact or has to abandon his track, Checkpoint 4 will be our rally point. Keyman, I'm glad you're so fucking worried about that zone because you, of course, will be taking the northernmost point near the slope. I'm south of you, then Abbot and Neech. Once in position, we'll set up the chemical alarms and have Webber and Deac establish an LP/OP just north of Red Two's position to supplement the GSR team and V Corps's scouts."

Usually the loaders from the wingman tanks would establish the listening post/observation post, but in this case it was better to use Deac, since he was a loader from the section closest to where the LP/OP would be set up, and

Webber, since he was comfortable with map-reading and communicating on the radiotelephone. "Are we straight?"

Neech and Abbot nodded, but Keyman barely moved his head, his eyes growing wider and wider.

"Let's get back," ordered Hansen.

As they pushed themselves up and started furtively toward their tracks, Hansen suddenly regretted what he had just done. He should have kept his cool. He should have done everything he could to make Keyman an ally, but he had stooped to the staff sergeant's level. And now, when the shit came down, would Keyman be the first to bolt?

Veterans would tell you that sometimes the hardest fight of all is the fight inside a man to do what he must, despite everything. Extreme situations brought out the best in men— and sometimes the worst (Hansen had already demonstrated that for himself). He could not expect every tanker in his charge to behave like a hero, nor could he expect all of them to piss their pants and run at the first sign of the enemy. Military urban legend had it that the poster boy type would fail and the screwup would succeed. However, that wasn't always true. The only truth was that all of them would, in his own way, surprise Hansen. Hopefully, the surprises would not get him killed.

Back at his tank, he cleared his throat, realizing only then that it had gone to cotton. "Crew report."

"Driver ready!"

"Weapon safe, HEAT loaded. Loader ready!"

"HEAT indexed. Gunner ready!"

"All right, boys. We've found some good BPs and hide positions."

"Uh, sir?" called Deac. "I just want to say for all of us that you've been the very best PL we've ever served with, bar none. And I just want to say—"

"Shut up, Deac. I don't know about you poor bastards, but I'm not getting killed on Christmas Day. No way.

So . . . save all that sappy crap for our twenty-year reunion, all right?"

"Yes, sir!"

"Driver, throw this beast in gear. We're going to the big show."

CHAPTER
ELEVEN

AS THEY ADVANCED steadily toward their hide position, working parallel to the heavily wooded slope on their right and leaving furrows of crushed snow behind them, Webber sat in his gunner's seat, contemplating what to do about Keyman. When the TC had returned from reconnoitering their battle positions, Webber had asked how they had made out. Keyman had replied, "Well, I hope you boys have had good lives. I hope you've all drank as much liquor and slept with as many women as you could. Driver, move out!"

Webber had tried to pry further, but Keyman would not elaborate, other than to give instructions to Morbid, who kept muttering, "My mom's going to cry when she finds out. She's going to cry real hard. Shit, I only had two months left. Two months. You believe that?"

Now, as they approached their hide position, Keyman dismounted to walk them into the best spot he could find. Meanwhile, Webber began to grow nauseous. The thought of going into battle with a man who had issues, a man who did not respect the LT, a man who was an overbearing ass-hole, was literally too much to stomach.

All at once, Webber leaned over and puked across the turret floor.

Smiley leaned out from his station and gasped. "Holy shit, Webber. You sick, man! You sick!"

"Yeah," Webber said, wincing as bile burned the back of his throat and vomit clogged his nostrils. He coughed hard.

"I help clean before Keyman see," said Smiley.

"Yeah, come on . . ."

But the tank rocked to a sudden halt, backed up a few meters, then remained stationary. They had reached their position, with the hull and turret concealed behind the ridgeline—and Keyman about to come back inside.

"Oh, shit," said Smiley. "You fucked."

"Hey, what is that on my turret floor?" the staff sergeant shouted, ducking down into the turret.

Webber eyed the puke, grimaced, and faced Keyman as it dawned on the TC.

"Aw, are you kidding me? You just puked inside my fucking track? This can not be possible."

Lowering his head, Webber coughed again.

"Webber? Are you going to be all right?" The staff sergeant's tone was anything but sympathetic.

Webber grunted. "Just give me a minute."

"Smiley, help him clean this up. God! The stench!"

"Yes, Sergeant." The loader went to fetch some rags.

As Webber rose from his chair, his cheeks caved in. He tried to hold it back.

Keyman's mouth fell open. "Webber!"

Too late.

"OH MY GOD!" screamed Hansen. *"Driver—"*

The SPANDREL missile struck the tank's turret, even as

Hansen, Deac, and Lee shrieked in agony. The resulting explosion was so powerful that it blew the turret fifty feet into the air and engulfed it in flames.

Gatch shuddered awake. Damn, they were only in their hide position a few minutes, and he had already dozed off. He had been sitting there, all cushy and reclined, with the engine switched off (all four tanks had completed that task simultaneously so as not to betray their number). For just a half second, Gatch had not given a shit if he lived or died. He had just wanted to close his eyes, just for that half second, just for a second, just for a few minutes . . .

Boom!

God damned dreams. Had to hate them, unless, of course, they involved college girls named Debbie who wore Celtic crosses. He sat there, his breath ragged as he tried to calm down and convince himself that his life and the lives of his buddies would not end that way.

"Oh my God!" screamed Hansen. "Driver—"

What had the lieutenant been trying to say? Move out? This is all your fucking fault? Driver, you just got us killed?

I can't die yet, Gatch thought. He had not gotten himself right with the Lord. He had been planning on doing that sometime when he was in his late sixties, you know, after he had banged so many women that his legs quivered when he walked. You got right with the Lord only then, when your time was coming to an end. You put a bumper sticker on your eight-cylinder Buick with spoked wheels that read, Jesus Is My Copilot or Got Jesus? or Jesus Buys His Buicks at McNamara Buick of Daytona. You went to church every Saturday night (because on Sunday mornings you went fishing—religiously), and you went to Bible study on Thursdays, where you had hit it off with that younger woman in her late fifties whose bed frame squeaked so loudly that it distracted you, made you lose

your concentration, made her use the Lord's name in vain.
Every night you watched the Christian Channel because
you had thumbed on the TV's sleep timer, and those
preachers sang you to sleep as they spoke in tongues and
cured arthritis. And when things went wrong for other people, you always said, "The good Lord will provide." And
when people asked how the hell you had survived Korean
War II, you said, "God had a hand on me and my crew. He
had a hand on us all. It was a miracle. . . ."

*I'm sorry, Jesus. I'm a wiseass motherfucker, I know
that. I need to be right with you. Old Dale was right with
you before he went. He respected you the way I should. And
I truly believe you won't let us down. I'm not shitting you.
Okay?*

HANSEN AND DEAC, along with the other TCs and
their crews, dismounted to help set up the platoon's two
chemical alarms, which had detector units attached to
alarm units by WD-1 telephone wire. They had to check
the wind direction and place the detectors upwind of their
hide positions and no more than four hundred meters from
the alarm units. Establishing those positions did not pose a
problem. However, the falling snow and the freezing temperatures could wreak havoc with the alarms, which was
why all of them would remain ready at MOPP 2 status,
wearing their overgarments, overboots, but carrying their
protective masks and gloves. The ROK scouts, positioned
on the east side of the pass, had most certainly set up their
own alarms and could also detect an NBC attack. While
Hansen and the others could don their masks and gloves
anyway, the gear severely limited their peripheral vision
and reduced their overall efficiency.

With the alarms in place, Hansen returned to his track,
where he and the other TCs established a hot loop between

their tracks, connecting wire between their AN/VIC 3 Vehicular Intercommunication Systems so they had an absolutely secure line of communication with each other. When that was finished, he met up with Webber and Deac, who were armed with pistols and M4s. In addition to the weapons, they carried a ruck containing a TA-312 radiotelephone with wire, some MREs, a two-quart bottle of water, NVGs, a copy of the map with overlay, and paper and pencil to make a sector sketch. They would also bring along their face masks and gloves. Before they left, they would attach their commo wire to Keyman's VIC 3, run the line out of the loader's hatch, and be hot-looped into the rest of the tanks.

"Guys, I need you to move out toward TRP 1 and attain the best possible view of the sector. Do a commo check and report when set, then update as needed." Hansen glanced at his watch. "ETA on the recon company is about eighty minutes. If we have to, we'll rotate you out. Don't try to play superman. I need guys who can function up there."

"Don't worry, sir," said Deac. "There's two kinds of blue balls, and we know the difference."

Hansen smiled, then narrowed his gaze on Webber. "You all right, Sergeant? You're looking really pale."

"I'm good to go, LT. Little queasy, that's all. I'm shaking it off."

"I hope so."

Webber's gaze tightened. "Don't worry, LT."

"I won't. So, once you're out there, do everything you can to improve the position. The current challenge is *kunsan* and the password is *cake*."

The challenge and password was a preestablished system of code words used throughout the theater and disseminated to the lowest levels among all coalition partners. Because of this, the system often contained some unusual Korean words along with standard English.

"You guys ready?" Hansen asked.

They were. And they jogged off, dematerializing into the raging storm.

Hansen directed his gaze over to the GSR team, who had parked their APC about thirty meters northeast of his track and were also hot-looped into the platoon's commo. The team had already set up their radar and were inside their vehicle, listening for the sounds of enemy movement.

With everyone and everything in place, Hansen hauled his cold and tired ass back to his tank. Inside, he reviewed his platoon fire plan—checking tank positions, target reference points, range lines, and the trigger point on his map and overlay. He would make further additions once Webber got him that sector sketch. Out of nowhere, though, a chill broke across his shoulders and made him look up. "Everybody okay?"

"I'm good," said Gatch.

"Me, too," Lee answered.

"Hang in there, guys. Won't be long now." Hansen returned to his map, tried to shake off the strange feeling, but it wouldn't go away. What was it? Perhaps a strong sense of déjà vu that might be attributed to having spent so much time in the turret. It seemed he had already fought the entire war, and now he had come back to do it again so that he could revise his mistakes. It was definitely weird, no mystical crap, just a warm rush that he could not ignore.

ABBOT KNEW THE men of Red Platoon very well, and he had been making some guesses about those who would rise to the occasion and those who would not. Of course, he wanted to believe that every man would perform admirably, but old Abbot had been there, done that, knew the real deal.

Keyman was, of course, an obvious choice for failure, but Abbot still had faith in him. The staff sergeant was the kind of man who remained cool and calculating as the intensity level grew, the kind of man you wanted at your side when the big guns started booming. He was a T-rex in the turret, a fierce competitor who, when commenting on the seriousness of a farting contest, had said, "I'll blow mud!" And when things went wrong, he was quick to problem-solve. He didn't ask, "Why did this go wrong?" He asked, "How can I fix this to stay alive?" And he reacted. Violently. Without equivocation.

But he was still the biggest asshole in the entire battalion. And sure, he had deserved the tongue-lashing he had received from Hansen. Enough was enough.

In fact, after the incident, Abbot had pulled the junior tank commander aside and given him a stern reminder that his actions were unacceptable and would not be tolerated. Though the lieutenant was the platoon leader, there was a common saying that the platoon leader *leads* the platoon while the platoon sergeant *runs* it. Abbot could not let one of his overaggressive and brash NCOs interfere with the combat effectiveness of the unit by questioning the LT—or all else would go to hell.

All of which was to say that despite his actions, Keyman did not top Abbot's list of potential meltdowns.

Hansen did.

Sure, Abbot liked the lieutenant, admired the man's determination and fortitude, and had continually been impressed by his skills as both a tank commander and a platoon leader. He especially liked Hansen's willingness to listen to suggestions and the respect he paid Abbot for all of his years of experience.

Yes, experience. That was the operative word. Hansen was just a kid, a twenty-three-year-old kid bearing a huge burden that would make most kids his age crack under the pressure. All right, so he had braved West Point, but that didn't prepare you for the sickly sweet stench of charred bodies or the gurgling cries of a man dying in your arms as his intestines poured into your lap, a man you knew better than any family member or spouse. That didn't prepare you for accidentally killing a friend or knowing that the orders you gave could result in the deaths of some or even all of your men. Hansen had not yet learned the trick of dehumanizing bodies and distancing himself in order to remain semisane. He was one, big, raw emotion waiting to get trounced on.

Thus, Abbott readied himself for that eventuality. He would do his best to avoid second-guessing the kid, but if he thought Hansen was wrong, he would employ his famous diplomatic skills to tell the kid he fucked up. Politely. Abbot needed to do that because Kim needed him to come home.

In regard to his own crew, he had complete and utter faith in Sparrow, whose mixture of brains and badass attitude honed by his L.A. hood were just what he needed to face the onslaught. Abbot imagined the driver bursting from his hole, leaping down from the tank, and shooting any North Koreans who refused to surrender and become productive citizens in a democratic society. Well, that meant all of them.

Park was all about honor and would not flinch an inch. Moreover, the KATUSA would want to prove to his ROK counterparts that he was as big a hard-ass as they were. Some ROK soldiers resented KATUSAs because they thought those guys were getting privileged and soft U.S. assignments. Recently, there had even been a few incidents between KATUSA and ROK soldiers, and Park had been quick to comment. "They want to beat shit out of me, but I am not afraid of them." No, he wasn't. Nor was he afraid of the North Koreans. He would fight with a vengeance.

And then there was Paz, good old Specialist Jeff Paskowsky, self-proclaimed loader extraordinaire and superstitious maniac.

When the tank had first come to a stop, ten minutes

prior, the loader had muttered, "Of course this happens to me on Christmas. Of course. What was I expecting? If I hadn't joined the Army, we wouldn't be going to war. I join. War starts. That's how it fuckin' works, see? Because I got shit for luck. I got nothing. You guys are lucky. Why? Because you're not me. But then again maybe you're not lucky because you're around me, and I'm bringing this all on you. Shit . . ."

"Paz, you just have to shut up," Abbot had ordered while getting ready to dismount to set up the chemical alarm. "All you have to do is keep loading that gun, loading that gun, loading that gun. That's your goal in life. Everything else is bullshit. Okay?"

"Okay, Sergeant. I'm good to go. And I'm not scared. Seriously. I'm just pissed off."

Park had cocked his brow and had regarded the loader. "Anger is good now. We will kick ass and break names."

"That's *take* names," Paz had said. "*Take* names."

"So we kick their asses, then *take* their names. What do we do with them? Make list? Where do we take list?"

Paz had shaken his head, started out of his hatch to help Abbot with the alarm, and continued to babble, but Abbot had thrown a mental switch to silence him. Just nerves talking.

Now seated at his station, Abbot looked down, checked his hands. Steady as a rock, even though his pulse was rising. He knew that in the hours to come, moments of exquisite bravery might separate the living from the dead.

NEECH WAS STILL in his hide position, but once he moved forward to occupy a good, hull-down battle position, he would have an unobstructed view of PL Volcano. He had positioned his track to cover TRP 3 in the southeast sector of the engagement area, and like everyone else in the platoon, he was observing all OPSEC measures to deny the enemy information regarding their position. He had already dismounted and gone forward with his NVGs to ensure that no light shone from their position. They had also tied down the antennas and had made sure no noise was coming from the radio's external speakers. Of course, they had turned off the engine, which unfortunately meant that the heater was also off, and the cold was quickly seeping into the interior of the vehicle.

To the untrained and somewhat distant eye, they were a mere mound among a thousand other mounds dotting the mountain pass. When the call came in to move up, Popeye Choi would dismount and move forward to observe the far side of the battle position and into the engagement area. They would then roll up from their hide position to their turret-down position, at which point they would pause while Popeye observed the engagement area and reported. Following that, they would shift forward to their primary battle position from where they would deliver their sermon of death. Fortunately, the ridgeline sank pretty low in several areas, providing some near-perfect terrain. Berms always attracted attention, so they always told you to dig down, not up, to create a hide position. There hadn't been any time to dig, but they had still lucked out or had tapped into a little Christmas magic.

Now they waited for the gutless, godless, communist bastards from the North to make their next move.

Which begged the question: What was worse? Waiting for the shit to happen or the shit actually happening? Neech wasn't sure. At the moment, an excruciating silence lingered inside the turret. Romeo had already said his prayers in Spanish. Popeye Choi was still scribbling in the journal he kept close to his side. He was writing a memoir that he hoped someday his children would read. Batman was doing whatever he did in the hole, though Neech had warned him to stay alert. The driver had assured him that once the bat signal lit the air, he would have them moving even before the order left Neech's mouth. Well, they wouldn't be starting that fast, but Neech appreciated the driver's confidence.

Seated at his station, with his gaze roaming the turret, Neech thought, *Some diet plan.* Yes, the Army had helped him take off the weight, but when you joined Weight Watchers or Jenny Craig, you didn't have to worry about a hundred thousand screaming North Koreans exploding out of your refrigerator when you sneaked down at two in the morning for a piece of chocolate cake. Some guys would tell you that they would rather face those North Koreans than wives bent on making them lose weight. Neech wasn't so sure about that.

Oh, who was he kidding? He loved what he did. He wouldn't trade it for the world. He was itching to give the command to fire. He was itching for the rush he received every time he watched a target explode. Nothing else could replace that feeling. If what a man drives is an extension of his penis, then Neech was the commander of one of the biggest, baddest phallic symbols in the land. Romeo would certainly appreciate that image.

Neech turned to the gunner, who sat with his arms folded over his chest, rocking to and fro, eyes closed. "Hey . . ."

The skinny man's eyes snapped open. "What's up?"

"How 'bout telling me your line of shit."

"To pick up women?"

"Yeah."

"Trade secret. You know that."

Neech smirked. "Come on, let's hear it. It must be good if it works for a guy like you."

"Not now, Sergeant. Just not in the mood."

"Okay. I hear you."

Romeo drew in a long breath. "You know what really sucks? I got a brand new Civic in my garage right now, tricked out and just waiting to go fast and furious. I was almost done with it before I left."

Neech could only nod. The gunner wasn't talking about his car, of course, but the ghost who might soon drive it.

WITH THEIR COMMO wire unfurling behind them, Webber and Deac dashed along the ridgeline and hit the deck for a moment to catch their breaths.

Behind them lay curtain after curtain of snow that completely obscured Keyman's tank. They rose and ran another dozen or so meters, nearing the edge of the northwest forest shielding them from the approaching brigade.

Seeing a decent little perch along the line, Webber waved on Deac and dropped to his gut. He shoved the night-vision goggles up to his eyes for a quick scan of PL Ice, the phase line marking the entrance into the engagement area. He was only about seven or eight hundred meters south-southwest of the area, though he could only see about two hundred meters up the defile. In the meantime, Deac held his rifle at the ready, his gaze sweeping the forest as he covered the full 180 degrees behind them.

Squinting even harder, Webber carefully focused the picture and panned along the trench; then he slowly shifted north, trying to free the jitters from his hands. Okay, he was getting a better picture, but it was still hard to discern anything within the grainy green image.

"You see those bastards?" Deac whispered, sounding more eager than afraid.

"Not yet. Let me dig in here."

Webber put his gloved hands to work, clearing away about a foot of snow to further conceal them against the slope while Deac continued to keep watch. Webber then booted more snow over the commo wire, going back a few meters before returning. He pulled out the TA-312 radiotelephone from his ruck, connected the commo wire, then called back to Hansen: "Red One, this is Red Two Golf, commo check, over."

"Red Two Golf, this is Red One. Read you loud and clear. Do you have good observation of the engagement area and defile?"

Once Webber sent a quick summary of what he could observe and informed the lieutenant that he was starting the sector sketch, he signed off. "Okay, wire's good," he reported softly to Deac.

"God damn, it's more frigid out here than a fifty-year-old spinster on a first date. This hawk ain't no joke either." The infamous "hawk" was the Army's euphemism for a biting wind.

Even as the loader finished, Webber was dry heaving again and failing miserably to hide his discomfort from Deac.

"Jesus, Sergeant, you lied back there. You're sick, man."

"Nah," Webber said, clearing his throat and jamming the NVGs to his eyes. "Shhh. Just queasy." He made a quick inspection, then lowered the goggles, pulled out his paper and pencil, and began his sector sketch, dividing his gaze between the image coming in through the goggles and the paper.

"I should call the LT. Tell him you're sick. Tell him to get somebody else."

"I'm fine. Just shut up."

"Sarge, you ain't fine. Come on."

Deac reached for the radiotelephone, and Webber seized his wrist. "You just keep an eye on the fucking woods. I got this."

Deac wrenched his arm free. "I'm calling."

"And you'll be breaking orders. We made the fuckin' commo check. We don't call again till we make contact. Now shut up and provide security—like you're supposed to. That's an order."

The big hillbilly frowned. "Yes, Sergeant."

"I'm fine, all right?"

"Yes, Sergeant."

"You don't believe me."

"No, Sergeant."

Webber continued making his sketch, while the loader never took his eyes from the surrounding terrain. "Deac, are you scared?"

"Well, when you think about it, anyone in his right mind would definitely be scared. But anyone in his right mind would not be out here."

"Deac, it hurts to figure out what you're saying. Yes or no, you dumb motherfucker . . ."

"I'm excited about fighting. Scared of dying."

"Me, too." The wind howled a little louder, then subsided for a moment, giving Webber a chance to voice one more curiosity. "Hey, any idea who put the lipstick on Keyman?"

"Shit, Sarge. I thought it was you."

"Not me. I bet it was Gatch."

"Don't give him all the credit. I was there, too."

Webber was impressed. "No, shit . . ."

"We took some digital pictures. Gatch says he's going to put one on his Web site. When you get a chance, you'll have to see them."

Webber smiled tightly. "Yeah, when I get a chance."

He dug his elbows deeper into the snow and finished working on his sketch as a sudden gust stung his eyes and nose.

Within five minutes, the brutal cold had settled into his bones. He sniffled, shivered, and strained to hear the sound of engines above that groaning wind.

Another five minutes passed. Then ten. Then Webber's thoughts began to run wild. He imagined thousands of special operations troops crouched in the forest behind them, just watching with amusement, their gazes sending gooseflesh across his shoulders. He whirled. "Deac, you hear something?"

"No, where?"

"I don't know. Somewhere back there."

Deac shifted a few meters along the ridge, then, after studying the forest intently, shook his head.

Webber just lay there, trying to catch his breath. *You're all right.*

CHAPTER
TWELVE

AS THE AGONIZING wait continued, Hansen thought back to some of those conversations he had had with Gutterson, who had been reading up on North Korean society and culture in an effort to keep his enemies closer than his friends. Hansen had suggested that his roommate spend as much time making friends as he did studying the enemy, but Gutterson had dismissed him with a wave of his hand.

Unsurprisingly, the North Koreans were not your average Joe six-pack soldiers. They clung to an ideal because that was all they had. Their country was a shit hole, with starvation running rampant and infant mortality and life expectancies plummeting. They obviously weren't fighting to preserve a way of life but for a "radiant socialist future," an idea kept alive by their "dear leader," who also kept them in squalor.

While the American military would spare no expense or effort to save lives by using machines to do the killing, the North Koreans would spare no amount of life to keep an irreplaceable machine intact and functioning. What's more,

North Korean soldiers would not dare make radical changes to a preconceived plan or express individuality in any form. They would much rather lose 10,000 men assaulting useless high ground that they could not hold rather than take the initiative to move around it. As crude as it might sound, Hansen considered them a colony of ants who attacked their enemies by exploiting their sheer numbers. They were, after all, the fourth largest army in the world.

And they had nothing to lose. If you didn't find that unsettling, then you didn't have a pulse.

Hansen shook off the thought, then leaned back and yawned. Communication over the hot loop had fallen off to the bare minimum, yielding to an electricity in the air that he had never experienced before. Something had to give. He checked his new pocket watch. Soon.

For a moment, he bowed his head and closed his eyes. *Will I be okay? Will I do what I need to do? Please, God, I can't let them down. . . .*

WEBBER AND DEAC were only in position at the LP/OP for thirty minutes when Hansen called to say they were being rotated out. The lieutenant's gunner, Sergeant Lee, along with Keyman's loader, Smiley, hurried over to replace them.

For the next thirty minutes, Webber flexed his aching muscles until the call came in again for Deac and him to replace Lee and Smiley.

Now, as he settled into position for his second round of listening and observing, with Deac just a meter to his left and eyeing the forest with an almost mechanical sweep, he thought he heard the low-pitched hum of engines.

He held his breath. Froze. Reached out. Listened. Hard.

The wind roared on through from the north, tree limbs rustling and tossing down accumulated snow.

Straining to hear through the racket, Webber finally detected them again. Engines. He focused his goggles toward the sound, realized that a stand of trees was in the way. "Deac?" He gestured that they move forward for a quick look.

The loader nodded, and they bolted off, beating a haphazard path farther north along the ridgeline, snow up to their calves, the commo wire rolling out again behind them. The energy drained from Webber's body as though someone had poked a hole in him. Still, they had enough strength and enough wire to reach the outcropping. There, they dropped to their bellies, and while Deac covered him, Webber leaned out for a better view up the defile.

"I hear 'em," Deac whispered, his words punctuated by the definite grumble of engines.

Webber worked his NVGs, and a pocket of visibility began to open in the storm, increasing his view to nearly a thousand meters, though the pocket began to deteriorate.

But then he saw them emerging from the grainy gloom.

"Hello, you motherfuckers," he sang, watching a platoon of three BRDM-2s whose boatlike bows and ATGM launchers jutted out from their snow-covered surfaces. They were part of the brigade's recon company and rolled slowly along the tree line on big tires. For a second they wove into the forest, ghosting away, then . . . they reemerged.

"What?" Deac demanded.

"Platoon of BRDMs. Losing them now. I think they just crossed Ice. They're about eight, maybe nine hundred meters out now. Moving real slow. Covering only a kilometer per hour. Maybe less." Webber reached for the radiotelephone. "Red One, this is Red Two Golf, over."

"Red Two Golf stand by," answered the lieutenant, sounding distracted.

* * *

HANSEN WAS RECEIVING a report from the GSR team, who had picked up the movement of three BRDM-2s heading down the center of the engagement area, about eight hundred meters north of Phase Line Warm. After jotting down the coordinates, he told Webber to go ahead.

"Red One, we have three BRDM-2s about eight hundred meters north of PL Warm, weaving in and out of the tree line, over."

"Roger, Red Two Golf. Night Stalker Two confirms. I have coordinates. Remain in position and continue to observe, out."

All right, they had visual and auditory contact with the enemy. Consequently, it was time to call the commander and request an artillery strike on that platoon through the company fire support team.

"Cobra Six, this is Red One. Observing three BRDM-2s vicinity PT978394 moving south at approximately one K per hour." He would let the artillery geeks figure out the time of flight for the rounds and the speed of the target to determine the actual spot at which to fire.

"Red One, Cobra Six. Roger. That's a good copy. Stand by, out."

Okay. Everything was set. But something nagged at Hansen. He wasn't sure what.

"YOU WATCH," WEBBER told Deac, still straining for another glimpse of the approaching BRDMs. "The LT's calling in the strike. Should be interesting."

They didn't wait long for the fireworks to begin. It was, Webber suspected, a battery three, consisting of six guns, three rounds per gun.

But the ordnance began flashing, rumbling, and echoing off the mountains, striking near the center of the engagement area about a kilometer east of the three BRDMs that Webber had identified.

"What the hell are they shooting at?" Deac asked.

Webber focused his night-vision goggles on the target area, but between the darkness, the wind, the snow, and the smoke, he couldn't see a damned thing. "Red One, this is Red Two Golf, over."

"Go ahead, Red Two Golf."

"Adjust fire! Target is approximately one kilometer west," Webber said.

"Are you sure? I have coordinates from Night Stalker Two. Fires should be on target."

Webber rattled off the last known grid coordinates for the BRDM-2s.

A long pause, then . . . "Stand by, Red Two Golf."

"OH MY GOD," Hansen muttered. Not one platoon but two. He had confused the reports, believing that both Webber and the GSR team had identified the same target. They had not. And now three BRDMs were drawing dangerously close to their location.

But the mistake had not cost them. Not yet. "Red Two Golf, do you still have visual contact, over?"

"Negative, Red One. Lost contact in the tree line, over."

"Continue observing. Regain contact, out."

They had to do everything they could to kill the enemy reconnaissance with indirect fires. If they got into a direct firefight, they would lose the element of surprise.

Hansen got on the hot loop, ordered the platoon to start up their tracks in unison. Once the tanks were running, he listened as Abbot made a radio check with the entire platoon. In the meantime, Deac kept his ear to the radiotelephone in case Webber had another report.

"Red, this is Red One. We have what appears to be enemy reconnaissance moving south of PL Ice. Range once they clear the tree line approximately eleven hundred meters. Stand by to move into BP, over."

The artillery continued flashing and reverberating across the mountain pass. Hansen called to Webber, who had yet to regain contact.

Yes, artillery was pounding the shit out of that other platoon, but those shells sounded more like hammers beating upon the nails of his coffin and the coffins of his brothers because . . . he had fucked up.

NO! He beat a palm into his fist. *Come on, Webber! I did you a favor! Help me out. Find those bastards!*

"**OH, I DON'T** like that," said Deac, turning to look around.

A grinding, almost gurgling noise resounded from the forest directly north of them as well as from another point farther west, seemingly from within the woods, though maybe that was an echo. Was it? Webber concentrated.

No, it wasn't. He craned his neck, eyes bugging out. Then he glanced back ahead, checked the tree line.

Two of the three BRDMs veered out for a moment, turned, then advanced behind some trees. They were moving much more quickly now, just five hundred meters out.

"Jesus Christ, he's coming right up toward us," cried Deac, rising to his feet and staring at the forest. "He's in there! He's coming right up!"

"Red One, this is Red Two Golf," Webber cried into the radiotelephone. "Two BRDMs advancing along tree line, five hundred meters north of our position. Believe third BRDM has broken off from platoon and is moving directly through the woods to flank Red Two."

HANSEN'S THOUGHTS FLEW in erratic orbits as he tried to process the information. He kept telling himself that his confidence was not blown—even though he had already made a mistake. He had to redeem himself. He would. "Red Two Golf, return immediately. Red Two, orient north to cover the woods, over."

"Roger," replied Keyman.

"THAT'S IT. WE'RE out of here," Webber told Deac as he stuffed the radiotelephone and NVGs into his ruck. Abandoning the commo wire, they started back toward the tanks, following their footsteps as best they could, bounding between snowdrifts that had grown nearly a foot since they had first passed them.

As they neared their original LP/OP, Webber's right boot hit a patch of ice beneath the snow and gave. At least his elbows and knees broke some of the fall, but he received a face full of the cold stuff. He cursed, cleared his eyes.

Deac, who was in the lead, kept on another few footsteps before chancing a look back. He stopped, turned, but Webber pulled himself onto his hands and knees and waved off the loader as the drone of that BRDM's engine grew even louder. He got up, dragged himself on, his arms and knees sore, his boots feeling like blocks of cement.

ABBOT WAS BITING his lip so hard that he thought it might bleed. He had been monitoring everything that had happened, and while his suspicions about Hansen were beginning to play out, he would give the young lieutenant the benefit of the doubt. At least for the moment. Abbot decided to politely remind the LT of the situation while at the same time boosting his confidence.

"Red One, this is Red Four, over."

"Go ahead, Four."

"If they have a platoon in the west and one coming up the middle, you can bet they got one to the east, where the ROK scouts are; those BRDMs won't meet any resistance, and that brigade commander might focus his breach force there. Break.

"GSR will pick up the lead battalion, probably fifteen minutes from now, with maybe a tank company leading them in. Break.

"They'll set up support by fire positions along those foothills just north of PL Warm, as well as on both sides of the engineers. Break.

"We'll be ready for them, over."

"Roger, Four. And thanks, out."

THE SECOND DEAC began to climb into the tank, Hansen announced over the platoon net, "Red, this is Red One. We've got reports of two platoons of BRDMs entering EA Slam. Alpha Section, move into a hull-down position and observe. Bravo Section, move forward to provide overwatch."

As the report left Hansen's mouth, Keyman hollered, "Contact! BRDM! two hundred meters east of TRP 1."

WEBBER WAS AT his station, watching through his sight as Keyman directed his .50 caliber machine gun at the oncoming enemy.

The BRDM neared the edge of the forest at a range of just 150 meters.

But then it suddenly stopped. Began to back up.

And Keyman reacted, squeezing off his first burst of fifteen armor-piercing incendiary rounds, the three tracers painting a crimson line out to the BRDM.

Keyman's gun fell silent for only heartbeat. A few rounds from his second burst caromed off the vehicle's 14 mm armor, kicking up sparks, while others burrowed into the crew compartment as brass casings dropped and rattled across his own turret. Webber had never seen the actual armor-piercing incendiary round fired from the commander's gun, since they usually trained with straight ball or ball and tracer. The silver-tipped ammo packed a staggering wallop.

A hatch on the right side of the BRDM's missile launcher swung open, and a soldier popped up, hoisting an RPG onto his shoulder.

He lasted a half second before Keyman's fire shredded his chest into a pink cloud while flailing him back, out of the hatch. Another salvo sent him and the RPG tumbling over the side.

"TC Complete!" announced Keyman.

None of them had ever witnessed a man die in combat, and for Webber, it was a moment he would remember for as long as he lived. He wondered if Keyman had even thought twice about it. Probably not. And that was probably for the better.

HANSEN COULD BARELY catch his breath as Gatch rolled them into their hull-down battle position.

"Are you guys ready to fuck up some North Koreans?"

"YES, SIR!"

Gatch nestled them into position. Then Hansen and Lee went to work, scanning for targets.

Just as Red Two's .50 cal went silent, two BRDM-2s rumbled into the open.

"There!" cried Lee. "Two PCs."

Hansen saw them, too, picking up the lead vehicle, only to notice the second just a few meters behind. "Right one first."

"Identified."

"Up!"

"Fire!"

"On the way!"

Crimson Death lived up to her name. The HEAT round

struck the BRDM center of mass, and a billowing ball of smoke and fire rushed up into the falling snow as pieces of flaming debris sparked and spat from the explosion.

"Target!" Hansen shouted as Deac was already beginning to reload the gun. "Left PC!"

"Identified."

"Up!"

"Fire!"

"On the way!"

Heady with adrenaline, Hansen squinted through his extension as the second BRDM lifted in a conflagration as hypnotizing as the last one. "Target! Cease fire!" He watched the vehicle burn for another few seconds, realizing only then that the EA had grown quiet. The artillery fire had ceased.

While Hansen ordered the platoon to send a SITREP, Lee muttered something angrily in Korean.

"Hey, Lee, that was for your parents, man," said Gatch from his hole. "Just for them!"

"Red One, this is Red Two. Engaged and destroyed one BRDM and air-conditioned one North Korean," reported Keyman.

"Roger, Two."

"Red One, this is Red Four," called Abbot.

"Go ahead, Four."

"Bravo Section's been observing the second recon platoon. Two PCs destroyed, one disabled, over."

"Roger, Four. Night Stalker Two? This is Red One. Any contact with possible third recon platoon, over?"

"Red One, this is Night Stalker Two," replied the GSR team's sergeant. "I've got contact with three BRDMs at Phase Line Warm. They are hugging the eastern wall. I'm also picking up what appears to be tracked vehicles from the lead battalion moving in. Grid coordinates to follow."

Hansen waited, then he took down the numbers and

plotted them on his map. He began to visualize the enemy force.

At the same time, Abbot was consolidating the battle damage assessment and the location of that third recon platoon. He would then relay the information to Captain Van Buren. Usually, he did the reporting on the company net, which allowed Hansen to focus on fighting his platoon. At times, though, Hansen would report to the commander himself. Likewise, the company XO talked to higher on via the battalion net while the company commander fought the company on his net.

"Cobra Six, this is Red Four, over," came Abbot's voice.

Van Buren responded quickly, "Go ahead, Red Four." He and the XO had no doubt been receiving reports across the company net regarding sporadic contact by the other platoons. The XO was consolidating those reports and forwarding them on to the ROKs.

"Red has engaged and destroyed three BRDMs in EA Slam. Artillery fire has destroyed two and disabled one from the second recon platoon. Night Stalker Two reports contact with what appears to be a third recon platoon and the lead battalion of the brigade." Abbot conveyed the coordinates, then added, "I want to use artillery to destroy that third platoon, over."

"Roger, Red Four. Coordinate fires through Cobra Death. Once the lead battalion establishes SBF positions, you will continue to defend BP C1 to destroy the enemy forces in your sector. Blue, White, and Renegade will engage companies at the breach point. Cobra Six, out."

Abbot passed on the information across the platoon net to keep Neech and Keyman abreast of the situation, since they did not monitor the company net.

A lot would happen within the next hour. That NKPA brigade commander had most likely received a report from the third recon platoon regarding the loss of the other two platoons. As Abbot had predicted, the commander would concentrate his breach force on the east side of the obstacle. Conducting a breach was one of the most difficult operations for a military unit because obstacles were only emplaced in locations where defending units could observe and place fires upon them. Because of this, a breaching force was naturally at a disadvantage.

The actual breach was typically conducted in four phases: suppress, obscure, secure, then reduce the obstacle (SOSR). The NKPA brigade commander would send in his lead battalion to establish support by fire positions to suppress any enemy forces. He would then use artillery-delivered smoke, mortar-delivered smoke, and any other form of smoke he had available to obscure the site in an attempt to prevent the U.S. and ROK forces from observing his assets. At the same time, dismounted infantry would advance along the mountainside so that they could secure both sides of the obstacle.

Once they did that, the brigade's engineers would move in to prepare the breach. They likely had ten to fourteen APCs carrying about 120 personnel. They also had some bulldozers, a couple of tank-launched bridges that were slow to deploy and highly vulnerable to enemy fire, and their version of MICLICs—Mine Clearing Line Charges—carried on trailers. The engineers would set up an MICLIC at the point of the breach, launch a rocket that would drag a rope of charges over the field, then they would detonate those charges, thereby detonating any mines emplaced within an eight-meter by one hundred–meter path. Since the obstacle at Phase Line Warm was two hundred meters deep, they would need to repeat the procedure. Then, tanks equipped with rollers would traverse their turrets over the side and proof the lane.

However, while all of that was going on, Hansen and the rest of the defense force would use their machines, their manpower, and their cunning to turn the engagement area into a graveyard.

And it would all start with more artillery. But damn, they weren't the only ones with big guns at their beck and call.

A shell abruptly detonated just a few hundred meters south of the burning BRDMs, a shell no doubt called in by that third recon platoon. Two more shells dropped right behind the first, and the detonation worked its way up, through Hansen's tank.

"Homey don't like this," said Gatch.

"Red, this is Red One. Shift to successive BPs. Night Stalker Two, shut down and follow. Move out!" Hansen ordered.

All four tanks would shift south approximately two hundred meters to the zone that Keyman had said might be unstable. However, if the ground proved suitable, Neech's track would wind up directly opposite PL Volcano, while the others would tighten up a bit more in an attempt to avoid becoming artillery toast. The GSR team would pack up their dish, further reducing the platoon's chances of becoming a magnet for fire.

As three more shells exploded in the woods a mere hundred meters north of Keyman's tank, the platoon turned right, running parallel with the ridgeline. Meanwhile, flashes erupted from the east side of PL Warm.

"HANG ON!" SHOUTED Batman.

But the call came too late. Neech banged his head against his hatch. The CVC helmet softened the blow, but just a little. Unknowingly, they had rolled down into a ditch about a meter deep and covered by a thick layer of snow. However, the track kept on moving, grinding a path south toward their next position.

Neech's head was just beginning to feel normal again when a second drop had him cursing. At least for the next minute the ground remained somewhat smooth. Eying the terrain through his extension, he said, "All right, that looks good right there, just past those trees. See it, Batman?"

"Got it, Sarge."

They rolled forward, up the reverse slope, then paused as their turret cleared. Neech traversed the gun left, keeping PL Warm in their sights. "Red One, this is Red Three. We're set, over."

"Roger, Red Three."

"How come he's not letting us shoot at that last recon platoon?" asked Romeo. "They're in range. Are we going to get in the fight or what?"

"We will, but not yet. We already drew artillery fire by taking out the platoon on our side. If we put direct fire on those other guys, we'll be waving at the lead battalion. They already know we're around here. They don't need any more help from us."

"I think they do. I think they need help dying. And I'm always willing to help."

"Me, too. Don't worry. We'll get our chance."

The gunner saw something through his sight and drew back. "Holy shit, Sarge. Here they come."

GATCH WAS STILL taking them toward their successive BP when Hansen spotted the first elements of the lead battalion moving into the engagement area.

Three mechanized infantry companies, each with about ten BTR60 or VTT 323 armored personnel carriers, were on a line, with three platoons abreast. A pair of T-62s rumbled out ahead of each company. Those tank commanders and their crews were identifying potential locations for their SBF positions, and once they and the PCs were in place, they would attempt to provide overwatch for the engineers as well as suppress potential and identified enemy targets. Additionally, they would control the flow of artillery on those targets and the flow of smoke to obscure the obstacle. Unfortunately, Hansen and his platoon were at the top of their target list.

While two companies broke away, shifting southwest, the other kept on in the east, barreling directly toward the obstacle.

Behind them, slowly materializing from the storm, came the pack of APCs from the engineer company, and though he couldn't see them yet because of their range and the heavily falling snow, Hansen knew their bulldozers, MICLICs, and other support vehicles were not far behind.

Abbot got on the company net and quickly relayed the grid coordinates for all three companies to Van Buren, even as from somewhere behind the lead battalion, rockets from the BM-21s came in and began exploding all around the obstacle, tossing up thick walls of smoke.

Finally, all four of Hansen's tanks were set in successive BPs, shielded behind the ridge's reverse slope and with turrets down. Enemy artillery was still pummeling the shit out of the area near the still-glowing BRDMs and the forest to their west, the booms echoing into each other and sending shudders through the tank.

Hansen quickly went through his "three-two-one" drill, reorienting the platoon on TRPs and sectors of fires. Then, for just a second, everything grew very quiet. The smell of cordite and a faint trace of smoke hung in the air. The heater blew steadily, and the engine idled. Hansen exchanged an odd look with Lee, then returned his gaze to his GPS extension. The shelling resumed. The companies continued bounding forward as the engagement area exploded around them, great torrents of mud, ice, and snow raining down, even as the storm continued to rage and grayish white smoke blew in great waves to the south. At any second the crews aboard the BTRs would open fire with their machine guns while some of the gunners on the VTTs would launch their AT-3 antitank missiles, should they ID Hansen and his men. With a minimum range of 400 meters and a maximum range of 3,000 meters, the wire-guided Saggers could penetrate armor in excess of 400 mm.

"Red, this is Red One. Tanks, PCs, direct front. Frontal at my command. Alpha, shoot sabot. Bravo, shoot HEAT."

Hansen paused, then called over the intercom. "Loader, battlecarry sabot."

Deac worked his reliable hillbilly magic by quickly removing the HEAT that was already loaded. He kneed open the ammo door, returned the round to the honeycomb of tubes, then grabbed the sabot and thrust it into the breach. "Sabot, loaded. Loader ready!"

Back on the platoon net, Hansen braced himself. "Red, Tophat, tophat, tophat!"

All four tanks in the platoon began pulling forward until gun tubes were clear of any obstructions and gunners were able to acquire targets.

After pausing long enough for his men to get into position, Hansen gave the order that would unleash simultaneous and unadulterated hell from all four tanks:

"FIRE!"

CHAPTER
THIRTEEN

WEBBER'S RETICLE FLOATED over the T-62 at their eleven o'clock. He had already lased the target. Range: 1,150 meters, give or take 10. While smoke, dust, and snow could degrade the range finder's accuracy, he trusted the reading based on the glowing tank's size.

With the lieutenant's order still echoing in his head, Webber squeezed the trigger on his Cadillacs. The sabot ripped away, punching him back into his seat.

Eyes widening, he held his breath as the penetrator struck the tank at the intended oblique angle, blasting off the domelike turret as columns of flames shot up from the hull and would continue to burn for a day, even two.

"Waxed that bastard!" Webber cried, unable to contain his enthusiasm. Yes, he was feeling better now. A whole lot better.

"Target," Keyman announced tersely.

Smiley opened the ammo door, grabbed the next round, but he banged it on the breach block before slamming it home.

"Careful, dude!" Webber hollered.

Smiley cursed in Korean. He wasn't smiling anymore. "Up!"

In the meantime, the lieutenant's tank had fired upon the other T-62 at their nine o'clock, which had lit up like a barbecue doused with gasoline. More voices sounded over the platoon net:

"Red Three!" Abbott hollered. "Your guy is shifting to three o'clock. Two hundred meters left of TRP 2."

"I got him!"

"I'm on the guy behind!"

"There he is!"

"Troops now. You see them?"

"Red Two, PC your ten o'clock. Right of TRP 1," Hansen ordered.

"Roger," Keyman responded, his eyes lit by his glowing extension as he traversed the gun tube, then released control to Webber.

Who sighted the target, lased it. "Identified!"

"Up!"

"Fire! Fire HEAT!" Keyman wanted Smiley to start loading HEAT rounds to fire at the APCs. They would save their sabots for the tanks.

"On the way!"

As the main gun shuddered and freed the round, Webber saw a flash come from the top of another VTT, about fifty meters. "Sagger incoming!"

"Driver, seek alternate position!"

Morbid throttled up and turned back north along the ridge. He suddenly sped up, then slowed down for a second before juking left and right in attempt to get the VTT's gunner to burn up all of his guidance fuel while trying to keep the missile on target. Additionally, the gunner's wire could get caught on the rocks and smaller trees along the ridge, breaking his line of control. Meanwhile, Smiley struggled to load the cumbersome HEAT round into the breech of the main gun.

An explosion resounded, seemingly from the tank itself, and showers of rock and dirt struck the turret.

"Oh, shit," Webber said under his breath.

"We're all right," yelled Keyman. "He missed." The staff sergeant traversed the gun tube toward the east, then returned control to Webber as Morbid slowed the tank near the base of the ridgeline, then rolled back up to a turret-down position. "Let's get him before he fires again!"

Webber began scanning.

"Come on, man!" Keyman urged him.

After blinking hard, Webber checked his primary sight again, searching for the glowing blip that would distinguish that VTT from the rest of the cold landscape. Nothing. And he wasn't doing anything wrong. Magnification was at ×3, wide angle. "Cannot identify."

"Traverse right," Keyman ordered.

Webber complied, kept scanning.

"Steady. On," said Keyman, indicating that Webber was near the target.

And there he was. "Identified." He switched to ×10 magnification.

"Up!"

"Fire!"

"On the way!"

The round streaked away as a fierce explosion—either from artillery fire or perhaps another Sagger—thundered from behind the tank.

"Target!" called Keyman as the VTT turned into an expanding hot spot. But immediately, he announced another target: "Moving PC!"

"Identified!"

"Up!"

"Fire!"

"On the way!"

The BTR-60 literally lifted off the snow as it succumbed to the explosion. In the moments to follow, it would melt to the ground, leaving only a rickety, blackened shell.

"Target. Cease fire," said Keyman; then he looked down at Webber, wearing a lopsided grin. "I hope you're feeling better now."

AS THEY ENGAGED the VTTs and BTRs, troops flooded from the vehicles, some of them desperately seeking cover behind the flaming personnel carriers and getting ready to shoulder their RPGs to take potshots at the platoon.

Hansen noted that he and his men had taken out the six VTTs and two of the four BTRs. The remaining two had reached the foothills about two hundred meters north of the phase line, and from his vantage point, he could no longer see them.

While Abbot was reporting their Battle Damage Assessment to Van Buren, Hansen concentrated on finding those personnel carriers.

"Red Two, this is Red One. Scanning for the last two BTRs. Can you identify, over?"

"Negative," answered Keyman. "Still scanning."

Damn. If they couldn't take out those vehicles, their crews would be joining the survivors of the other APCs and advancing toward Red's position.

Hansen spoke through clenched teeth. "Gunner, find me those targets."

"Sir, they must be behind the foothills," said Lee. "We can fire near to flush them out."

Wearing a grimace, Hansen answered, "I want to make every shot count. Keep scanning." He squinted through his extension, twice imagining that he had spotted those enemy vehicles.

* * *

NEECH, WHO HAD been monitoring the platoon net, knew that from his position he could see farther down the ridgeline. Hell, he might even find the missing BTRs, get off a flank shot, and call himself a hero for five minutes. "Romeo," he began slowly, spacing his words for effect. "Find those targets!"

"Scanning."

"Driver, move up ten meters."

"Moving up," answered Batman.

The tank had rolled but two meters when Romeo shouted, "Got him, Sarge! Identified!"

"Up!"

"Fire!"

"On the way!"

The BTR swallowed the HEAT round and belched a decent and correct fireball that made the entire crew cheer. "Target! Cease fire!"

But Neech cut his own celebration short as he spotted a squad of dismounts dashing toward them. They must have been following the ridgeline south, past the obstacle, in an attempt to ambush the platoon. One guy reached the crest of a hill, where he fought against the wind and snow, trying to take aim with his RPG. "Troops!"

"Identified!"

"Fire!"

"On the way."

The coax sang and spat death, blasting holes into snow, earth, and men whose audacity, though admirable, had cost them their lives. Through the thermals they saw what appeared to be a starburst of light that in actuality was flesh and blood spraying the countryside. The North Korean with the RPG managed to squeeze his trigger before a round drop-kicked him back, over the hill. The rocket zoomed off on a wild trajectory, detonating somewhere in the trees south of them. "Target!"

"I see the second BTR," said Romeo as Batman brought them to a stop. "He's rolling forward, firing at us!"

"Fire!"

"On the way!"

As the BTR's machine gun fire pinged off the hull and turret, Neech crossed mental fingers, held his breath, saw the vehicle vanish behind a sphere of light that fluctuated as though in slow motion. "Target! Cease fire!"

"Yeah!" hollered Romeo. "Take that, motherfucker!"

ABBOT KNEW BETTER than to get too cocky, even after the platoon had taken out ten APCs and two tanks. Dismounts were swarming all over the place, darting along the ridge, searching for little channels and hogbacks that would conceal their advance west, past Red's position. He was worried about a squad or two reaching the woods, only to come around and attack them from behind. He had to believe that the lieutenant was concerned about that, too. He decided to confirm. "Red One, this is Red Four."

"Go ahead, Four."

"I'm keeping a close eye on our six for dismounts, over."

"Roger. I'm calling up Cobra Six now, out."

As Abbot continued probing the area around his track, Hansen's voice rose steadily over the company net. "Cobra Six, this is Red One. Red has engaged and destroyed two tanks and ten PCs in EA Slam. There is an unknown number of dismounts still in sector. We have shifted to successive BPs approximately two hundred meters south our last location. Class I green, Class V amber, over."

"Roger, Red One. White, Blue, and Renegade are still engaging companies at the breach." Van Buren then addressed the entire company: "Guidons, ROK scouts report enemy has successfully deployed MICLICs to clear the field. Second echelon forces appear to be moving in to attempt a breach in the west. The ROKs are taking heavy artillery fire. I see six burning vehicles from my position. Division may put all tubes on counterbattery duty since the corridor forces are getting hammered."

Abbot's heart sank over that news, though what did he expect? Murphy's Law dictated that when you needed artillery fire the most, you would not get it. They had to take on those second echelon forces without indirect fire, even while they took the same from the enemy. They faced at least another battalion.

Van Buren continued, "Renegade, continue to put TOWs on the breach. Bradleys will hold until forces begin to cross the obstacle. Blue and White, target forces that make it through the obstacle and any supporting forces as they near PL Volcano, out."

Abbot felt a little better about getting more help from the infantry boys and their Tube-Launched, Optically Tracked, Wire-Guided Missiles.

Another wave of enemy artillery fire came in, dropping north of them, and Abbot glanced down to Paz, who had his face in his hands. "Hey, man. Take it easy."

STANDING TALL IN his hatch, Second Lieutenant Suh squinted into the darkness and swirling snow. His platoon, along with two others and the company commander, were part of the brigade's reserve force and positioned about two kilometers northwest of the breach in the enemy's minefield.

According to the radio reports, two tanks with plows were beginning to proof the lane, while the second battalion of thirty-one APCs and six tanks was just fifteen minutes out, ready to assault through and engage the enemy. Before that battalion lay a path of fire and death that Suh felt certain would unnerve those crews. His men, however, were in excellent spirits, and Suh knew he had to further boost their morale.

He would remind them that dismounted infantry had secured both sides of the breach.

He would tell them that the lead battalion had already destroyed the enemy and was covering the second battalion's passage. All of the flashes west and east of the obstacle were enemy forces being destroyed—not elements of the brigade.

And he would point out that their revolutionary spirit was more powerful than anything on earth. They would listen. They would believe him.

Suh smiled bitterly. The truth was always subjective.

No matter. At least life had become a simple equation without philosophy or politics to complicate matters. There was only himself and the enemy.

If he had one desire left, it was to meet the enemy on the battlefield and destroy him. He wanted to unload all of his ammunition, kill as many as he could, and bathe in one small victory. He did not want to die inside his tank from a round fired by an enemy he had never seen. Were it up to him, they would all be riding horses and carrying swords. They would engage like cavalry should. They would die with honor and dignity. They would see the face of their enemy, draw blood, and watch the light fade from their eyes.

"*So-wi,* there are many fires ahead," called Corporal Kang, his voice shaky for the first time.

"I see them! They are lighting the path to victory!"

"Yes, *So-wi.* The path to victory."

HANSEN WAS SCANNING for targets through his extension when a shell dropped like a piece of hell, torn off and flung by the devil himself. Still flinching, he panned right to see the GSR team's shattered M113 blazing in the wind, pieces of the APC strewn about the ridgeline. Those intelligence guys had remained close, intending to withdraw with Red once the platoon returned to the company.

"Red One, this is Red Four," called Abbot. "We just lost Night Stalker Two!"

"Roger," Hansen answered gravely. He kept searching the wreckage for survivors, though he doubted anyone could have lived through that.

ABBOT TOOK A few seconds to gather his thoughts before keying his mike. "Cobra Seven, this is Red Four, over." His voice had cracked. Even though he was the most experienced soldier in the platoon, nothing could prepare a man to lose fellow soldiers.

"Go ahead, Red One," came First Sergeant Westman's voice.

"Night Stalker Two has taken indirect fire. Vehicle destroyed. Believe crew are causalities, over."

"Roger, Red Four. We are unable to conduct CASEVAC at this time. It's too hot up there. Will notify ASAP when we can come up, out."

The company first sergeant would usually ride in the medic track to evacuate the causalities. As tough as it sounded, it didn't make sense to risk more injuries or deaths to move into such a ferocious firefight. The first sergeant had made a very difficult decision, and Abbot did not envy the man's position.

INSIDE HANSEN'S TANK, Van Buren's voice sounded from the radio. "Red One, this is Cobra Six, over."

"Cobra Six, Red One. Go ahead," Hansen responded.

"ROK scouts report second echelon forces are nearing the breach. As expected, our tubes are now on counterbattery. Continue to engage, out."

Hansen cleared his throat. "All right, boys. They killed the GSR team. You know what that means. . . ."

"Payback, sir," yelled Deac.

"You're fuckin' right." Hansen seized the mike. "Red, this is Red One. Second echelon forces are hitting the breach. Tanks, PCs. Frontal. Alpha section, fire sabot. Bravo section—"

"Troops! Troops!" cried Lee as a horde of about thirty infantrymen came bounding over the ridge, about two hundred meters out. Two or three halted in their tracks to shoulder their grenade launchers.

"Red, stand by! Troops in sector," Hansen reported.

Lee didn't wait for a fire command. As far as Hansen was concerned, the gunner didn't need one. "On the way!"

Rounds from the coax dropped men to the snow as though their legs were snapping like twigs. One bad guy got off an RPG that came within a meter or two of the turret. Hansen's jaw was just going slack as the rocket hurtled by.

"Target! Cease fire! Cease Fire!"

"Red One, this is Red Four. Checking our three and six," Abbot reported.

"Red One, this is Red Two, no dismounts sighted here, continuing to scan. Lead company of the assault force is crossing PL Warm now, over."

"Roger," Hansen replied.

ABBOT FIGURED THE frontal attack by those troops was merely a diversion, and he had already traversed the turret toward the northwest woods behind them, where he spotted a squad of guys moving in from about five hundred meters, crawling on their hands and knees, RPGs slung over their shoulders.

"Troops!"

"Identified," answered Park.

"Fire!"

"On the way!"

Showers of snow lifted from the ground as Park's coax dished out an early morning death to those dismounts. He continued to fire a moment more as Abbot studied the area. "Target! Cease fire!" No movement. But he would continue to scan.

"Red, this is Red One. Tanks, PCs. Frontal. Alpha fire sabot. Bravo fire HEAT. Tophat, tophat! Fire!"

SECOND LIEUTENANT SUH watched the distant flashes from his turret, his mouth growing dry, his stomach tightening into a knot. TOW fire flashed like red fireflies across the mountain pass, while more rockets carrying smoke continued to strike points along the breach, though the screen was repeatedly diffused by the powerful winds. As expected, the enemy force situated on the west side of the pass had just massed fires on the second battalion, their guns flashing and booming from the darkness.

"*So-wi,* will we get our chance to fight?" asked Corporal Kang.

"We will, *Sambyong.* Patience."

"Yes, *So-wi.* But we are the reserve. By the time we are used, all may be lost."

"Not so, *Sambyong!* If matters become desperate, we will be the heroes who will save the battle!"

Suh could only hope that they would be called upon soon.

AS HANSEN'S ORDER to fire echoed in his ears, Neech took a deep breath, eyeing the VTT as it rolled through the minefield. The monsters had not stopped coming, and he wondered how many more were waiting behind this horde.

As Romeo shouted his "On the way!" four simultaneous cracks of thunder echoed across the ridgeline. A gasp later, two tanks and two PCs from the second echelon's second company came to fiery halts before they even reached the breach, their crews giving up their ghosts.

The actions of Neech's men had been so smooth that it seemed they were all a single entity, an M1A1 Abrams Main Battle Tank with a life of its own.

He was already sighting his next target when another flurry of TOW missiles, perhaps fourteen in all, raced from his right to left, leaving flashes in their wakes. Multiple explosions bubbled near the breach, and the VTT Neech had been sighting took one in the ass, rolled, and disassembled the hard way, more than likely killing the two-man crew and all thirteen soldiers on board.

"Troops! Troops!" called Romeo. "Identified!"

Neech ordered a cease fire of the main gun, then cried, "Troops. Fire!"

"On the way!"

The gunner swept across a squad of dismounts that had decided to launch an attack from the northwest side of the ridge. Why they fired their rifles at a tank was beyond Neech. Perhaps it made them feel better to put up a fight before they sacrificed themselves for that maniac in Pyongyang.

On the other hand, yet another (and requisite) North Korean with an RPG had dropped to one knee and fired, just as a round punched a gaping hole in his heart. The rocket streaked toward the turret.

And for a millisecond, Neech felt utterly helpless.

But then the rocket suddenly dove in the wind to strike the ridge right in the front of the track. A wave of rocks, ice, and snow broke over the tank's hull.

"Yo, Romeo," Batman called from his hole. "You suck, man. You let that fuckin' guy get too close. Shit, man! My life was flashing!"

"Hey, fuck you! You fuckin' geek!"

"Shut up! BTR!" Neech shouted.

A pause.

"Romeo!"

"I got him. Identified!"

THEY HAD PICKED an appropriate name for the engagement area. The enemy was, in fact, getting slammed in EA Slam. Hansen marveled over the growing graveyard of burning vehicles, dozens of fires strewn across the pass and bending hard in the wind and snow. He had never witnessed anything as hauntingly surreal.

As he gave the order for Lee to take out what appeared to be the last VTT of the first company, he reminded himself that by now Abbot and Neech were getting low on HEAT rounds, since they had been targeting most of the PCs while he and Keyman had been servicing the T-62s. They each had started off with a full load of twenty-seven sabot, thirteen HEAT.

After watching the VTT add its dying fire to the battlefield, Hansen cried, "Target!" Then he kept surveying the breach, saw the next company bounding forward, led by another pair of tanks. "Red, this is Red One. Make sure you're watching your ammo count. We'll need to transfer rounds soon."

"I don't know, LT, I'm beginning to think coon hunting is harder than this," said Deac as he finished reloading the main gun. "They come. We shoot. They die. We don't need no stinkin' artillery to help us."

"Yeah," said Gatch. "This is turning out to be a good Christmas after all. Look at all the pretty lights out there."

"Don't let it go to your heads," Hansen warned, spotting their next targets. "Moving PCs. Near one first!"

But Lee did not cry out, "Identified!"

Instead, he spoke three simple letters: "RPG!"

Hansen saw only a flash before a terrible blast ripped into the left side of the turret, throwing him against his extension and shattering two of his rectangular vision blocks.

"Holy shit! They got us!" shouted Deac.

"We've been hit! We've been hit!" Gatch added.

Lee rattled off something in Korean, then all three screamed at once, voices blending into a meaningless cry of terror: "Fucking shoot them . . . I don't see . . . let's get the hell . . . they must be everywhere! Get ready for—holy shit!"

Trying to remain calm—and failing—Hansen screamed, "Everybody shut the fuck up! Gunner, coax troops!"

Although Hansen did not see where the rocket had originated, and at the moment, the ridgeline looked barren, that didn't matter. He wanted Lee to give those dismounts pause. The coax beat its warning rhythm while Deac muttered, "Shoot 'em, shoot 'em, shoot 'em."

After three more salvos, Hansen shouted, "Cease fire! Cease fire! Crew report!"

"Driver ready. No damage."

"Weapon safe, HEAT loaded, loader ready."

"HEAT indexed. I'm doing a quick MRS update and a computer self-test, sir. One moment."

Not a single dead infantryman lay along the ridge, and as Hansen strained once more to find one, frigid air poured in through shattered vision blocks above his head while a warm, wet sensation suddenly came over the left side of his face. Reflexively, he ran a finger over his cheek. Blood.

Lee finished the MRS update and self-test. "Sir, we're good." Then he frowned at Hansen. "Lieutenant, you're bleeding!"

Suddenly, Hansen felt faint, and not from the loss of blood. Hell, he hadn't bled out that much. It was the Grim Reaper's breath that had made him feel dizzy. He blinked hard, regained his balance. Flames still flickered where Deac's machine gun had been blown off the tank. That bad guy had assumedly fired an RPG-7, whose rocket-assisted HEAT round was highly susceptible to even mild crosswinds and weakened by the angle it struck its target. The round had made more of a glancing blow than a direct hit to their flank, but somehow it had still shattered his vision blocks.

"LT, you're bleeding! You all right?" asked Deac.

Hansen ran his fingers along his cheek and felt the cut near his sideburn. "It's not deep. Must look worse than it is. Get me the extinguisher! Now!"

While Deac fetched the fire extinguisher that was strapped to the support bar under his seat, Hansen called on the platoon net. "Red Four, this is Red One. I've sustained RPG fire. Loader's weapon is gone, otherwise minor damage. Red, continue to engage targets, out."

With the extinguisher in hand, Hansen popped his hatch and quickly put out the fire while Lee was ready to gun down any bastard who thought twice of taking another shot at them.

As Murphy would have it, a round of artillery struck the ridge just a hundred meters away, sending Hansen ducking down. He shut the hatch, turned to face Lee, who traded him the first aid kit for the extinguisher. "Can I help?"

"Yeah," Hansen answered, his voice just shy of a whisper. "You can find me a target."

SECOND LIEUTENANT SUH listened attentively and excitedly to his company commander over the radio. The brigade's reserve force of ten tanks had just been ordered to push west, into the forest. They would find and follow some of the cuts and trails blazed by the men who had fought the original Korean War. The company's mission was to advance behind the enemy armor flanking the breach. Once in position, Suh and his men would move up and destroy those tanks.

While he would never get the chance to stare into his enemy's eyes, he might destroy one of their tanks at close range, perhaps within 150 meters. Given his position and the circumstances, Suh could not ask for anything more. He replied that he and the rest of his platoon were ready for the mission.

"And now, crew, we are in the fight!" he told his men, who followed with a resounding cheer.

The ten tanks shifted into a staggered column formation, with Suh's platoon in the rear. They would maintain that formation until they bridged the one kilometer gap of rolling hills to the western woods. There, they would shift into a column, and, as stealthily as the snake they resembled, they would slither up behind their prey, expose their fangs, then wait patiently for the perfect moment to strike.

CHAPTER
FOURTEEN

"**OF COURSE HE'D** be the first one to get hit," Keyman was saying as they hunted their next target. "What was he doing when that guy took a shot? Picking his ass? Damn. Top Tank means nothing out here."

Webber lifted a brow. "Then why are you still talking about it?"

"I'm just saying—"

"What? That you have more combat experience?"

"What are you? On his side?"

"I thought we all were."

"Hey, man. This is fucking war. I'll do whatever it takes to keep myself and my crew alive. Whatever it takes."

"That's supposed to make me feel good?"

"Why wouldn't it?"

"You're implying that you'll disobey his orders if you don't like them."

"I'm not implying anything."

"Then what *are* you saying?"

"I'm saying you should thank God you're not on his track."

Webber shook his head. "Hansen's the PL—"

"That's right. And the Army's desperate these days."

"Come on, you know what I'm getting at. He's not your older brother. But that's all fucked up in your head."

"Don't give me that shit now."

Amid the many fires and leaning pillars of smoke came the glowing outline of a personnel carrier. "Moving BTR—identified," said Webber.

"Up!"

"Fire!"

"On the way!"

The BTR disappeared inside a roiling ball of flames. Webber whispered, "Boom." Then he sang, "And another one gone, another one gone, another one bites the dust." Just as he switched back to ×3 magnification, a squadron of troops reached the edge of the ridge, kneeing and elbowing their way up to within twenty meters of the tank. For a split second, no words would come out of his mouth. Then he screamed, "TROOPS!" and switched his fire control to coax.

"Fire!"

"On the way!" Webber opened up, maintaining a white-knuckled grip on his control handle.

Two soldiers pitched grenades that exploded ineffectually over the forward hull. Webber took out those bastards as a third was getting ready to aim his RPG.

Keyman, whose frustration had clearly gotten the best of him, was firing his .50 caliber machine gun. He hollered at the enemy, "Aren't you motherfuckers getting tired of this?"

Then he let Ma Deuce do a little shaking, rattling, and rolling. Between volleys he added, "This is a goddamned tank, you assholes!"

After sighing in disgust, the staff sergeant muttered,

"Dumb as stumps, man. Dumb as fuckin' stumps." He looked at Smiley, as though the KATUSA wasn't any different.

Webber glanced back at the loader, whose gaze found the turret floor.

"Aw, I'm not talking about Korean people in general," Keyman explained, beginning a half-assed apology. "Just those meatheads out there."

Webber smirked. "It's nice to know you care."

"Get off my back! Next target!"

A thought struck Webber just then, not an epiphany but a bitter conclusion: Keyman would not die.

Why? Because life was unfair. Assholes like him would live through the night, while the good would die hard and young.

In a way, Webber was secretly glad for his loan-sharking and misbehavior. Although he had turned over a new leaf, he was still pretty much an asshole, too. The unfairness of life would play in his favor. Maybe.

"**CHRIST, IT'S RAINING** anvils outside," said Gatch. "Now Dale, I need you to get on your cell phone, call the man upstairs, and put in a good word for me, all right? Just a good word. Okay, I know it's not safe to talk on the phone while you're driving, but just do this for me."

"Hey, what about us?" Hansen asked, flinching as the tape and gauze tightened across his cheek.

"You heard the man, Dale. For all of us."

The enemy howitzers were, as Gatch had noted, pumping out rounds like there was no tomorrow—in an effort to make sure there would be no tomorrow for Hansen and his men. Most of their fire had been drifting farther west, behind the platoon, though the occasional round dropped just over the ridge.

So far, the platoon, along with the help of those TOWs

from Renegade to their south, had destroyed all elements of the second company. Since the first echelon had been a battalion-size force, Hansen assumed the same of the second echelon. Despite losing two companies already, the brigade commander would send in the third and presumably final company because once the North Koreans committed to a breach, they simply did not give up.

And sure enough, Hansen spotted a T-62 leading two platoons of VTTs toward the minefield at PL Warm. "Red Four, this is Red One, over."

"Go ahead, One," Abbot replied.

"Is your ammo transfer complete, over?"

"Five more minutes."

"Roger. The third company is heading toward the breach. Let's speed it up, out."

In addition to pitching aft caps out the hatches to clear the turret floor, Abbot and Neech were both transferring rounds of main gun ammunition from the semiready rack behind the TC's station to the ready rack behind the loader's station. The semiready rack held seventeen rounds, as did the ready rack, while six additional rounds were stored in the hull near the driver. Moving ammo from one storage place to another sounded much easier than it was.

First, the TC manually opened the door sealing off the semiready rack, pulled out the forty-six-pound sabot or fifty-plus-pound HEAT round, handed it off to the loader, then closed the semiready rack's door, because only then could the loader manually slide open his ammo door and shove the round home into its storage tube. Then he shut his door so the TC could reopen the semiready rack door to grab another round.

Loaders could arrange the ammo however they liked, though many kept the heavier HEAT rounds toward the middle and top of the rack to save their backs. Repeatedly closing and reopening those doors and carefully passing off all that ammunition in a confined, smoky space reeking of cordite and sweat was a task you didn't see in the Army's recruitment videos.

Hansen had ordered Bravo section to transfer first while he and Keyman of Alpha continued to scan and overwatch Bravo's sector. Now that the third company was moving in, he and Keyman desperately needed to transfer their own rounds.

"Red One, this is Red Two. Request permission to transfer ammo, over."

"Stand by, Two. Bravo section is still transferring." Hansen did not need to remind Keyman of that; the TC had heard Abbot's voice over the platoon net. Conclusion? Keyman was just busting balls and probably enjoying it.

"I say again, the third company will be assaulting through the breach any time now. Request permission to begin transferring ammo!"

"Negative."

"Red One, this is Red Four," Abbot called after getting a report from Neech. "Bravo section has completed transfer, over."

"Roger, Four. We're going to transfer now. Red Two, begin transferring ammo, over."

"Transferring ammo," snapped Keyman. "Out."

Hansen opened the semiready rack's door, slid out the first sabot, then pushed it into Deac's waiting hands.

Suddenly, Abbot's voice shattered the silence on the platoon net. "Contact! Tanks!"

THE MECHANIZED BRIGADE'S reserve force had ascended into the forest and had found a winding, narrow trail leading south but turning lazily about one thousand meters west of the ridgeline and the enemy's suspected position. Decades had passed since those first combatants had cut through with their vehicles. Trees had sprouted up in the path, yet most were thin and fell quickly, providing a bit more stability beneath the tanks' tracks.

Suh, whose T-62 rumbled just ahead of the company commander's, ordered Corporal Kang to increase speed as they approached the well-trodden base of the next hill.

With the diesel engine wailing, they charged forward, but then Kang jerked right, toward a path adjacent to the rest of the company's. Whether he had seen something at the foot of the hill or had simply decided to alter course, Suh did not know.

With an appreciable thud they hit the base of the hill, then splashed loudly into a deep puddle of broken ice, mud, and snow. Waves lapped at the tank's sides.

"*Sambyong* Kang!"

The engine balked even louder as Kang tried to push through the muck. The tank started up the hill, rose several meters, then slid back, the tracks spinning futilely and showering the path behind.

Suh opened his hatch and ascended with his flashlight. Mud rose halfway up the tank's road wheels. As his breath quickened, he began to mutter Kang's name, a name that had become a curse.

The company commander's tank edged around them, and, standing in his hatch, the captain glanced over at Suh. "We have no time to help you."

"I understand," said Suh, his heart sinking with the tank.

Sans second glance, the commander moved on, leaving Suh standing there, feeling pathetic, inept.

"Corporal Kang, why did you turn?"

"Because, *So-wi,* I was afraid the other tanks had made the path too unstable."

"Too unstable? Look now! The battle will go on—and we will be here, in the mud!" Suh climbed out of his hatch, crawled forward onto the tank's hull, and pounded on the driver's hatch until the driver swung it open. He seized

Corporal Kang by the collar of his coveralls. Then, his face hot with rage, Suh dragged the driver out of the hole and lay him across the tank, unsure what he would do next. He drew back a fist.

"So-wi," cried Sergeant Yoon, sticking his head out from the TC's hatch. "Please!"

Suh glanced at the gunner, at Kang, then up at the hill, where the commander's track had just now vanished. His breath came heavy but began to slow.

Kang's eyes pleaded for release.

Abruptly, Suh lowered his fist and freed the driver, letting him shrink onto the hull.

"So-wi, we cannot not give up now. We must try to free ourselves," said Yoon.

Suh nodded slowly. *"Sambyong* Kang, get back in your hole. You *will* get us out of here."

The driver's voice came so softly and thinly that Suh could hardly hear it above the wind. "Yes, *So-wi."*

NEECH DID NOT have time to deal with Popeye Choi, but it was damned distracting to listen to the loader crying as he slammed rounds into the breach block.

"Yo, Popeye, come on, man," said Romeo. "Get it together."

"Two PCs," Neech announced. "Near one first."

"Identified!"

Choi remained silent.

"Loader!" Neech yelled.

"Up!"

"Fire!"

"On the way!"

After the main gun's boom faded, Choi slammed another round into the open breech while muttering, "I'm worried about family."

"Dude, they'll be all right!" Romeo shouted.

As the first BTR took a direct hit, Neech called out, "Target! Far PC."

Romeo identified the BTR, and Popeye Choi issued his "Up!" without delay, raising the lever to arm the main gun. Neech gave the command, Romeo launched the next round, and the PC became yet another NKPA statistic.

"Popeye, if you can't do this, you let me know right here, right now," said Neech.

The young KATUSA wiped tears from his eyes. "I can do it, Sergeant. I just can't stop think about family. What can happen to them. What can happen—"

"You're helping to save them right now. That's what you're doing. So come on!"

BUTTONED-UP OPERATIONS COULD reduce a tank crew's ability to acquire targets by nearly 50 percent; however, Abbot always reminded his crew that reduced ability did not always mean reduced effectiveness. The crew was meeting the challenge admirably, having already picked off a T-62 and a pair of VTTs. Abbot was just laying the gun on the next target, and Paz was just opening the ammo door to grab his next round, when Abbot spotted some rustling trees out near the northernmost part of the ridge, where Webber and Deac had set up their LP/OP.

He glanced again, figured the wind had picked up, but then he did a double take. Squinted. Wanted to believe he wasn't seeing things. No, he was not.

A familiar silhouette with sloping wings and a bubble-shaped canopy appeared beside the trees, robbing him of breath. "Red air!" That was a term often used in training and informed everyone that enemy aircraft were in their battle space.

An Mi-24 Hind attack helicopter hovered in the high winds, its pilot wrestling to keep the craft stable, its four under-wing pylons weighted down by some nasty weaponry including two pairs of tube-launched 9M17P antitank missiles.

The Hind's pilot was clearly insane, trying to keep that bird aloft in a snowstorm, though he would probably rather face the weather than U.S. and coalition forces aircraft, which were still grounded but would have easily gained air superiority by now.

Abbot remembered that Hinds usually flew in pairs and were capable of dropping off infantry into the sector. Maybe this pilot was covering his buddy, who was doing just that on the other side of the outcropping.

"Identified," announced Park.

"Up!"

"Fire!"

"On the way!"

Their HEAT round streaked past the chopper.

"Fuck, we missed!" Abbot cried. "MPAT air!"

The Multi-Purpose Anti-Tank round, pronounced *m-pat,* was one of the newest rounds fielded and had two modes of operation that were set by turning a dial on the tip before loading. In ground mode, the MPAT acted like a conventional HEAT round. In air mode, a proximity fuse was activated, and when the round neared an object such as a helicopter, it detonated to obliterate the lightly skinned target.

Paz was already opening the ammo door to grab one of the two MPAT rounds they were carrying. Ironically, during the ammo transfer, he had made a comment about the crew not needing the rounds to engage air targets in a raging snowstorm, so he had placed them on the bottom of the rack and knew exactly where they were. However, prior to loading the round, he still needed to rotate the dial near the nose to Air and announce that he had done so. Only then could he slam the round home and shout, *"Up!"*

At the same time, Park placed the ammunition select switch to MPAT, laid the sight reticle on the helicopter's visible center of mass, then lásed the target. He also accounted for deflection and elevation offset because once the round was fired, it would target almost any object it detected, including the nearby trees. He would use an alternate aiming point, just to the right of chopper. "Identified!"

The Hind lowered its nose and both wingtips flashed.

"Fire!" ordered Abbot.

"On the way!"

As the chopper began to gain altitude, a thunderclap came from the main gun, followed by a black puff of smoke out near the trees as the round detonated.

Almost instantly, the Hind burst into multiple fireballs trailing lines of flickering debris tumbling down into the mountain pass.

Before Abbot could say anything, the Hind's missiles drummed in succession along the ridgeline, blasting up snow and mud and sewing a heart-stopping path to within a hundred meters of the tank. Abbot clutched his armrest as the ground continued to rumble. Then the booming finally died off.

"Target," he gasped.

"Good shot!" Park hollered, obviously amazed that he had hit his mark. "Good shot! I got another one!"

Abbot spotted the second Hind as well, but the bird was turning back around, heading north up the defile.

"He scared!" Park said. "He run!"

Paz, whose sector of responsibility lay to the rear of the turret during buttoned-up operations, removed his gaze from his vision block. "We got troops behind us!"

Clever bastards, Abbot thought. They had known that the tank crew was busy engaging the chopper and had exploited the moment to shift their position.

"RPG!" Paz added.

Suddenly, a massive impact shook the turret, knocking all of them to the floor as a shriek of tortured metal came from behind the ammo door. Several more detonations rattled through the tank, followed by several more, making it feel as though the entire track might explode.

BEFORE THEY HAD even engaged the second echelon's third company, Keyman had noticed that the artillery fire that had been falling behind them had ceased, and he had voiced that observation to Webber, who, in turn, reminded Smiley to continue scanning to the rear. In the meantime, they and the rest of the platoon had finished off the ten PCs assaulting through the breach.

Hansen was on the platoon net, trying to raise Abbot. The smoke from the tanks and diminished artillery was mixing with the snow and making it impossible for Neech and the lieutenant to see Abbot's track.

"What do you think? Radio problems?" Webber asked Keyman.

"No. Something's up. Something bad. We may have lost him."

"No way!"

"Fuck this shit." Keyman seized control of the turret, swung them around to the rear, then popped his hatch.

"Where you going?"

"Shut up. Loader, arm the gun! Webber, engage the Cadillacs and stand by. I might be putting you on a target very, very fast. Driver, back up and hold your right." Keyman was reorienting their thick, frontal armor toward the threat. The ridge they were sitting behind would provide cover from vehicles down in the engagement area.

Oh, shit, Webber thought. *Here we go again.*

"RED FOUR, THIS is Red One, over. Red Four, this is Red One, over. . . ."

Hansen had reported the Hind's destruction to Captain Van Buren, but now, for some reason, he could not raise

Abbot on the net. Should he call back Van Buren? Report that he had lost contact with one of his tanks? Not yet. He would give the platoon sergeant a few more minutes. Abbot was a good man. And he was not responding for a damned good reason.

"Sir?" Deac called while looking intently through his vision block. "I thought I saw something."

"What do you got? Troops?"

"Negative. For just a second, I thought I saw just this blur of movement."

"Jesus, Deac, I need more than that." Hansen used his TC's override to rotate the turret so that he could observe the sector with his extension as he listened to his fellow platoon leaders calling in more reports to the company commander. He panned slowly along the tree line, letting his gaze probe the hills out to nearly a thousand meters. If he identified a threat, he would have to quickly get Gatch turned around to face the enemy.

"**NOW THIS IS** getting boring," said Romeo, pushing his arms out for a stretch as he gave a deep yawn. "I almost wish those troops would attack. I need something to shoot at!"

"LT says we're waiting to see if that brigade commander decides to send in his reserve," Neech reminded the gunner. "Haven't you blown up enough stuff already?"

"I guess so."

"Sergeant, I see something," said Popeye Choi, leaning out from his station.

"Something like . . ."

"I don't know. Maybe nothing. Maybe something."

"Maybe it's a guy dressed up in a chicken suit, waving a white flag of surrender," said Romeo.

Neech silenced the gunner with a look.

"Sergeant, please look," urged Popeye.

"All right," said Neech, bringing the turret around, where several stands of trees seemed to shiver in the wind.

WEBBER'S LEG WAS shaking. He looked down at it. Shit. He glanced over at Smiley, who looked exhausted. Then he resumed his gaze through his thermal sight, scrutinizing the frozen hills behind them.

"They're in there," said Keyman. "I just know it. I think I can hear them." Keyman ducked back into the turret and grabbed the mike. "Red One, this is Red Two, over."

"Go ahead, Two."

"I believe we've got enemy armor moving to our rear."

"Roger, Two. We're scanning as well."

"Recommend I conduct a recon by fire to draw them into the open while you engage them from your position, over."

"Stand by, Red Two."

"He always tells me to fucking stand by! Why can't he make a decision right now? Jesus, God!"

"Negative, Red Two. I cannot effectively cover the hills behind you from my position."

Keyman dragged a hand across his face, then scowled at the microphone without keying it. "So what do you want me to do, motherfucker? Sit here and get shot at?" He keyed the mike, opened his mouth, then bolted back into his hatch.

"Sergeant, the lieutenant's calling you," said Webber.

Keyman answered in the strange lilt of a preacher standing atop his sixty-eight ton altar. "The lieutenant is calling me? Well, hallelujah!"

"I'm not kidding, Sergeant!"

"Well, neither am I! Webber, get ready! Morbid, any dismounts ahead of us may have a shit fit in a few seconds, so keep sharp eyes and be ready to move. Smiley, I'll need you to work as fast as you can. Remember, every time they fire, they lose power traverse while their cartridge ejects, so they can't track targets the way we can. We're going to use that to our advantage. Do you understand?"

"Yes, Sergeant."

"Keyman, you heard the LT," Webber warned. "If they're back there and you draw their fire, he can't cover us."

"We'll cover ourselves."

Keyman fired a burst of .50 caliber fire into the woods behind their position; then he fired a second volley as Webber pressed his face so tightly to his eyepiece that it hurt.

And then he saw them: a platoon of three glowing tanks positioned roughly fifty meters apart, moving up into hull-down battle positions at a range of just over a thousand meters.

Keyman fired again, then hollered, "Webber?"

"I got 'em! Three tanks!"

CHAPTER
FIFTEEN

HANSEN'S EYES BURNED, and his pulse raced. His command was slipping through his trembling fingers, and as he scanned the forest, searching for Deac's "blur of motion," he knew he had to call Cobra Six to report a loss of contact with both Red Two and Red Four.

Damn it. The battle had, up to the moment, been a turkey shoot, one that had made him feel like a serious badass. He was an M1A1 tank commander deciding who lived and who died.

What was he now? A shivering idiot staring bleary eyed into his extension. "Deac? I don't see a fucking thing!"

Before the loader could respond, Keyman's agitated voice sounded over the net: "Red One, this is Red Two. We've got three tanks to the rear! I'm about to engage!"

"Tanks!" Deac cried.

"Red One, this is Red Three! I have enemy movement to my rear," Neech reported. "At least two tanks. Wait. Three!"

"Red, this is Red One! Reposition to orient fires from far left of TRP 1 to TRP 2. Destroy those tanks!" Hansen ordered. Through the intercom he added, "Driver, pull forward and hold your left."

ALTHOUGH ABBOT KNEW what had just happened, he was so shaken that he thought he could be wrong, could be dreaming, could be dead . . .

Had an RPG really struck them? No. Something much more powerful had, probably a sabot whose penetrator had pierced the thinner back armor of the turret, had moved on to the ammunition compartment, and had ignited the ammo stored there, sending a horrific blast of shrapnel upward through the blow-off panels, venting the explosion away from the crew.

Thank God the ammo door had been closed at the time and had protected them from the blast, but the temperature inside the turret had shot up more than ten degrees, accompanied by a haze of dust and a terrible, gag-inducing stench created by all that ammo blasting off.

Some unburned primers were still popping as Abbot dragged himself to his feet, noticing that the track's familiar vibration was gone. The tank had aborted. The engine was off.

As he turned his head, a drop of blood fell from his nose. His ears felt wet. He tasted blood at the back of his tongue.

Paz and Park were also bleeding from their noses as they dragged themselves back to their seats. "Are you all right?"

"What?" Paz asked, banging the side of his CVC helmet. "Can't hear too good!"

"Everybody mask up!" Abbot ordered, gesturing with a palm over his face.

From down in his driver's station, Sparrow yelled that he was getting out to check on things.

"Sparrow, stay in your hole!" Abbot boomed. "Reset your circuit breakers. See if you can get us started."

"You got it, Sarge."

"Park, get the gun tube over the side to keep that shit from going off into the engine compartment."

Since they had lost power and assumedly hydraulics, the gunner relied upon his manual traversing handle to carry out the order.

In the meantime, the crew would have also used the tank's overpressure system to help clear out the dust and potentially toxic fumes, but the power failure precluded that. For the moment, their chemical protective masks would suffice.

Fearing now that the fire up top made them an even more vulnerable target, Abbot, yelled, "Driver, hurry up! I need to know if we can move."

"Okay! Fire in the hole!"

As the tank's engine spun back to life, Abbot told Sparrow to move out, veering southeast along the ridgeline in search of a hide position. Yes, they were supposed to stop and wait at least sixty minutes because any remaining ammo might still cook off, but suggestions made in the field manuals could not account for all of the variables of real combat. Right now, stopping might get them killed.

Abbot grabbed the mike. "Red One, this is Red Four, over?"

Silence.

"Red One, this is Red Four, over?"

"Sarge, our radio lines—"

"Yeah, I know," Abbot said, cutting off Paz before he could finish. "Shit." The lines had obviously been severed by the explosion.

Paz slammed a fist against the turret wall. "Fuckin' curse again!"

"Shut up. Listen. I'm pretty sure a sabot hit us. And if that's the case, then there's enemy armor back there. Park, do a computer self-test and an MRS update. We need to see if we can still shoot. Sparrow, forget that hide position.

Keep heading south, toward Red Three. Maybe we can get to him before they do."

"You got it, Sarge."

"Paz, is HEAT loaded?"

"HEAT loaded, Sarge."

"All right. As soon as we can, we'll see how the ammo well looks and see about getting the rest of those rounds out of the hull, but for now, we got one shot. You hear that, Park?"

"Yes, Sergeant. We make shot count!"

"Sarge, we're staying in the fight?" asked Paz.

Abbot backhanded the blood from his mouth. "You're damned right we are."

"But we got no commo. Shouldn't we fall back to the rally point? Checkpoint Four, right? Wasn't that part of the LT's plan?"

"It's part of his plan. But we're not leaving until we're out of ammo—or we're dead." Abbot lowered his tone to warning depths. "Good to go?"

The loader glanced over at Park, who nodded and gave a thumbs-up.

"Okay, Sarge," Paz finally said. "Good to go."

"**COBRA SIX, THIS** is Red One. Engaging nine tanks vicinity grid PT968386. Class III amber. Class V red. Slant three. Continuing mission, over."

"Roger, Red One. Tubes still on counterbattery duty. Will advise if they become available. Destroy enemy armor, then fall back behind Renegade's position, out."

Three distinct flashes appeared in Hansen's extension, followed a heartbeat later by a loud scraping noise from outside the turret.

"Holy shit," said Deac. "Just glanced off. Their angle sucked. Missed us by inches!"

The three T-62s they were targeting had assumed

hull-down positions behind a long hump with several stands of trees on both sides. They had already massed fires once, and now Hansen and his crew would race against the clock to take out all three before the bastards could reload.

"Right tank! Identified," said Lee.

"Fire!"

"On the way!"

Hansen gritted his teeth as the sabot hit its mark, ripping the turret clean off the enemy track below multiple rings of fire. "Target! Left tank!"

Perhaps the crew sensed Hansen's panic—or maybe even his fear. Whatever the case, they put him at ease and reminded him that they were Top Tank. Lee was on the target, and Deac had the round loaded and the gun armed even as Hansen announced the left tank. Within three seconds, their next sabot was cutting through the snow on a one-way collision course with North Korean armor.

But the round struck the hump about one hundred meters in front of the tank. "Short!" Hansen screamed.

"Wrong ammo," said Lee.

They had just fired the heavier, bulkier HEAT round using the computer's ballistic solution for the lighter, streamlined sabot round. Hansen shot a hard look to Deac.

The loader's jaw dropped in realization of what he had done. "Damn it, you stupid hillbilly," he shouted at himself, then rapped a fist on his CVC helmet as he kneed open the ammo door. He grabbed the next round, uttered, "Sabot" to confirm to himself, then punched it into the breach.

Hansen turned back to his extension. "Reengage left tank!"

"Identified," Lee answered.

"Up!"

"Fire!"

"On the way!"

Their round struck the enemy tank and tore into the base of its turret just a second before its cannon flashed. As the resulting flames clawed at the trees, Hansen felt a shudder from the enemy's round, which must have struck within twenty meters. "Target!"

"Sir, I'm sorry. I don't know—"

Hansen raised a palm. "Save it, Deac."

"Center tank's going to fire!" shouted Lee.

"Driver, back up!" Hansen ordered. No doubt that last T-62 had had enough time to reload, but Hansen and his men would slip farther back where they had found a supplemental BP.

They had moved no more than two meters when the ground shook violently just ahead.

"He fired and missed!" said Lee.

"Gatch, stop! Get us back up there, same spot," ordered Hansen. "We're going to kill him now!"

"**WHERE'D HE GO?** Where'd he go?"

"Scanning," Webber told Keyman, who was barking like a Doberman and probably drooling like one, too.

They had taken out two of the three T-62s before the third one had vanished like a ghost tank into the gusting snow. Despite losing that track, they had done pretty well for themselves, attacking the platoon before the enemy had had a chance to mass fire.

"Red One, this is Red Two. Engaged and destroyed two T-62s. Scanning for the third, over."

"Roger. Find and destroy that track, then rally on Checkpoint Four, out."

"Webber?" Keyman sang, sounding more than a little deranged. "Where's my enemy tank?"

"I'm scanning, God damn it!"

"Driver, move out!"

"What are you doing?" Webber demanded. "He's just looking for an alternate BP. You want to close the gap? We're less than a thousand meters already!"

"He's not looking for another position. He's on the run," said Keyman. "And we're going to ram our gun tube right up his ass!"

WHEN NEECH HAD spotted the platoon of tanks moving up on his position, he had cried, "Three moving tanks! Right tank first!"

"Identified!"

But then something improbable had happened.

At least two dozen dismounts had begun to attack them with small arms fire and RPG-7s. Two grenades had struck and exploded over the turret, and Neech felt certain that both his machine gun and Popeye Choi's were history. Yet another grenade hit them from behind, igniting the extra small arms ammo they kept stored in the bustle rack, creating a hellacious hailstorm whose clanging, pinging, and reverberating had all of them swearing against the racket.

"Driver, back up!"

And then, ironically, just as Batman was attempting to turn some of the dismounts into track grease, all three T-62s had opened fire. One sabot drew within three or four meters, while the other two fell short. Still, one of the short rounds took out two RPG-wielding bad guys who were torn to crimson ribbons by the projectile.

Only then did the dismounts realize they had stumbled into a tank battle and should get their highly vulnerable asses out of there. It would seem they had a communication breakdown with their armored buddies.

As they fled, the little, refrigerator-sized lightbulb in Neech's head began to flicker, then it burned brilliantly. He saw how he could skirt around to the south, completely hidden by the meandering foothills. He could turn west and either fully flank or get a really good oblique angle on all three tanks before they could ID him. Sounded good in theory. Time to put it into practice.

And so the batmobile was off and running, grinding along the foothills, sliding a bit here and there as they struck heavy ice that had accumulated in furrows and strings of ditches.

"Ground's a little unstable," Batman reported.

"We'll make it," Neech said through his teeth.

"We should have engaged them head-on," said Romeo as he squinted into his sight. "They saw us move. Now they'll move, too. Fuckin' cat and mouse. I don't like it. And with Abbot gone—"

"He's not gone," Neech corrected. "He's too smart to die. Too damned smart."

"That's a good one, Sarge."

"It's not a joke."

"If you say so."

"Fuck, Romeo. We're all exhausted. Just do your job, all right?"

"I'm trying, Sarge. But you're getting me paranoid, you know? I just want to get this done and go home."

"So you've changed your tune, huh? Not bored anymore?"

"No way. Like you said. Just—wait. Hold on. I think I got a target. Can we stop?"

"Driver, stop!"

Romeo pursed his lips. "You see him?"

Neech squinted through his own extension. "Yeah. Fuckin' monster dead ahead."

HANSEN WHISPERED, "YES!" as the final tank of the attacking platoon blasted apart, debris arcing in all directions to drop and burn like fallen stars against a cold blanket of snow.

"Red Two, this is Red One. I have engaged and destroyed three T-62s, over."

"Roger."

Expecting Keyman to issue his own situation report, Hansen waited. Nothing.

"Red Two, this is Red One. SITREP, over."

WEBBER WONDERED IF Keyman was going to answer the lieutenant. Of course if he did, he would have to admit that they were still looking for one of their tanks while the lieutenant had wiped out all three of his bad guys.

Keyman was second best. Once again.

And that did not bode well for Webber's life expectancy. Not well at all.

"The lieutenant's calling," said Webber, mimicking the preacherlike tone Keyman had used earlier. "Hallelujah?"

The TC's face grew flushed as he keyed the mike. "Red One, we are moving up to engage and destroy enemy tank, out." Then he aimed an index finger at Webber. "You have to decide which is worse: dying here with me in battle or dealing with me after this is over."

Webber turned quickly away from his primary sight, puckered up, and winked. "I love you, too."

But Keyman wasn't looking. Or listening.

As they came up and over the next hill, skating slightly along the thirty-degree grade, Webber returned to scanning.

Oh, shit.

Right there, just two hundred meters out, sat a shimmering hot spot in his thermal sight. It was, without question, the last T-62. The tank's turret jutted up from behind a fallen tree sitting atop a slight hill. The son of a bitch's gun tube was elevating. And they were out in the open, rolling directly toward him.

NEECH SAW THAT they had a perfect angle on the T-62 as Batman ascended to the crest of a steep hill, then turned to work parallel along the edge. They were heading toward a lower portion of the crest where their hull would be better protected. Neech used his override to lay the gun tube on target. Romeo lased and identified the tank, and as he armed the main gun, Popeye issued the requisite "Up!"

Drawing in a deep breath, Neech roared, "Fire!"

"On the way!"

"Whoa, whoa, whoa!" cried Batman a half second after the tank rocked back and the main gun fired.

Although the T-62 took a direct hit at a perfect angle, Neech could only enjoy the light show for a second before he was tossed back into his seat, then shoved left.

The tank had hit a deep depression and was sliding sideways down the hill.

"Aw, shit!" groaned Batman. "End connectors are popping! We're going to throw a track!"

A breath-robbing thud jerked them again, then Neech felt a steady vibration as Batman tried to countersteer into the slide in an attempt to walk the track back on. If they weren't carrying the plow, the driver might have had an easier time. After a few seconds, he shouted, "It's no good!"

"Driver, stop!"

Batman hit the brakes, but the tank slid several more meters, then came to an abrupt halt. Save for the humming engine, the turret grew excruciatingly quiet. They were lying sideways on the hill, on about a forty-five degree grade, with, Neech suspected, one track thrown to the inside.

And they were sitting ducks.

"My tank becomes disabled twice in one fucking night!" Neech screamed. "I don't fucking believe this! This ain't happening!"

"Hey, Sarge?" Romeo called in a low, even voice. "Who's the fuckin' monster now?"

* * *

WEBBER'S VOICE CRACKED as he shouted, "Tank!" and brought the gun on target. Every hair stood on end. Every muscle was flexed.

But he still believed that they were too late. They had been ambushed, been bested, been lured into death because Keyman had been too eager to save the world from communist aggression. Oh, yes. The tables had turned, and now *they* would be getting a gun tube enema from Mr. T-62.

Just as Webber was lasing the tank, a blinding flash swallowed the entire hill, including the enemy tank. Had someone called in artillery fire? Impossible? Had another tank taken out the T-62? Who? Hansen?

"God damn, did you see that?" Keyman said, mouth falling open as he further scrutinized his extension. "They're so scared they've blown themselves up!"

Webber recoiled. "Bullshit!"

"No, shit," argued Keyman. "I saw no incoming round. No one else shot them!"

After looking again, Webber shrugged. The TC was probably right. An error on behalf of that enemy loader had resulted in an internal explosion. "He was getting ready to fire," Webber then pointed out, his breath still uneven. "We would've been dead."

"No way. We had him."

Webber shook his head but wouldn't argue further. Chalk up their survival to the unfairness of life.

Now it would be interesting to hear how Keyman reported the incident. "Red One, this is Red Two. Third enemy tank has been destroyed," he said carefully. "Rallying back to CP Four, over."

"Roger. While en route, scan for Red Four. He may be disabled. I've already pushed about three hundred meters southwest en route to CP Four and am scanning myself, out."

* * *

HANSEN WAS ABOUT to set down the mike when Neech called urgently over the platoon net. "Go ahead, Red Three."

As the report came in, Hansen closed his eyes. Not another problem. Yes, a problem. Thrown track. *Shit!*

"Red One, this is Red Two. Since you've pushed southwest, I can get to Red Three's position before you can. Request permission to assist, over."

"Roger, Red Two. Expedite your move to Red Three's position. Have your guys assist with the thrown track and help with security. I'll meet you there, over."

"Red One, be advised there are at least two enemy tanks and possible dismounts in my sector," said Neech. "I suspect they're closing in on my position. My fifty and loader's M240 are history, over."

"Just hang in there, Three, we'll get to you, out."

Hansen glanced wearily at Lee and Deac, who sat quietly in their seats, Deac scanning through his vision blocks, Lee peering through his sight. The ride grew even bumpier as they hit a rocky saddle between hills.

"Hey, Deac?"

"Yes, sir?"

"We all make mistakes. Even tank commanders, right?"

The loader turned, nodded solemnly.

"Don't let it happen again."

"No, sir."

"Neither will I."

"Sir, you think they got Abbot?"

Hansen shrugged and began to choke up. "I just can't believe that."

"Uh, Lieutenant. Possible contact in the woods, eight hundred meters northwest."

Hansen grabbed his extension and studied the images that Lee had found. The gunner went to ×10 and panned around. Six hot spots. Two fuel trucks, one ammo truck, and three NKPA tanks.

"We got a resupply point," Hansen thought aloud. "But why is it over there, so far west of the defile?"

"I don't know," said Lee. "But I don't like mystery—especially in combat."

"No, shit, buddy. Gatch, take us around to the tree line, about five hundred meters up, then I want a hide position over there."

"Yes, sir," answered Gatch.

"What are you thinking, sir?" asked Deac.

"I'm thinking we don't blow them to hell. Not yet, anyway. Let's find out what they're doing way over there."

SECOND LIEUTENANT SUH had, after an exhausting half hour, freed his track. He and his men were rolling south through the mountain trail. He had been monitoring the radio traffic and knew there was only his and two other tanks still communicating on the company's channel. He would link up with his brothers and take the fight as far south as they could.

Indeed, the battle had not fully passed him by. He would still get his chance to draw blood. He could barely catch his breath.

As they rolled forward into a broad, flat clearing surrounded by higher ground, he instructed Corporal Kang to keep them close to the western tree line, where they could find better cover. They turned, and suddenly Sergeant Yoon's voice came sharply over the intercom. "Possible enemy tank. Range: twenty-eight hundred meters. He's moving toward the tree line. Losing him now."

"We won't lose him. Kang? Increase speed. Get us within range, and then we will teach him how to die."

* * *

NEECH LEFT ROMEO inside the turret to man the coax, while Popeye Choi stood in his hatch, brandishing his M4 rifle. Batman, rifle also in hand, hunkered down near the thrown track to inspect the damage.

With a growing sense of dread, Neech worked his way back up the hill, keeping hunched over, then dropping to his gut as he reached the top. He brought his NVGs to his eyes, searched the hills, thought he saw one of the enemy tanks, then flinched as automatic fire sewed across the snow to his right, less than a meter away.

"I got skinny, all right," he whispered to himself. "Now I'm going to get dead. Fuck . . ."

The squeaks, clicks, and humming of that approaching tank got louder, and Neech hazarded a second glance over the hill.

A North Korean soldier appeared from behind a mound no more than fifty meters away and lifted his RPG.

Neech rolled back down the hillside.

As the weapon whooshed, the grenade struck, and his former position blossomed into a fiery rose.

Twenty meters to his left, four more enemy troops came charging down the hill, firing at Batman and Choi, both of whom returned fire, as did Neech.

Three of four bad guys hit the ground, convulsing, while the last guy met up with Romeo's coax fire, which hammered him into hamburger.

And then . . . a lull. A strange lull, with just the hiss of falling snow, the steady idle of their tank's engine, and then the abruptly louder addition of that approaching tank.

Once more, Neech crawled up, carefully peered over the hill, saw the T-62 just two hundred meters out, closing in for the point-blank kill. And then the second tank appeared, about five hundred meters beyond, moving in the same direction. Where the fuck was Keyman?

* * *

"**HE HAS TO** be around here, somewhere," said Webber, his eyes so heavy and sore that he could barely keep them open.

"Damn, Neech, man. I used to like him," said Keyman. "Before he hooked up with the world's worst driver. That goddamned kid got his license at Wal-Mart."

"Wait. Think I got something moving ahead."

"Do you have a fucking contact? Or do you have a fucking something?"

"I got a tank. Close in. Eight hundred meters, moving away."

"One of ours?"

"Negative. Second contact. Tank. Range: thirteen twenty. Moving away."

"Near tank!"

"Identified!"

"Up!"

"Fire!"

"On the way!" Webber sensed the sabot as it flew in its flat trajectory and exploded about ten meters behind the moving tank.

"Short!" said Keyman. "God damn it!"

"They're hauling ass," said Webber.

"Yeah, and I'm betting we just found Neech, sitting ahead of them. Near tank!"

"Identified!"

"Up!"

"Fire!"

NEECH STOLE A quick glance at Keyman's approaching M1A1 behind the conflagration of the enemy tank that the staff sergeant had just destroyed. All right. It was about fucking time. Neech scurried down the hill. He made it about halfway back to the tank when shots rang out, and for some damned reason, his right leg gave way.

Then he felt the sharp sting in his calf.

"Sarge!" screamed Batman. "TC's down! TC's down!"

Neech glanced up, could barely see the tank as the wind picked up, driving snow into his eyes. He thought he saw Batman rushing toward him, wanted to wave the kid off, but it was no use. He got onto his hands and knees as Popeye Choi and Romeo began firing at the wood line, trying to provide covering fire.

For a somewhat scrawny kid whose face still seemed ravaged by puberty, even at nineteen, Batman was suddenly a being of pure muscle. He seized Neech's arm, draped it around his shoulders, then in one powerful motion hauled Neech to his feet.

They started for the tank, despite the rounds ricocheting off the armor. When they got to the rear deck, Batman laid him behind the tank, then sat down himself.

Neech wiped snow from his eyes, looked at the kid, whose eyes seemed vague. "Sarge? Sorry about getting high-centered. Sorry about throwing the track."

"Aw, shit. Don't worry about—"

Batman's eyes rolled into his head. He collapsed onto his back.

"No!" Neech shoved himself to Batman's side, lifted the boy's arm, and saw the bullet hole in his NOMEX. "No, not him. He's nineteen for God's sake!" Neech checked the driver's neck for a carotid pulse. No thump. Nothing. He checked again, never wanting to feel something as badly. He gripped Batman's head in his hands, put his ear to the kid's mouth, listening for breath signs.

But the clanking and grinding noise of that enemy T-62 stole his attention.

He took a breath of his own. Looked up.

The tank neared the crest of the hill, less than fifty meters above them.

But its turret was facing away, toward Keyman.

"Sarge, come on. Have to get inside," said Popeye Choi,

slinging his rifle over his shoulder, then pulling Neech away from Batman. The KATUSA grimaced at the driver's limp form.

"I think he's dead," said Neech.

"Batman . . ." Popeye whispered, fighting against the tears as he tugged harder on Neech's arm.

Wincing and feeling his ankle growing damp as the blood seeped into his boot, Neech mounted the tank, rifle in one hand.

But then a horde of troops came bounding over the hill, perhaps thirty in all. Neech and Popeye dropped to the back deck as so much incoming fire clanged against the tank that Neech felt certain his number was up.

Although Romeo began cutting down the troops with his coax, another platoon-size force came in from the west, shifting like shadow warriors in the dim light. Neech figured that Romeo did not see the new threat.

"We die here," said Popeye, clutching Neech's hand. "But we are brothers."

"We're brothers, but we're not dead yet. I got a full mag."

"Me, too!"

"Then we'll take a few of these motherfuckers with us—for Batman!"

Popeye nodded, showed his teeth, rolled, then let out a horrific cry as he fired upon the enemy.

Neech joined him, and together they were monsters killing monsters, victims of what Nietzsche had warned them about, but ironically, Neech had never felt more alive.

CHAPTER
SIXTEEN

ABBOT WAS THE kind of man who, had he not joined the Army, would still be very regimented about his life. He was neat to a fault and so punctual that he drove Kim insane. He liked to tell her that timing was everything—especially while making love . . . and while on the battle-field.

Right now, good timing meant the difference between saving a fellow tank commander's life or watching him die.

As Abbot's tank dropped farther down the hill, coming within one hundred meters of Neech's disabled track, he barked an order: "Gunner, coax troops!"

Firing the main gun while his buddies were still outside was far too dangerous, given the ranges, so Abbot had Park going to town on the dismounts to the west. Most of them hit the snow under his withering onslaught, and only spo-radic fire came toward Neech's tank.

"Now put some fire on that tank," Abbot said.

The strangely beautiful line of tracers lit the hill and ter-minated in showers of sparks as Park's rounds knocked on the enemy's door and asked if he would like to come out and die. Hopefully that enemy tank crew would stay buttoned up, buying Neech and Popeye Choi some time.

What're they waiting for? Abbot thought. *Come on, guys. Get back in that fucking turret!*

"**HE'S GOING TO** fire at us," said Webber.

"Then we have to kill his ass."

"What if Neech is on the other—"

"Red Three, this is Red Two, over," Keyman said, not waiting for Webber to finish.

"Red Three, we are engaging troops," answered Romeo, the sound of gunfire clearly echoing in the background. "There's an enemy track just above us, fifty meters! Somebody's hitting him with small arms. Is that you?"

"Negative. Closing in. Can we take out that track?"

"No, don't fire! Neech and Choi are still up top! I gotta go!"

Webber exchanged a confused look with Keyman, who said, "Damned if we do, damned if we don't? Fuck this shit!"

HANSEN AND DEAC reached the woods, then stole their way through the trees, closing in on the enemy resupply point. Meanwhile, Gatch and Lee waited for them in a hide position, but they couldn't stay there long without their heat signature being picked up. When Hansen had told Deac that they were dismounting for a closer look, the loader had simply closed his eyes and nodded.

Good old Deac. He had spent almost as much time outside the tank as he had in it. But he was a coon hunter, a self-proclaimed woodsman. He could take it. Maybe.

They drew up on a rocky, ice-slick cliff overlooking the valley where the fuel and ammo trucks stood idling. While

Deac covered their asses, Hansen surveyed the operation with his goggles. The three T-55s sat in column formation beside the two fuel trucks. Apparently, they had just finished refueling and began to roll off toward the southwest. Hansen's frown deepened.

"Are we done?" Deac whispered in a broken voice, then began a fit of sniffling.

"Almost." Hansen worked his way north with the NVGs until his gaze settled upon long lines of vehicles about eight hundred meters west and shimmering in the night-vision sight. He saw T-55s, T-62s, BTRs, VTTs, and BRDMs pushing steadily south, vanishing just behind the next row of hills, with some veering off toward the narrower defile of the resupply point. The numbers were staggering. "Jesus Christ, Deac. There's a shitload of armor out there, heading right toward the TDC corridor. Could be part of an entire division."

"So what are we doing here? Come on, LT. We got a hot tank out there. Any of these assholes point in the right direction, we're history."

Hansen was still lost in thought. "I wonder if Brigade knows about this."

"Of course they do. Come on, LT."

"Give me one of those grenades."

Deac sighed. "I knew it. I just knew you were going to do this. I shouldn't have packed them."

"But you're a good guy. You followed orders."

"And now what?"

"You'll see. Abbot told me about a little trick he learned during the first Gulf War, and if he's dead, then this is for him. Besides, we'd have to get our track in too close to get a shot down there. It's too risky. This is better."

"Uh, sir? You're fucking nuts." Deac handed him the thermite grenade.

"You got that hundred-mile-an-hour tape?"

The loader produced the roll, and Hansen began wrapping tape around the body of the grenade, securing the spoon with a half-inch-thick wad of the same. "All right. Most of those guys will be staying warm in their cabs until the next customers arrive."

"You're telling me they got no security down there? Bullshit."

"I'm not worried. I think I can get in close enough."

"LT, come on. Fuck these guys."

"Listen to me, Deac. We can slow them down. At least a little. Now you watch. But you don't fire. You don't give up your location. If I don't make it back, you make sure Lee rallies to CP Four. You tell him about that armor out there. The mechanized brigade was obviously the feint. They sold us the attack we were expecting. And now they're heading down to pound the shit out of the battalion. Got it?"

Deac averted his gaze. "Yeah, roger. I got it."

As Hansen turned to leave, the loader added weakly, "Hurry back."

Hansen gave him a tight smile, then slipped off toward a path beside the cliff. He carefully picked his way down through the snow, shifting toward the nearest cluster of trees. He figured it would take him about five minutes to reach the edge of the clearing. No. He would do it in three.

"CHOI, GET INSIDE," Neech said as the small arms fire from somewhere behind the tank continued to keep the dismounts pinned down. "I'm going back for Batman."

"Me, too," said the loader.

"Negative, get in that fucking turret right now!"

"Okay, Sarge."

Tentatively, Neech inched across the deck, reached the edge, then slid down. He threw Batman's body over his shoulder, tried to stand, but dropped onto one knee. His wounded leg would not support him, let alone Batman as well. He realized he would have to leave the driver outside. He hated doing that. Hated it. But he had no choice. Holding his breath, he climbed up in one quick movement. Damn, he nearly slipped off the turret, recovered, then reached his hatch. Several rounds clanged off the gun tube as he dropped down and buttoned up.

"Keyman! Shoot this motherfucker! Now!" Romeo cried over the platoon net.

SEEING THAT NEECH was safely inside and that smoke was already billowing from the back of the T-62's turret, Abbot gave the command to fire.

Their last HEAT round tore into enemy tank, sending flames and pieces of shattered armor surging into the night sky.

"Target!"

A VERY CONFUSED Webber watched the tank light up. "Who shot that track?" he asked Keyman. "Wasn't Neech."

"No, I saw a flash out past his position."

"Yeah, I did, too."

"Couldn't be the LT. He's behind us."

"Maybe you can call him. See if the rest of the company has moved up."

"Red One, this is Red Two, over?"

"Red Two, this is Red One, go ahead," answered Lee.

"Has the rest of the company moved up, over?"

"Uh, negative Two."

"Where's the LT?"

"He has dismounted. We'll rally on your position soon, out."

"Well, that was abrupt," said Webber.

"That fucking Hansen, man. Now he's dismounted? What's he doing?"

"I don't know," answered Webber. "But it can't be any more stupid than trying to run a gun tube up some North Korean's ass."

COVERED IN SNOW, Hansen crawled about five meters across the clearing and reached the second fuel truck, which was parked between the first one and the ammo truck. He crept beneath the idling vehicle, then peered up toward the windshield of the ammo truck. He knew the guys inside might get a look at him, even through their foggy windshield, but he had already come too far.

Maybe it was stupid. Maybe he didn't have to do it. But he kept seeing Abbot sitting there, telling him the story, telling him how to do it, and making him feel proud and honored to be in the presence of a man who had seen real combat. If the platoon sergeant was really gone, then he deserved no less.

Before Hansen made his move, he reached down and felt the watch at his hip. He had known the love of a beautiful woman, which was more than some people could say. A tremendous sense of peace washed over him.

He was ready.

And the approaching whine of more tracks signaled his move. He crawled out, mounted the side of the truck, then opened the fuel hatch on top. He pulled the pin on the thermite grenade and dropped it in. Then he leapt down from the truck and hauled extreme ass toward the forest as the ammo truck's doors swung open and men shouted.

Gunfire ripped into the trees as he bolted up the hill, imagining how the fuel was now eating away at the adhesive of the tape securing the spoon. At any second that spoon would fly off, and three seconds later . . .

More rounds dropped snow from overhanging branches as Hansen neared Deac's position. The loader was there, perched on one knee, his M4 trained on the valley. He just looked at Hansen and said, "I don't believe it."

Barely two seconds after he spoke, the rear fuel truck blew up in one of the most impressive fireballs Hansen had ever seen. Fluctuating walls of orange and pale yellow devoured men on the ground and at once reached the other vehicles. The glare left Hansen squinting, and the heat came like hands pressing hard on his cheeks.

As the fire continued swelling, he turned away from the mesmerizing image, reminding himself that the other two trucks were about to blow. He waved Deac on, and they started back toward their waiting track, jolting as a second, then a third explosion rocked the hills, followed by the sound of ammo cooking off like popcorn in a microwave.

With Deac taking the lead, Hansen found himself replaying the moment in his head, unsure whether he had actually gone through with it. He kept seeing himself get shot as he tossed in the grenade, and he wondered if what he was experiencing now was, in fact, the afterlife, where things went right. Or was he just tired beyond belief?

"WELL, THERE'S A sight for sore eyes," Neech muttered as he watched Abbot's tank roll toward his. The platoon sergeant situated his track behind Neech's so that he could tow them down to level ground and begin work on the thrown track. Above them, the T-62 sat lifeless and flying a long pennant of black smoke. "Red One, this is Red Three," Neech called Hansen.

"Go ahead," answered Lee.

"LT's not back yet?"

"I expect him any minute."

"All right, inform him that Red Four has found us. Looks like he took an ammo compartment hit. He has no

comms and is black on main gun ammo. He and Red Two
are assisting with the thrown track. We have one casualty,
over."

"What're you talking about?" asked Romeo.

Neech shushed the gunner as Lee answered, "Roger,
will relay. And we will rally your position, out."

"Red Three, this is Red Two, over," said Keyman.

"Go ahead, Two."

"We're coming up there. We'll set up on the crest for
overwatch. I need positions of the dismounts, over."

Neech relayed what he knew, adding that he suspected
those soldiers had already moved.

"There's Keyman," said Romeo, watching the TC's approach through his sight. "Webber's laying down some fire
to the west."

"Good, I'm going up top. Choi? Get in the hole. You're
driving."

The loader, whose face was once again tearstained, nodded. Although KATUSAs did not typically drive U.S. military vehicles, Choi had been around long enough to
understand how to do so. Neech trusted that the Korean
would not let them down.

"What's going on?" Romeo asked. "Batman's not back
in his . . . we have . . . one casualty?"

Neech had assumed that Choi had told the gunner.
"Yeah, we do." Neech's lip began to quiver.

"No, no, you're not fucking serious. Oh, no, man."
Romeo began shaking his head and hyperventilating.

"Romeo, look at me," Neech said sharply. "We're okay.
Me and you? We're okay. We're going to make it. All
right?"

"Yeah. All right." Romeo dragged fingers over his face,
then glanced down. "What about your leg? Let me get the
first aid kit."

"Not now. I'll live." Taking in one of the longest breaths
of his life, Neech grimaced as he climbed up into his hatch.

Outside, Abbot was already on the back deck. Paz handed off Batman's body to the platoon sergeant, who carried him carefully over to Choi's hatch. There, Romeo accepted the body, helping to slide it into the turret.

"Jesus, Neech, I'm sorry," said Abbot. "I thought I had good timing. I should have been here sooner."

"He saved me," Neech said, unable to hold back the tears. "That fucking kid down there saved me."

Abbot lifted his chin at the hatch. "He was a good kid. But now we have to focus. I'm going to tow you down. That track don't look too bad. We'll get it on, and we'll get the fuck out of here."

"Abbot?"

As the platoon sergeant cocked his brow, Neech wanted to ask him if he knew how to deal with losing a man and if there was something, anything, that would ease the pain.

But all Neech could manage was a word: "Nothing."

HANSEN AND DEAC reached the tank and made record time getting into the turret.

"Sir," Lee began as Hansen shut his hatch. "Neech called. He found Abbot."

Hansen closed his eyes, balled his hands into fists. "Is he alive?"

"Yes, his ammo compartment exploded. He lost his commo. But he's alive."

Eyes snapping open, Hansen waved a fist. "Fuckin' A! All right!"

"Uh, yes, but Neech says he has one casualty."

Hansen's grin faded. "Oh, no. Who?"

"He did not say."

"Shit. Let's get over there. Driver, move out."

"Thought you'd never ask," said Gatch.

As they rolled off, Hansen called Cobra Six. He conveyed the news regarding the resupply point's destruction and the enemy armor moving south toward TDC. Then he relayed the platoon's status. They had found Abbot, were working on Neech's track, and would link up with the rest of the company ASAP. He ended with the worst news of all, and could hardly bring himself to say it, but he had to: they had lost a man.

SECOND LIEUTENANT SUH'S eyes grew wide, but was he staring at a phantom? They had been searching for the enemy tank for the past fifteen minutes, and while it had seemingly vanished, it had suddenly reappeared, as though its commander were taunting him. "There he is!"

"Eighteen hundred meters," reported Sergeant Yoon. "He is still out of range."

"Driver, increase speed!"

"Yes, *So-wi,*" replied Corporal Kang.

"We could attempt a shot," said Yoon.

"Not yet," Suh told the gunner. "If we miss, he will turn—and we are in his range."

"*So-wi,* he is going over the next hill. We may lose him. I do not think he sees us yet. Do you want to fire?"

Suh clenched his teeth. If the moment slipped through his grasp, he would never forgive himself. But if they missed . . .

GATCH WAS BEGINNING to nod out. And that was bad. Falling asleep at the wheel of your car was one thing, but falling asleep at the controls of a sixty-eight-ton tank bouncing along a mountain pass was . . . well, then again, both would get you killed. He concentrated on the next hill. Not much of a grade, maybe twenty degrees. He wished he could make better time, but the terrain seemed to get shittier the closer they got to Neech. Probably why Batman had thrown a track. Gatch had told the kid over and over how to walk the track back on, but it just hadn't sunk in yet. Maybe someday. He veered a little to the right, aiming for the lowest part of the hill, where snow had drifted into several peaks along the edge.

Two soldiers shot up from behind those drifts and launched their RPGs in unison.

Gatch narrowed his gaze, tensed up on the T-bar, and rolled up the acceleration as the rockets exploded over the forward hull.

As the lieutenant gave the order to coax the troops, Gatch turned sharply toward the snowdrift, smashed through it, and came charging after the running soldiers. He mowed down one, even as Lee tore him up with the coax. Then he caught the second guy, gave him an express burial, wished he could hear the scream. How dare these motherfuckers attempt to destroy his nice ride!

Another squad of troops was abandoning their positions, and once again, Lee rolled out the red carpet for Gatch, who proceeded to grit his teeth as he rolled over the bodies. He was taking it all out on them: his anger, frustration, lack of sleep, and all of the fear that had worn him down to a nub. He wanted to make them pay, but as they fell pathetically to the ground, he saw they had nothing left to give. He saw that they were . . . just boys.

Suddenly, it was all very grotesque. What the hell was he doing?

He turned slightly, taking them around the bloody soldiers, and finally began to relax. He was not a sick bastard. Not anymore at least.

With steady hands he guided them up and over a small mound, tapping the brakes to control their descent.

But then a wave of mud and snow crashed over the hull, knocking back the forward mud flaps and dousing his hatch and vision blocks.

Suddenly, they were beginning to sink into a streambed

between the hills. The water had frozen over, allowing the snow to accumulate and make the whole trail appear gradual and smooth when it was anything but.

"Gatch, back up!" the lieutenant ordered.

Although he was already on the brakes, the tank slid a few more meters. They pitched down about thirty degrees, and the water reached the top of the hull, though Gatch believed that only the forward portion of the tank was submerged. He threw it in reverse and slowly twisted the throttle. "All right, guys, I stop for blondes and brunettes, but I back up for redheads. Here we go."

"*SO-WI!* HE IS not moving," said Sergeant Yoon.

Suh ordered Kang to keep on the throttle, and the ride grew very rough as they churned their way through the snow, narrowing the gap between them and the enemy tank.

"You are right," Suh finally said, seeing that the tank stood on the side of a hill, trying to slowly back away from what might be a watery furrow. Suh smiled so widely that it hurt. "He is stuck! And now we move in for the kill!"

HAD HANSEN NOT popped his hatch to view their predicament, he would have missed the faint but discernable resonance of a diesel engine over the high-pitched whir of their own turbine engine. "Gatch! Hold up a second!"

The driver eased off the throttle as Hansen called for Deac to hand him his NVGs. He swung around, panned the landscape in the general direction of that sound, and saw it, a lone T-62 coming at them, range about fifteen or sixteen hundred meters and closing fast. Where was the rest of his platoon? Hansen could not find them, and that chilled him even more. He glanced back at his tank. Even if they swung the turret around, they could not get the gun tube low enough because of the incline. They needed to back out and rise to level ground.

"Tank to the rear!" he reported. "Gatch, you have to get us the fuck out of here so we can shoot this bastard!"

"I'm on it, LT. I'm on it. Dale, I need you now, buddy! I need you now!"

As Gatch attempted once more to free them from what might become their watery graves, Hansen swung the turret around and put them in the general direction of the tank. The second they moved up, they would have him. If they failed, well, they were already showing him their more weakly armored ass and would simply bend over and kiss it good-bye.

The tracks spun. Torrents of mud shot out across the streambed.

"Come on, Gatch!" Deac howled. "You got this! Been there, done that! Get us out of here, you fuckin' biker dwarf! I'll come down there and kick your midget ass!"

"Fuck you, Deac, you dumb-ass redneck," Gatch said, gunning the engine, once, twice, a third time.

"Why hasn't he fired?" Lee asked. "He is most definitely within range."

Hansen peered through his goggles once more, estimating the tank's range at just a thousand meters now. "He knows we're stuck. And he's fucking with us. Maybe he'll come in closer, stop, take his time, make sure everything's perfect, then take his shot."

"Sir, if we cannot get free, should we abandon the tank?" asked Lee.

That question sounded unreal to Hansen. He could not believe it would come to that. "Gatch!"

"Hold on!" cried the driver as he cut the T-bar, throttled up high, and then . . . the tank jerked, spun a second, and finally began clawing a path to the right, still slipping a little but gaining ground.

"Come on, Gatch," Hansen growled. "Go! Go! Go!"

Another roar from the engine, and a whoop from Gatch pushed them over the edge.

But now they were showing the enemy their full flank. Gatch knew that, and he was already turning hard left as Lee kept the Cadillacs engaged and the target in their sights. Gatch turned harder, and they faced their thick frontal armor toward the bastard.

"Tank!" Hansen cried.

"Identified!"

"Up!"

"Fire!"

"On the way!"

The second Hansen called to fire, the T-62 fired and abruptly dove behind a hill—not to evade but simply because the tank's driver was following the terrain.

In that millisecond, Hansen realized his shot would miss and that the enemy's would not.

We're done.

The forward hull rang out like a colossal church bell, sending shudders into every part of the track.

The explosion would come in the next second.

What the hell?

The tank grew quieter, and Hansen laughed in disbelief. He wasn't sure what the hell had happened, but at the moment, he didn't care. He checked his extension, saw the tank coming up over the hill. Range: seven hundred meters.

"Aft cap, aft cap, aft cap!" Deac shouted.

That call sent Hansen's heated gaze toward the loader's station. "What the fuck now?"

"I'll get it out," said Deac.

The aft cap of the round they had just fired was stuck

between the aft cap deflector and the breach because Deac had thrown the arming lever too quickly to safe. He now had to remove the deflector and free the jammed cap.

"Come on, Deac! This isn't gunnery," Hansen yelled. "We can't stop the clock! Get that fucking cap out of there!"

Wearing a tortured expression, Deac got to work, while Hansen turned back to his extension.

"He's reloading," said Lee in an eerily calm voice.

"No, shit! Gatch, go right to that little knoll there. See if we can get behind it."

"Oh, I know we can," said the driver. "Let me show you what this bitch has under the hood!"

"*SO-WI*, HE HAS not fired back," said a stunned Sergeant Yoon. "I do not understand!"

"I do," answered Suh. "He is out of ammo!"

"We are losing him again, behind that hill," Yoon reported.

Suh smote a fist on the turret wall. "Kang, keep closing in! Move left to come around the hill."

"Yes, *So-wi!*"

"We will shoot them at five hundred meters," Suh announced. "It is impossible to miss."

"DRIVER, STOP!" HANSEN ordered.

As the tank rocked to a halt, Lee shook his head. "We can hide here, but he is still coming."

"Deac, God damn it!"

"Shit, LT, this fuckin' cap is really stuck!"

Hansen was almost out of breath. "Listen to me, Deac. If you don't get that cap out of there and get another round loaded, we're going to die right here—on Christmas Day.

Do you understand? Is that the kind of present you want to give to your mother?"

Deac glanced up from the breach. His wounded-boy expression tightened into one of sheer determination, and he seemed to age right there in front of Hansen. He was no longer a hard-drinking, skirt-chasing hillbilly. He was a man. "I'm going to do this, sir!"

Working furiously, Deac suddenly freed the cap, let it clang to the turret floor. He reinserted the deflector plate, then kneed open the ammo door, grabbed the next sabot, and drove it home into the breech. "Loader ready!"

"You're damned right you are! Good job!" Hansen yelled. "All right, Gatch. He knows we're here. Let's come around to the right, get a good angle on him. Lee, the second we move, I need a target."

"Yes, sir."

"Guys, we're First Tank. And he ain't shit. Hooah!"

"HOOAH!"

"Driver, move out!"

As they thundered alongside the hill, Hansen said a prayer for the crew. They had worked so hard—all of them. And there wasn't even time to say thanks.

SUH COULD ALMOST taste the enemy's blood. His entire life had led up to this moment. Years of training would culminate in a single word: the command to fire. The tank and crew were ready. All he needed was his target, his first enemy kill.

"*So-wi!* He is there!" yelled Sergeant Yoon.

HANSEN'S TANK HIT a bump that jostled them. He was just resuming his glance through the extension when he glimpsed a flickering silhouette: the T-62. The crazy bastard was less than five hundred meters out. "Tank!"

"Identified!"

"Up!"

"Fire!"

"On the way!"

SECOND LIEUTENANT SUH saw the enemy's gun tube flash.

And he knew.

While Yoon threw up his arms in terror, Suh sat there proudly, his chest thrust out in a final act of defiance. "For our dear leader!"

THE SABOT'S PENETRATOR slammed into the right side of the enemy tank's turret, tore through the entire dome, and pounded into the hillside.

Yet even as it did, the turret blew off and shattered in the air, pieces of armor and flaming flesh hurtling in all directions as more flames rose and sputtered from the hull.

"Target!" Hansen screamed. "Gatch! Turn around. Let's get out of here before his buddies show up."

"You got it, LT!"

Hansen reached down and offered his hand to Lee, who shook it heartily, though he seemed too tired to smile.

"Hey, LT. Get up top," Gatch said. "Santa left us a present outside."

Furrowing his brows, Hansen popped his hatch then rose to see a long rod penetrator jutting from their frontal armor like an arrow stuck in an apple. "Holy shit!"

"Yeah, wait till Keyman and his assholes see that!"

As Hansen gaped at the battle damage, a chill reminded him of just how close they had brushed with death. He ducked down into the turret, shut his hatch, then he turned his attention to Deac, who just sat in his seat, rubbing his temples and staring a thousand yards away.

"Hey, Deac?"

"Yes, sir?"

"Hang in there, buddy, all right?"

"I'm trying. It happened again. I promised it wouldn't."

"So what? It's the end result that counts. Anyway, thanks. All of you . . . thanks a lot. Good job."

"Hey, sir?" Deac called. "Merry Christmas."

"You, too, man. You, too."

CHAPTER
SEVENTEEN

BY THE TIME Hansen and his men reached Neech's position, Abbot had already towed the tank onto level ground while Keyman continued his overwatch. The presence of all that armor apparently gave the scattered dismounts a case of the runs. Their occasional fire fell off to nothing as the wind did likewise, and the first hint of sunrise began to outline the mountains. The snow continued to fall, but it seemed the blizzardlike conditions were behind them.

As Abbot attached a tow cable to the left front of Neech's tank, Hansen hooked up another to the right rear. They served as anchors while Choi neutral-steered in order to shift the weight of the tank and force the track back onto the sprocket. After a few minutes of trying, the track finally popped on; however, because it had been stretched, they still needed to adjust the track tension before they could get under way.

The entire operation, from towing the tank to level ground to finally tightening up the track, took about two hours, following which they conducted their rearward passage of lines through the remaining element of A/2-9 IN (M)'s position and advanced another five kilometers to Assembly Area Cobra for refitting and resupply. As the old cavalry saying went, first the horse, then the saddle, finally the man. They joined Blue, White, and Renegade Platoons in forming a circular perimeter, with support and command vehicles positioned inside the circle. The haggard dismounted infantrymen from Renegade were already conducting security patrols outside their perimeter. The company XO was coordinating with the battalion maintenance officer and battalion XO to obtain a replacement tank for Abbot.

While the cut on his cheek was being treated by a medic, Hansen learned that First Sergeant Westman had just returned from the GSR team's location and had recovered the bodies. He also took Batman, while the entire platoon stood there, watching in silence. It was nine A.M. Christmas morning.

Afterward, Hansen caught Keyman staring at the sabot sticking out of the front of *Crimson Death*. If the staff sergeant was impressed, he did a good job of hiding it. Without a word, he strutted back to his tank.

GATCH AND DEAC had finished loading rounds and stood outside for a breather. Though it was still bitter cold and the sky had brightened to only a sooty gray, they were sweating and getting the chills.

"Hey, how many guys you think we killed?" Deac asked.

Gatch looked at the loader like he was nuts. "Who cares?"

"You think we're going to hell?"

"Fuck no. It's war. Jesus gets that."

"Maybe he don't."

"Look, all you have to be is right with the Lord and you're not going to hell, okay?"

"Are you're right with him?"

"By the time this is over, I will be."

Deac snickered. "Maybe it's easier for you. All you did was drive."

"Fuck you. All you did was load. And you're saying I'm not responsible? I ran right over some of those motherfuckers. Killed 'em. Watched 'em bleed."

Deac slowly shook his head. "No one will ever understand this—except us."

"That's cool. And that's why we're sticking together, me and you, bud. We're going to ride this out and do what we have to do. Don't feel bad about it, okay?"

"I don't know . . . maybe this was a really big mistake."

"What?"

"Joining the Army. What am I doing with my life besides killing people? And I can't even do that very well. I load the wrong round, I throw the arming lever too fast—"

"You asshole. Everybody on our crew made mistakes, even the LT."

"What about Lee?"

"He doesn't count. He's a fucking machine."

"I don't know. I just don't know anymore. . . ."

"Well, do me a favor? Get your head on straight before we roll out again, okay?"

Deac nodded; then suddenly, out of nowhere, his hands went to his face and he broke down.

"Aw, don't cry, you big fuck. You're going to make me do it, too. Shit."

AS THEY SAT on a couple folding chairs, stealing a few minutes of rest, Hansen finished telling Abbot about how he had rigged the thermite grenade, just like the platoon sergeant had told him. "But Lieutenant, we only did that with a captured fuel truck," Abbot explained. "I never did anything like you did, especially with all those guys running around."

"I got a confession. I'm not sure I would have done it if I knew for sure you were alive."

"What do you mean?"

Hansen released a long breath. "It's a long story. I'll tell you after we win the war, okay?"

"Sounds good. So, uh, what did you think?"

"About what?"

"About the real deal."

"I don't know yet. It just happened so fast, you know? I'm still trying to figure it out. One minute I feel bad, then guilty, then the next I'm like, damn, that was exciting; let's do it again. And then that makes me feel like shit because this isn't a ride at Disney. We lost a man."

"I know what you mean. They say combat changes your outlook on life. It makes you appreciate the little things, and it makes you question all the decisions you made that got you here."

"You have any regrets?"

"Who doesn't? But you go on, because you're proud of the work and proud of the people. Speaking of which, have you talked to your crew?"

"About what?"

"Just make sure they're all right." Abbot tapped his temple. "You know, upstairs."

"Yeah, I hear that. It's been one hell of a night."

Abbot nodded. "You know, most guys will tell you they don't miss shit holes like this place. But they do miss the people—unless, of course, we're talking about Keyman."

Hansen grinned knowingly. "I think he and I will have a little talk before we head out."

* * *

NEECH LAY ON the stretcher, staring up at the ceiling as the medics worked on his leg. Clear entry and exit wound. No major damage. They would bandage him up and send him to the battalion aid station for treatment by the unit's physician assistant or battalion surgeon, who would then determine whether he needed to be evacuated farther back for following treatment or observation. He would receive the Purple Heart, even though he should have received a bullet, the one that had killed Batman.

He did not have to write the letter to the kid's parents. Captain Van Buren would do so, and maybe that was good, because that father and mother deserved a letter from the real deal. It wasn't as if Neech had dreamed of commanding a tank from the time he was a little boy. Sure, he had played with little green Army men, but he had had no dreams of riding on tanks. The Army had been his weight loss program.

And, dear God, he had lost so much.

WEBBER DID NOT know that a cup of hot chocolate could taste so good. He sat, shivering, trying to get the cup back to his lips. His stomach was already growling, but he was afraid to eat anything, given his little episode. So he sat there on the tank's warm back deck, trying to relax, but it wouldn't happen.

He kept seeing Keyman give him that hard look and Smiley offering his trademark smile weakened by the war. He kept hearing the heater and the voices, over and over: *Tank! Identified! Up! Fire! On the way! Target!*

"God, I can't wait to get back out there," Keyman said, ambling over.

"You're not tired? Not sick? After all you had to drink? You don't even remember what you did at the party, do you?"

"Doesn't matter. What we did out there is what counts."

"But it wasn't good enough, was it? You still need more. You still think he's better than you."

"And you're a fucking coward, puking your guts up inside my track. You'd better find your balls, buddy. Otherwise you're going to lose them."

Webber sipped his hot chocolate and watched the asshole walk away. They knew how to push each other's buttons. That was what happened when men with big egos worked closely together for long periods of time. Other consequences included developing a mutual respect and committing murder.

"I'm not a fucking coward," Webber muttered. "I'm not."

For the most part he had done all right out there. But Keyman saw through him. In his heart of hearts, Webber had been scared shitless, but he had managed to suppress his fear to get the job done. Could he do it again? He had seen firsthand how fragile human life really was, even when it was shielded by guns and armor. It was just so easy to die. Too easy.

Maybe he could cut a deal with the man upstairs and get a loan on some courage. The interest rate for former loan sharks like him was currently 100 percent.

He finished his hot chocolate, climbed down from the tank, and glanced across the assembly area. It wouldn't be long now before the company moved out. He took a deep breath, glanced skyward, and accepted the terms of his agreement.

KEYMAN, COFFEE IN hand, was heading back toward his track when Hansen intercepted him. "Let's talk."

"Yes, sir," the staff sergeant grumbled.

Hansen led his wingman over to *Crimson Death*, where

Captain Van Buren was taking some digital photographs of the sabot before the maintenance crew hacked it off the hull.

"You were pretty lucky," Keyman observed.

"Yeah. For a second, we all saw God."

The staff sergeant hoisted a brow. "So . . . what is it I can do for you, sir?"

"Did you fire out there—after I denied your request?"

Wearing a sarcastic grin, Keyman did not hesitate. "Yes, sir, I did. I assume you've already questioned my crew?"

"No, I haven't. Should I?"

"It's your platoon, Lieutenant. You can do whatever you want."

"No, actually, I can't. And neither can you."

"You call it insubordination. I call it survival. I will do whatever it takes to keep myself and my crew alive. I've said it before, and I will say it again."

"What's your fucking problem?"

Keyman looked surprised. "You want the truth?"

"I'm asking for it."

Breathing a heavy sigh, Keyman took a step back. "Oh, man, this is . . . yeah."

"Are you going to answer the question?"

"No. The answer's obvious, and if you haven't figured it out by now, then . . . I don't know."

"I'm going to tell you something. I don't need to earn your respect. I demand it. Do you understand?"

"Sir—"

"Do you understand?"

"Yes, sir."

"Good. Because we're not fucking around anymore, understood? This is the big show."

"Yeah, it is, sir, but the fight last night was just the warm-up. You'll either prove me right or wrong."

"You don't think I can lead this platoon."

"I'll take the Fifth."

"I want to hear you say it."

"Okay. You can't lead this platoon. And do you know why? Because a good platoon leader would've never put up with my bullshit. You've been stringing me along, cutting me slack the way you cut Webber slack. You want to be our buddy, just a regular guy. But the weak get nothing but killed."

Hansen was a breath away from raising his fists. "You think I'm weak?"

Keyman's cocky grin grew even wider. "Uh, no, sir. I'm just kidding. I'm a team player."

Hansen snorted. "Keyman, you're so full of shit they can smell it in Pyongyang."

"I hope they can, sir."

A flurry of artillery fire began to pop and rumble to the south, drawing their gazes.

"Are we finished here?" asked Keyman.

"You know what? We are. You're dismissed."

Hansen began to lose his breath as he imagined himself swinging around, grabbing Keyman by the collar, and delivering a roundhouse that would send teeth flying and the staff sergeant toppling to the snow. There was just no talking to him, so Hansen decided that he wouldn't try anymore. Yes, they were finished.

He turned back for his tank, then he hesitated, his breath growing steady.

Across the way, Gary Gutterson assisted his crew in loading ammo into his tank's bustle rack. And off to the left, Neech was back on his feet, chatting with some maintenance personnel who were working on his damaged machine gun mounts. In a few minutes, he would leave for the aid station. Meanwhile, Abbot walked around, talking to his men, assessing their ability to continue fighting after successfully facing death head-on. The rest of the company buzzed about, each man with a job, a purpose, a direction.

And there he stood, First Lieutenant Jack Hansen, Red Platoon Leader, Charlie Company, 1st Battalion, 72nd Armor, watching it all unfold. He was just twenty-three years old.

His life had just begun.

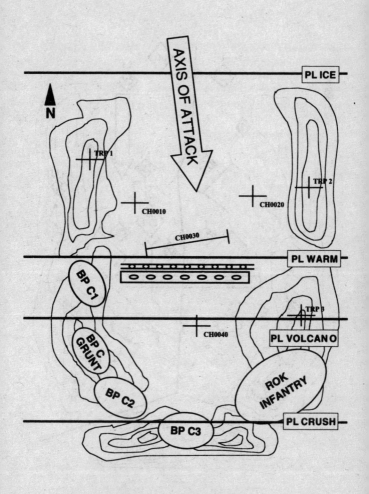

**Map of Friendly forces
by Captain Keith Wilson and Shown T. O. Priest**

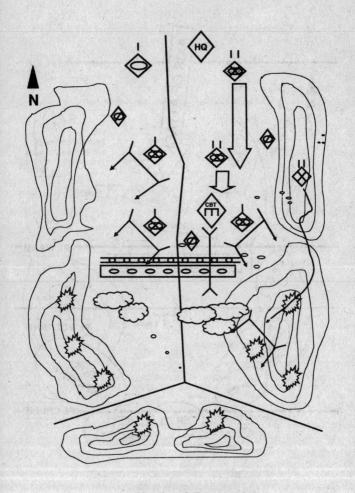

Map of NKPA breach force
by Major Mark J. Aitken

NKPA Breach Force
Enemy Unit and Map Symbols

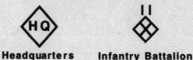

Headquarters

Infantry Battalion

Each company is led in by two tanks (not shown on map)

Mechanized IN Battalion

Mechanized IN Company (BTRs and VTTs)

Reserve company is shown on map

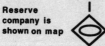

Tank Company (T-62s)

Combat Engineers

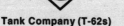

Recon Platoon (BRDM-2s)

Lane

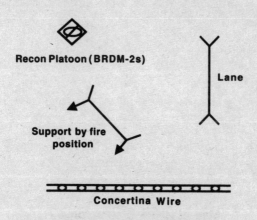

Support by fire position

Concertina Wire

Minefield

GLOSSARY

Compiled by Shawn T. O. Priest and Captain Keith Wilson

A

AA avenue of approach; assembly area

AAR after-action review

ABF attack by fire (position)

ACE armored combat earthmover

ACR armored cavalry regiment

active air defense direct defensive action taken to destroy attacking enemy aircraft or missiles

ADA air defense artillery

adashi Korean: *uncle,* GI slang for any adult male Korean

ajima Korean: *aunt,* GI slang for any adult female Korean

A/L administrative/logistics

ammo ammunition

AO area of operation

AOI area of interest

AOR area of responsibility

APC armored personnel carrier

APFSDS-T Armor Piercing Fin Stabilized Discarding Sabot with Tracer (ammunition); a high-velocity inert projectile of depleted uranium

ARTEP Army Training and Evaluation Program

ASLT POS assault position (abbreviation on overlays)

AT antitank
ATGM antitank guided missile
ATK POS attack position (abbreviation on overlays)
AVLB armored vehicle launched bridge
AXP ambulance transfer point

B

BAS battalion aid station
BDA Battle Damage Assessment
BDE brigade
BFV Bradley (infantry) fighting vehicle, equipped with 25 mm cannon and TOW launcher, battle-proven in both Gulf Wars
BHL battle handover line
BII basic issue items
BMNT begin morning nautical twilight; time of day when enough light is available to identify the general outlines of ground objects
BMP *Boyeveya Machina Pyekhota;* Russian-designed infantry personnel carrier; used by the North Korean People's Army
BN battalion
BP Battle Position
BSA brigade support area
BSFV Bradley Stinger (missile) fighting vehicle, modified to fire the Stinger for antiaircraft defense

C

CA civil affairs
cal caliber
CAM chemical agent monitor
CAS close air support
CASEVAC casualty evacuation
CBT combat
CBU cluster bomb unit
CCA close combat attack; attack helicopter aviation in support of ground combat operations

CCIR commander's critical information requirements; composed of EEFI, FFIR, and PIR

CCP casualty collection point; preestablished point to consolidate casualties and prepare for evacuation

CDR commander

CEV combat engineer vehicle

CFC Combined Forces Command

CFL coordinated fire line; a line beyond which conventional fire support may fire at any time within the zone established by higher headquarters without additional coordination

CFV cavalry fighting vehicle

CIP combat identification panel

CMD command

cml chemical

CMO civil-military operations

CO commanding officer; company

CO TM company team; company-sized combat element that includes attachments such as engineers, aviation, air defense, etc.

coax coaxially mounted (machine gun)

COLT combat observation and lasing team

CP command post; checkpoint

CS combat support

CSS combat service support

CSM command sergeant major

CTCP combat trains command post

CVC combat vehicle crewman

CWS commander's weapon station, from which he can engage targets with the main gun, coax, or the M2HB .50 cal machine gun

D

DA Department of the Army

DD, DoD Department of Defense

DMZ demilitarized zone; space created to neutralize certain areas from military occupation and activity

DOA direction of attack (abbreviation on overlays)
DP decision point
DPICM dual-purpose improved conventional munitions
DS direct support
DS/R direct support/reinforcing
DTG date-time group

E

EA engagement area
EEFI essential elements of friendly information, critical aspects of a friendly operation that, if known by the enemy, would compromise, lead to failure, or limit success of the operation
EENT end evening nautical twilight; there is no further sunlight visible
ELINT electronic intelligence
EPLRS enhanced position locating and reporting system
EPW enemy prisoner of war
ETAC enlisted terminal attack controller; enlisted Air Force personnel assigned to provide close air support/terminal guidance control for exercise and contingency operations, on a permanent and continuous basis
EW electronic warfare

F

1SG first sergeant
FA field artillery
FAAD forward area air defense
FASCAM family of scatterable mines
FDC fire direction center
FEBA forward edge of the battle area; foremost limits of area in which ground combat units are deployed
FFIR friendly force information requirement; information the commander and his staff need about the forces available for an operation
FIST fire support team
FIST-V fire support team vehicle

FLE forward logistics element

FLOT forward line of own troops; a line that indicates the most forward positions of friendly forces at a specific time

FM frequency modulation (radio); field manual

FO forward observer

FPF final protective fires

FRAGO fragmentary order

FROKA First Republic of Korea Army, mission is to defend the eastern section of the DMZ; the VII ROK Corps defends the eastern coastal invasion route; and the VIII ROK Corps is responsible for the coastal defense of Kangwon Province

FS fire support

FSCL fire support coordination line

FSE fire support element

FSO fire support officer

FTCP field trains command post

G

GEMSS ground-emplaced mine scattering system

GPS global positioning system; gunner's primary sight

GS general support

GSR ground surveillance radar; efficient system for tracking enemy troop and vehicle movement in near-zero visibility

H

HE high explosive

HEAT high explosive antitank (ammunition)

HHC headquarters and headquarters company

HMMWV high-mobility multipurpose wheeled vehicle (Humvee); the able replacement for the military jeep

HPT high-payoff target; a target whose loss to the threat will contribute to the success of an operation

HQ headquarters

HUMINT human intelligence

HVT high-value target; assets that the threat commander requires for the successful completion of a specific action

I

IAW in accordance with
ICM improved conventional munitions
ID identification
IED improvised explosives device
IFF identification, friend or foe
IFV infantry fighting vehicle
IN infantry
IN (M) mechanized infantry
IPB intelligence preparation of the battlefield
IR infrared; intelligence requirements
IVIS intervehicular information system

J

JAAT joint air attack team
JCATF joint civil affairs task force
JPOTF joint psychological operations task force

K

KIA killed in action
klick one kilometer

L

LBE load-bearing equipment
LBV load-bearing vest
LD line of departure; a line used to coordinate the departure of
    attack elements
LNO liaison officer
LOA limit of advance; a terrain feature beyond which attacking
    forces will not advance
LOC line of communications
LOGPAC logistics package
LOM line of movement
LP/OP listening post/observation post
LRF laser range finder
LRP logistic release point

LT lieutenant (2LT, second lieutenant; 1LT, first lieutenant)
LTC lieutenant colonel
LTG lieutenant general

M

MACOM U.S. Army Major Command
MAJ major
MANPADS man-portable air defense system
MBA main battle area
mech mechanized
MEDEVAC medical evacuation
METL mission-essential task list
METT-TC mission, enemy, terrain (and weather), troops, time available, and civilian considerations (factors in situational analysis)
MG major general
MICLIC Mine Clearing Line Charge
MOPP mission-oriented protective posture; consists of seven levels of preparation for chemical or biological attack, MOPP READY being the least protected and MOPP 4 the most protected
MPAT Multi-Purpose Anti-Tank (ammunition)
MRE meals, ready to eat; also referred to by troops as Meals Rejected by Everyone, brown bags, or bag nasties
MRS muzzle reference system; a system enabling tank crews to adjust the gun alignment quickly in combat to compensate for gun tube droop caused by the heat from firing
MSR main supply route
MST maintenance support team

N

N-Hour an unspecified time that commences notification and outload for rapid, no-notice deployment
NAAK nerve agent antidote kit
NAI named area of interest; point or area through which enemy activity is expected to occur

NBC Nuclear, Biological, Chemical
NCO noncommissioned officer
NCOIC noncommissioned officer in charge
NCS net control station
NEO noncombatant evacuation operations
NFA no fire area; an area into which no direct or indirect fires or effects are allowed without specific authorization
NGO nongovernmental organization
NLT not later than
NOD night observation device
NVG night-vision goggles

O

OAK-OC obstacles; avenues of approach; key terrain; observation and fields of fire; and cover and concealment (considerations in evaluating terrain as part of METT-T analysis)
OBJ objective
OIC officer in charge
OP observation post
OPCON operational control
OPLAN operation plan
OPORD operation order
OPSEC operations security
OPTEMP operational tempo

P

passive air defense all measures, other than active air defense, taken to minimize the effects of enemy air action
PCC precombat check
PCI precombat inspection
PEWS platoon early warning system
PFC private first class
PIR priority intelligence requirements
PL phase line; platoon leader
PLL prescribed load list
PLT platoon

PMCS preventive maintenance checks and services
POL petroleum, oils, and lubricants
POS position
POSNAV position navigation (system)
PSG platoon sergeant
PSYOPS psychological operations
PVT private (buck)
PV2 private

R

R3P rearm, refuel, and resupply point
RAAM remote antiarmor mine
recon reconnaissance
REDCON readiness condition
REMS remotely employed sensors
retrans retransmission
RFL restrictive fire line; line between two converging friendly
forces that prohibits direct or indirect fires or effects of fires
without prior coordination
ROE rules of engagement
ROK Republic of Korea
ROKA Republic of Korea Army
ROM refuel on the move
RP release point
RTE route

S

S1 adjutant (U.S. Army)
S2 intelligence officer (U.S. Army)
S3 operations and training officer (U.S. Army)
S4 supply officer (U.S. Army)
SALUTE size, activity, location, unit identification, time, and
equipment (format for report of enemy information); abbrevi-
ated format is SALT or size, activity, location, and time
SAM surface-to-air missile
SAW squad automatic weapon

SBF support by fire (position)

SFC sergeant first class

SGT sergeant

SGM sergeant major

SHORAD short-range air defense

SINCGARS Single-Channel Ground and Airborne Radio System

SITREP situation report

SITTEMP situational template

SOFA Status of Force Agreement; an agreement that defines the legal position of a visiting military force deployed in the territory of a friendly state

SOI signal operation instructions, a code book for encrypting and decrypting coded messages

SOP standing operating procedure

SOSR suppression, obscuration, security, and reduction (actions executed during breaching operations)

SP start point

SPC specialist

SPOTREP spot report

SROKA Second Republic of Korea Army; responsible for defending the rear area extending from the rear of the front area to the coastline, and consists of an army command, several corps commands, divisions, and brigades; the Second Army has operational command over all army reserve units, the Homeland Reserve Force, logistics, and training bases located in the six southernmost provinces

SSG staff sergeant

STAFF smart target activated fire and forget (ammunition)

T

TAA tactical assembly area

TAC or **TAC CP** tactical command post

tac idle tactical idle (speed), keeping the engine at high rpms for maximum efficiency of hydraulic systems and electrical output

TC tank commander

TCP traffic control post
TF task force
TIS thermal imaging system
TM team
TOC tactical operations center
TOE table(s) of organization and equipment
TOW Tube-Launched, Optically Tracked, Wire-Guided Missile
TRADOC U.S. Army Training and Doctrine Command
TROKA Third Republic of Korea Army; South Korea's largest and most diversified combat organization; responsible for guarding the most likely potential attack routes from North Korea to Seoul—the Munsan, Chorwon, and Tongduch'on corridors
TRP target reference point
TSOP tactical standing operating procedure
TTP tactics, techniques, and procedures

U
UAV unmanned aerial vehicle
UMCP unit maintenance collection point
UN United Nations
UNC United Nations Command
USFK United States Forces, Korea

W
WIA wounded in action
WARNO warning order
WP white phosphorus, also called willie pete

X
X-Hour an unspecified time that commences unit notification for planning and deployment preparation in support of operations not involving rapid, no-notice deployment
XO executive officer

Z
Zulu (time reference) Greenwich Mean Time

ABOUT THE AUTHOR

Pete Callahan is the pseudonym for a popular author of fantasy; science fiction; medical drama; movie, television, and computer game tie-ins; and military action/adventure novels. His heavily researched work has been sold worldwide and translated into Spanish, German, French, and Japanese. He invites readers to contact him at

armoredcorps@aol.com.

FROM THE AUTHOR OF
The Sixth Fleet

DAVID E. MEADOWS

A "VISIONARY" (JOE BUFF) IN THE WORLD OF MILITARY
FICTION, PENTAGON STAFF MEMBER AND U.S. NAVY
CAPTAIN DAVID E. MEADOWS
PRESENTS A BOLD SERIES THAT TAKES AMERICA INTO
THE NEXT ERA OF MODERN WARFARE.

JOINT TASK FORCE: LIBERIA
0-425-19206-7

JOINT TASK FORCE: AMERICA
0-425-19482-5

JOINT TASK FORCE: FRANCE
0-425-19799-9

"ON PAR WITH TOM CLANCY."
—MILOS STANKOVIC

One man has just discovered an
international threat that no one could
have prepared for—or imagined...

Unit Omega
by
Jim Grand

In charge of investigating unusual
scientific phenomena for the UN,
Jim Thompson is the world's authority
on the unexplained.

But when a world-renowned scientist
reports a sighting of the legendary
Loch Ness Monster, the disturbance
turns out to be much bigger—and more
dangerous—than the folklore
ever suggested.

0-425-19321-7

**Available wherever books are sold
or at www.penguin.com**